# HIS MEMORY IN ASHES

## AN AMERICAN INJUSTICE NOVEL

S M REINE

# CONTENT NOTES

This book contains depictions of eating disorders,
substance abuse, gun violence, sexual assault against adults
and minors, domestic violence.

You can find more info on this series on my website:
americaninjust.us

*For the ones who keep screaming when others would prefer silence.*

# HIS MEMORY IN ASHES

# PROLOGUE

**Hank**

I spotted Evangeline Ashe at a hospital seven years ago and knew instantly I'd marry her. I worked for the Reno Police Department back then. Meeting my future wife on the job was the last thing I expected to happen, especially considering I'd closed out a shift by hauling a junkie into the emergency room. That's how I spent most shifts in those days. Any addict who couldn't be cleared up with naloxone got cuffed to a bed before getting tossed to the jail uptown.

When I finally dropped off the trash, Eve had been pacing outside the doors, just far enough from the entrance that she could smoke. Back then, she smoked all the time, walking around in a cloud so I could never quite see through to her face.

I only glimpsed her profile as she paced away from the door, lit in red tones by the cherry of her cigarette when she inhaled. She wore lipstick that left a ring of dark-red on the filter. "Did you know you can't smoke that here?" I asked.

She confessed that she knew, but needed to relax. "My brother's in the hospital." Eve's voice was both raspy and velvet.

"I'm sorry to hear that," I said. "But you can't smoke here."

The breeze picked up. Her hair was blown back, so I finally got a clear look at her gorgeous features, from the sinuous curve of a bottom lip begging to be nipped, to calf-eyes rimmed by fatigue. Her eyelashes were long enough to trap tears. Her hair fell in wispy locks, styled to give softness to an angular face.

She asked, "Can I finish this cigarette?"

I'd never wanted to tell someone yes before so badly.

I walked away without answering. As long as I didn't have to see it, I didn't have to tell her to stop.

* * *

After divorcing my first wife, a fat stuffy bitch named Alice, I spent a few years' worth of weekends playing poker at the Atlantis. I was a high roller. They gave me a room, drinks, food—all gratis. All I had to do was keep putting money on the table. I never went home in the red except that weekend I first met my queen of hearts. I was so distracted thinking about the specter of Evangeline Ashe, I burned through my chips before church on Sunday morning. It's hard to break a losing streak when you start with a loss as spectacular as the one that had just hit me.

When I returned to St. Mary's on Monday—another patrol, another addict—I found Eve walking the halls, haloed by the scent of tobacco. She seemed more waifish in

the hospital lighting. I could have lost myself in the
shadows of her collarbones.

"Still here?" I asked.

"Here again." Eve stopped outside an open door. Aaron was
arguing with a nurse inside, and I'd arrested enough
addicts to recognize a man chasing dragons.

Eve had been quick to make excuses. "Childhood trauma,"
she said. "It's not his fault he has demons."

"You should come to my church. They know what to do
with demons there," I said, surprised to hear myself joking.
"I mean, they have addiction groups. Come on Sunday. You
can ask Pastor Johns about it."

"I don't think Aaron will be out by Sunday. West Hills is
taking him this afternoon, and they never hold him less
than a week." Eve was still convinced that Aaron would be
okay once he got into the mental hospital. Once his meds
stabilized. Once they got him back off opioids.

The nurse left the room looking angry. Aaron remained in
his hospital bed like some Jabba-looking asshole sprawled
over the sheets watching TV with a Big Gulp in hand. Eve
gazed at him with love. Big eyes glistening with tears, the
smallest smile, fondness in the tilt of her shoulders. Even
her bony knees knocked together like she was overcome
just looking at him and needed help standing up.

"You can come to church without Aaron, too," I said. "I'd
love to see you there."

"Okay," she said.

Eve showed up the next Sunday. She talked to Pastor Johns and let me take her to brunch afterward. Eve ate dainty nibbles of fruit and gave her phone number to me.

We went on three dates while Aaron was in the hospital. The first time, we hiked Oxbow. The second time was dinner and a movie. The third time started at the Atlantis, passed through my hotel room, and ended with another Sunday at church together. Eve fucked with the wild abandon of a woman with something to prove, and she unraveled when she was naked on my dick. I could actually *see* her behind the mask of constant composure.

Once Aaron was discharged from the hospital, he returned home to Carson City, and Eve stopped agreeing to dates at night. "Reno is too far away. Who'll manage Aaron's medication?" she asked. "He'll need help for at least a few months before we can get new home care."

Just like that, my weekends at the Atlantis ended. I stayed over with Eve instead. The habits my first wife hadn't been able to beat out of me, I relinquished willingly just to be with the queen. And it wasn't that long before we got married. Like I said…once you know, you know.

# CHAPTER 1
# EVE

**Years later.**

Aaron Ashe is a large man by any standards. He's over six feet tall and almost four hundred pounds. He carries it in the tire around his neck, the slabs of his arms, and his belly like a bear's. He barely fits through the trailer's front door, more biblical Leviathan than man.

Deputy Jobson's body camera footage shakes as he takes quick steps back. "Put your hands over your head!" His voice is nasal.

Aaron's response booms out of his chest. "You don't see it. You won't look, so you don't *see* it!" His rapid-fire words run into each other, one after the other. He keeps stuttering the syllables in a whispered echo. His fingers flutter over his temples, eyes squeezing shut. *Y-you won't-t look, you won't l-look, you won't, y-you won't...* He only stutters when distress has taken him beyond reason.

"Hands over your head, *now!*" In front of the body camera, a pair of hands lift a Taser.

Aaron doesn't hear the deputy. He swings around to glare at nothing. "I told you, it's all right there. *Fuck!*" He pitches down the stairs, steps creaking under his bare feet. "It's the manifesto. If you see it, I won't have to do it!"

Deputy Jobson doesn't warn him again.

A pop-sizzle and my brother is falling. The Taser has been fired. Aaron doesn't land gracefully. He strikes the ground on his shoulder, stiff as the dead. Slender coils connect the gun to Aaron's chest, bouncing between them as the deputy approaches at an angle.

Aaron isn't dead. Not yet.

Nor is he down for very long. He's a hardened addict used to trauma. And he's an electrician who has experienced a few shocks. He recovers from the jolt, swiping the pins off his chest to roll onto all fours.

"Stay down! Stay down, or you'll get it again!" Deputy Jobson is panicking now. The body camera footage nods up and down frantically.

"You don't see him, but he's always watching," Aaron says. I'm uncertain those are the exact words. The audio is muffled by the deputy's uniform shifting. "The manifesto. Ten twenty-seven, find the manifesto! Mack! Ten twenty-seven!" Those numbers are clear.

He lunges at Deputy Jobson. Aaron's face swells in the camera lens, moon-pale and just as round. His mouth is open. He's slick with drool. His eyes are unfocused. My heart splashes into my stomach.

"Stop!" cries Jobson.

They collide.

The body camera footage goes black with occasional flashes of light. Scraping floods the speakers.

My husband, Hank Everhardt, stands over my left shoulder with his arms folded. Hank is wearing his deputy sergeant uniform, sidearm and all. Carolina blue eyes have narrowed to slits as he watches the footage over my shoulder. When he told me there was a video, I insisted that he bring it home. Hank has seen it at least twice. If it hurts him the way it hurts me, he doesn't show it.

The video ends with a shot of Deputy Jobson pressing one knee into Aaron's back. My brother is facedown on the dirt. It's the end of the file.

"Where's the rest?" I ask.

"Isn't that enough?" Hank scrapes a hand through his hair. "Jesus, Eve. That's more than enough."

"Aaron." My trembling fingertips trace his shoulders on the screen. I don't recognize the mobile home. My brother lives in a little brick house in West Carson. It's where we grew up. "Where did it happen?"

"The incident occurred at a known drug house in Crest View Mobile Home Park." He's using his professional voice, emotionless and authoritative, and Hank is undiminished by taking the chair next to mine. Our home office is cozy, tucked away in the third bedroom. We're sitting near enough that I can smell his aftershave and the starch on his uniform.

"What was Aaron doing at a trailer park?"

"Trespassing," Hank says. "Nobody else was there. Odds are good that Aaron broke in for drugs and couldn't wait to leave before getting high."

My body hums with cold. "Aaron's not like that."

"You can see on the video that he's 'like that.' It's incontrovertible proof. Christ, I could get into trouble for showing you this. The least you could do is believe me."

Aaron's dying words are trapped in my ears like the vibrations have imprinted my eardrums. *The manifesto. Ten twenty-seven. Mack. Y-you don't-t look so you d-don't see it...*

Anything could send him skittering off on a manic relapse with delusions. It happened if he forgot his medicine. It could also happen with too high a dose or the wrong pills. Long-term stress or panic attacks brought the stutter to the surface, too.

None of those things have been worries for a while. Aaron's been getting better. He's been going to the psychiatrist regularly. He attends the sobriety meetings. Aaron hasn't been inside a hospital for three months except for physical therapy.

My brother will never be in a hospital again. At last, he's completely sober.

* * *

Going downstairs, I'm hyperaware of my husband's footfalls on the stair behind me and the carpet under my bare feet even as my mind swims with Aaron's muddied words.

*Ten twenty-seven. Mack. The manifesto.*

Once we're in the brighter lights of the kitchen, the upstairs office becomes a distant dreamscape, adrift from reality. Everything looks normal. It's a cramped space, but

I've replaced the appliances with the best we can fit. I also repainted the cabinets last spring, updating light oak with masculine stormy gray. It's my safe space, somewhere created with my hands, tailored to my husband's taste.

Hank grabs a beer out of the stainless-steel fridge I selected for him. I turn on my Keurig to preheat water and pick a tea pod out of the basket.

This is a normal evening. News plays on the living room TV, which we never turn off. Our front curtains gap enough to see neighborhood children riding bicycles under a red-orange sky. There are wildfires east of town, out on Highway 50, but the wind's blowing away from us. It's not too smoky for the little ones to be out.

At any moment, my phone will buzz. Aaron will demand that I bring dinner to him. He'll eat a Whopper while I read, then we'll jump on a video game together for a few hours. I'll medicate him before heading back home. He can't control his pain pills, or else he'll take the whole bottle at one time, you see. I administer them every day. Twice a day. Three times a day. Whenever he needs it and can safely have it.

Normal.

Hank opens his beer with a snap-hiss so sudden that I flinch. "SE&G filed a police report the day before Aaron died." He takes a swig. "He stole corporate property." SE&G is Sierra Energy and Gas, our local power utility. Aaron worked for them until two years ago. He hasn't had a key to their offices since the accident. "We've also got a reason to think Aaron started the VC Fire."

"Really?" I'm as cool-voiced as my husband but with none of the authority. We're having a casual conversation.

"Really," says Hank.

The Keurig is ready. I move to grab a coffee mug, then realize I already put one on the base. "Can I see that evidence, too?"

He takes another drink of beer. Condensation glistens on his fingertips like spit on Aaron's chin. "I can't be involved in the investigation, honey. He's my brother-in-law. The sheriff won't let me near it."

I'm supposed to agree. *All right. Thank you, honey. I love you, Hank.*

I say, "He was terrified of fires. Why would he start one?"

My husband shakes his head, silently disagreeing, or maybe silently lamenting what an idiot he married. "Eve," he says in *that* tone. It feels like I've disappointed a stern teacher. The fifteen-year age difference between us doesn't feel significant when things are good, but things often aren't good. "I've told you a thousand times. I saw this coming from miles away."

This is our oldest, most enduring conflict. It plays out at least four nights a week, beginning when Aaron texts me for dinner. Hank gets angry that I'm leaving again, neglecting us-time to care for "a junkie loser." Hank's words. They weigh in the zero space between us every time we repeat this fight.

I settle my hands on my necklace, a little diamond pendant on a gold chain. I've worn the setting smooth by fingering it too often. Aaron gave me that necklace. My throat aches, it's so tight. "However you feel about Aaron, we both know he was afraid of fire. There is no reason to think he was involved."

Hank's holding his breath like he does before showing his hand in blackjack. "They found his old pickup on the road by the VC Fire."

Now that's a surprise to me.

The fire's a good drive out of town. It started in Virginia City Highlands two days ago, in the middle of the night, and wind spread it across Moundhouse. There's no risk of it reaching Carson City, where we live. How would Aaron drive that far? The anxiety medicine he took after the fire made him fall asleep sitting up. He lost his driver's license nine months ago. The pickup hasn't gone anywhere since.

"You heard him talking about a manifesto on the video," Hank continues. "It's possible that Jobson prevented Aaron from committing a bigger act of violence. Sheriff Wilkes will put someone good on the case. We'll know the truth once they've found it."

"You're the sergeant. Can you pull some strings? Find out more about the arson investigation at least?"

Hank drains the beer bottle. "Seriously, Eve?"

I'm very serious. I'm filled up with it from my tingling toes to the swimming crown of my skull. "Remember the time we went to Davis Creek and he cried in the camper all night because of the campfire?"

"Yeah. A real chickenshit. It's hard to imagine Aaron getting his shit together to commit arson. But he *was* pissed at SE&G." He surveys me with suspicious eyes. "If I can pull a few strings, show you the proof that it was him, you'll move on?"

I massage my temples, seeking to relieve pressure that only builds. "Move on from my brother?"

His jaw's so tight that I think his teeth might shatter. "You'll *try?*"

*Junkie loser.*

"He's my *brother*, Hank." My mug is filled. The Keurig beeps again, prompting me to drink. I hold Hank's gaze, exposing what emotions I have to offer. There aren't many. I'm in shock.

Hank puts his empty drink into recycling, then lifts the bin to take to the garage. "Fine. Anything you want. As always. I'm your slave." Hank bends down to kiss my forehead, and when I lift my face, he kisses me on the lips. "I'm sorry, Eve. I love you."

I didn't know I needed to hear that. I brush my forehead against his shoulder, letting my eyes shut as I wait for the surge of emotions.

I should be grieving. Aaron is gone.

Yet the feelings won't come. My soul is holding its breath for something that will never happen. Hank walks out. He opens the garage door and the faint scent of smoke wafts into the kitchen. I crave a cigarette, but I drink the tea.

# CHAPTER 2
# EVE

Little has changed at my childhood home since my father walked out seventeen years ago. My parents' bedroom has the same wood paneling, and Aaron sleeps on the same sunken mattress my mom never replaced, set atop a brass bedframe from 1982. The bathroom counters are still pink. The refrigerator is green. The heart of the house has exposed brick walls offset by white carpet which is never clean.

The only difference is the laundry room.

It used to be painted white with white appliances. The tiles had been the same as in the kitchen, white linoleum interspersed by black diamonds. There was a narrow gap between the stacked washer/dryer and the wall, just big enough for Ronnie and me to hide. Ronnie was my best friend. We played every day in summer and after school the rest of the year. When it was too cold to disappear into the foothills, we whispered secrets behind dusty pipes and wires, shielded by the handle of Mom's mop.

That was where I saw someone die the first time.

Ronnie and I were going through a shoebox that had been hidden in the linen drawer. Dad's six-shooter was in that shoebox. I remember so many details about that day, but not the gunmaker's name engraved on the grip. I can recall the feel but not letters.

Later, they told me it's normal to forget parts of traumatic events. I don't think I'd remember any of it if I hadn't repeated the same story a thousand times. "We were playing," I said in therapy, to my school counselor, to police. "Ronnie was acting like Bugs Bunny. She pretended to shoot herself, and the gun went off."

I forgot much of the day, but I remember the blood.

When Ronnie's skull came apart, there was enough force to splatter blood on my shirt, my feet, the laundry room's white walls. With the knee-jerk judgment of a nine-year-old, I grabbed the gun to hide it. I knew we'd get in trouble if they discovered we were playing with it. But that got me bloodier still, and Ronnie wasn't getting up, and I realized I couldn't hide anything.

Mom found us because I was screaming.

Ronnie was the first person I saw die. That was the last gun I ever touched.

Dad left the same night.

My mother wallpapered the laundry room in gold and bought new appliances on credit that week.

* * *

Dad missed Ronnie's funeral. By the time that date arrived, he'd emptied his drawers, taken our cash, and left a note saying he wouldn't come back. He was going to start over across the country. There was no number, no address. He was just…gone.

Nobody was angrier about his disappearance than Ronnie's parents. Dad had been friends with her dad. His gun had killed her, and he never apologized for leaving it unsecured.

My mom used to tell me to forgive him. "Most people can't cope with that kind of guilt," she explained.

But I felt no forgiveness standing over Ronnie's casket alone while her parents wept.

Dad should have been there, but he wasn't, and it was all his fault.

If we'd had a funeral service for Mom, Dad wouldn't have been there either. Nobody in Mom's family wanted to hold a service for a woman who killed herself.

And Dad isn't at Aaron's funeral, either.

* * *

I stand with my husband and my other brother, Wyatt Ashe, beside a tombstone. We're shaded by a flimsy awning that flaps in the wind. Two of Aaron's former coworkers stand behind us, politely aloof now that we've exchanged condolences. The only other person in attendance is Johnny, a wiry guy in a black wife beater and tattered jeans. Hank's not grateful to see one of Aaron's addict friends around, but I am.

"From the dust we came, and to dust we return," says the priest.

The words are literal. I'm holding the box of Aaron's cremains against my chest. This whole human being—a once-competitive gamer, a clever wit, and my best friend— now fits into a square the size of our childhood portable TV.

"Let's have a moment of silence," says the priest.

Only Wyatt audibly sniffles. He rubs his hand in circles over my shoulders like I'm a cat present for his comfort. On my other side, Hank's hand cradles my elbow. He thinks that's what he should do to make his wife feel better. He's sent me flowers every day since I saw the video, too. He hasn't sent me flowers in years.

"It's time to inter his ashes," Hank tells me. He's not choked up. His mouth is pinched at the corners.

Wyatt lifts the lid off Aaron's box, and I pour the contents neatly into a hole in the ground. It's six feet deep but only a square foot across. A tiny oubliette. Aaron's world is getting all the smaller.

We pour.

He's gone.

* * *

It won't take much time to close a grave this small, so the cemetery staff packs the awning and promises to close the grave in an hour. I can stay to grieve until then. I'm the only one who wants to. I stand alone at the headstone while coworkers leave. Hank and Wyatt talk under a gnarled tree scraping its branches at an ashen sky. Half the town is covered in old cottonwoods, and the other half is brushy desert—the strange duality of living in a high desert tucked against the Sierra Nevada Mountains. Lone Mountain Cemetery is on the desert half. The only things growing around my husband and brother are foxtails.

My throat hurts from breathing the smoky air. Weather systems shifted over the Sierras, the VC Fire is funneling toward us, and the heaviness of the air makes it feel like Aaron's ashes have coated my skin. Hank and Wyatt's voices are distant, rendered incoherent by wind. There's nothing but me and these last scraps of my brother.

I've been waiting for the shock to wear off so that the grief can set in. Yet now I'm at Aaron's gravestone, looking at his name, his birthday, his picture engraved in gray scale, and I feel…nothing.

Wyatt appears silently behind me. "Hey, Evie." He stares into Aaron's grave, jaw clenched tight so that his cheekbones furrow to marionette lines. Unlike Aaron and me, Wyatt is an average healthy individual. He exceeds the FBI's fitness standards. It must be easy to take care of yourself when you don't have anyone else to worry about.

"What can we do about this?" I ask, tipping my head back to study my eldest brother.

"Aaron is beyond help," Wyatt says.

My French tips scrape his jacket when I grip the sleeve. "A deputy killed him. There has to be some justice."

Wyatt squeezes my hand. He's browner than me, thanks to sun exposure and different genetic expression. Otherwise, we look much the same. Same hazel eyes. Same blond hair.

His is clipped professionally short; mine falls straight to my shoulders. "I know what you're thinking," he says quietly enough that Hank won't be able to hear us. My husband is on his phone by the tree. "You can't get involved, Evie. Follow the rules, trust the process, and let the system work."

"You mean the system that killed Aaron? The system you're still working for?"

He rubs his puffy eyes and wipes a hand down his face. "His addiction isn't the system's fault. That's always rested squarely on Aaron's broad shoulders."

"Did you know half of people with severe mental illness fight substance abuse? Half of them, Wyatt. That's a coin flip, not culpability." But that's not the point. "He wasn't using again. I told you, Aaron was keeping up on appointments."

"You also told me that he was avoiding you last month. He wouldn't do that if he were clean. Grief gives the bereaved selective memories, but…at some point, you'll have to accept this is all Aaron. Accept it and move on." Wyatt kisses me on the forehead. "I have to go. Don't stay here too long. I'll call you later."

He waves to Hank before heading for the gates.

A young woman stands inside the fence, a few feet off the path from Wyatt. She's a curvy little thing. Whiter-skinned than I am, but darker-haired too. Underneath all the makeup, her face says teenager, but she's dressed in a tiny skirt I'd never let a daughter wear. She might be from one of Aaron's addiction groups. She's wearing enough eyeliner for it.

She's staring at me.

"Hey," I say, lifting a hand.

Her eyes go wide when I take a step in her direction. She bolts like a deer fleeing the bark of a dog. By the time I reach the gates, the woman is gone.

# CHAPTER 3
# HANK

From the first time I visited his house, Aaron hated me. He didn't meet my eyes when we talked. Snorted derisively after every sentence I spoke. Answered my questions monosyllabically. He spent more time looking at his computer screen than getting to know me.

On the second visit, I brought cards so we could play a few hands of twenty-one. It was an activity all three of us liked. It became a routine. We played a hundred games as the months wore on. "Lost again," I said, grinning at Aaron's cards. He'd reached twenty-three with a king on top of his nine and four. Busted. He always busted hitting too aggressively. "I don't think you know how to win at this."

Aaron gave me a flat look and shrugged. "I win enough."

He was even easier to beat at Hold'em because he got a stutter when he bluffed. "I'm g-going all in," he'd say, pushing in his chips while meeting my eye. It meant he had nothing. A pair, maybe. "Are y-you going to risk-k it?"

I always risked it. And I always won.

Couldn't tell you which day it was, or which game we were playing, but there was a time Aaron got sick of playing nice with me. A timer had gone off, and Eve stood from our blackjack table like an automaton. "I'll get your meds," she said.

"Took you long enough," Aaron growled. "I've only been hurting for an hour. My back is killing me!"

"You couldn't have more until now."

"But I'm hurting! The nurse said it's reasonable to hope for a pain score of zero."

"I know, and I'm sorry. You just can't have more than the doctor prescribed." Eve left the room.

"The doctor didn't prescribe enough!" he called, leaning back in bed so he could watch her go. "I'm tall so I need more! They never give me enough!"

She didn't reply. She had to open a locked safe in the spare bedroom to get his pills, which took her across the house, too far to hear his verbal abuse.

I was left sitting with Aaron alone. The man was ambulatory but didn't like getting out of bed. I almost never saw him standing unless he was heading to relieve his bladder after another seventy-two ounce Big Gulp of Mountain Dew. So we were playing cards on his bedside table.

I'll never forget what he said then. Aaron scowled at me, right? And he said, "You never defend Evie. I make demands, and you sit there quietly."

"It's not for me to get in between siblings," I said.

"So you'd let me do whatever to your girlfriend? What kind of man are you?" Aaron asked.

In that moment, I was an *angry* man. But more impor-
tantly… "I'm a Catholic man who fears God and loves
Evangeline Ashe. That means I love you like a brother.
Maybe I would defend Eve if I weren't trying to make
friends with you. I can't seem to win you over. Is it that
hard to get along with the guy your sister loves?"

"We're never going to be friends, *Hank*," he said, meeting
my gaze. Another first for the night. The whites of his eyes
were bloodshot, his pupils dilated.

When I got back to my apartment on Sunday night, I
discovered a hundred bucks missing from my wallet.
Turned out the asshole would be ambulatory to steal from
me, too.

Aaron relapsed the same day. One of a dozen relapses
while I was with Eve. It was the same every time—acting
weird, stealing money, buying drugs, going to the hospital.
Again and again. I wasn't upset after the first couple times.
I threw trash like Aaron in the back of my car for a ride
more shifts than not. I knew his type. Aaron Ashe was a
dead man walking all along.

* * *

It's a decent approximation of Aaron's ugly face on the
tombstone. He's looking up at me with a triple-chinned
smile. His lips are fat sausages. "Game over, bastard," I
whisper to his headstone. "Lost again. You shouldn't have
kept hitting."

My wife returns to the grave, squinting against a brassy
bar of sunlight. She's wearing a simple black dress that fits
her like a paper bag, and the diamond necklace hangs
from a slender neck. Her hair is pinned over her left ear

with a cheap black bow. Something else that Aaron
gave her.

"Where'd you go?" I ask.

She gestures to the fence with fragile fingers tipped by
white nails. "I thought I saw someone I knew."

"Who would *you* know?" Eve doesn't get out of the house
except to take care of Aaron and attend church.

"Nobody, I guess." She clutches the straps of her purse. It's
the same purse she always carries, some huge bag that
hangs to her waist. She stands close enough to Aaron's
headstone that her shoes overlap the edge, and she stares at
her brother's face.

He's dead, and he's the only thing she wants to see.

"I've gotta go, honey. The sheriff called me into work," I lie.
I've been trying to reach Sheriff Wilkes about the investigation on Aaron. Five calls and he hasn't answered. I'd
rather hunt him down than stand in the cemetery another
minute.

"Okay. I understand." Her stiff nod is bird-like. "I'll run
errands."

That's the same quiet, velvety tone she always uses. Eve has
one purse for every occasion, and one emotion for every
occasion. I haven't seen her shed a single tear for Aaron. I
wish she would. I can understand grief. I grieved when my
father died; I grieved when my mother turned into a shell
of herself; I grieved the loss of the family I once knew. But
not Eve. That's not her style.

"You want me to take the afternoon?" I ask. "Stay with
you?"

She shakes her head. "Thank you, Hank. You're so good to me." I *am* good to her. So much better than her brother ever was. "But I'd rather you go to work and see what else you can find out."

"I'll have something to show you tonight," I promise.

Eve isn't looking away from the headstone.

"Evidence," I say. "About Aaron. If you still want to know everything."

"I do." She kneels, kisses her fingers, and presses them to Aaron's face on the headstone.

Our hands link as we walk to the parking lot. Eve brushes a kiss over my cheek. It smells minty, like gum, rather than the toxic tobacco kisses I used to get. And when she leaves, she still hasn't cried. She's just like Aaron in so many ways. She's already lost, a chance for victory long gone, and she won't even get upset about it.

* * *

Living in Carson City is all right. It's less urban than Reno and feels like a proper small town, even with the highway bypass. You can walk just about anywhere. Lone Mountain Cemetery is near enough to the Sheriff's Office that you could probably hit a baseball from one to break a window at the other. The road clears for a patrol car even with its lights off, which makes it a quicker drive yet. I've got a couple twisty blocks past by-the-week motels, a cramped little library, and a few Victorians, and I'm there.

The Carson City Sheriff's Office is in quiet chaos when I arrive. The patrol deputies are clustered in a whispering group, and Gina's crying at the front desk. For the first time, I consider the possibility Wilkes hasn't been ignoring my phone calls. "What's going on?" I ask Gina.

She grabs another tissue. "Wilkes retired." Gina honks into her Kleenex.

"Retired?" He's getting up there in years. He won't run for another term, but the election isn't until next year.

"He stepped down," she says so quietly that she's practically mouthing the words.

"Is he all right? Did he get hurt?" Wilkes is a sixty-something cowboy with a penchant for fixing roofs, digging trenches, and hauling rocks around his property for fun on the weekends. He won't cancel lunch plans, much less the final year of his career.

"No, he's not injured. I know that much, thank God." She crosses herself. Gina goes to my church, St. Teresa of Avila, and she relishes the gesture. "I can't believe Sheriff Wilkes would go like this unless something's wrong. I'm going to pray for him, Sergeant Everhardt. Would you join me?"

I take her hand to say a few words, our heads bowed, hearts with God. "Lord, we ask for your blessing. May Sheriff Wilkes be in good health, with peace in heart and mind, from this day forward and each that follows. Amen."

"Amen," she says fiercely, squeezing my fingers.

Casually, I ask, "Is Bregan in today?" She's a younger secretary, fresh out of Western Nevada College. Bregan has a perfect recall for conversations and such light feet you never know she's listening in. Wilkes jokes we should put a cowbell on her. If anyone knows what happened, it's Bregan.

"Oh no, the fire's getting down toward her house," Gina says. "Bregan's got to relocate the horses."

"Is she in the Highlands?"

"Moundhouse. They're evacuating now, too."

I blow a whistle through my teeth. That's a lot of land for a wildfire to cover, but with the wind whipping the trees halfway to the ground outside the window, I'm not surprised. "Hope Bregan can get out."

"Her mom's got a ranch in Minden," Gina says. "Bregan will be fine if she can get down there. I don't know where everyone else in Moundhouse will go."

"The Emergency Management Division's got it in hand." Their plan for the evacuation sits in my inbox. We've got half the patrol division doing door-to-door checks. Aaron couldn't have died during a less convenient week. "Where's your house, Gina? Are you safe?"

"Oh, I'm in town, right by the old hospital. Not far from Deputy Jobson in fact." She smiles at me with wrinkled eyes. I think she's forgotten that Jobson's out of the office, and it's my brother-in-law's fault. "You don't think the fire's going to come this way, do you?"

"Not a chance."

"That's a relief. I don't know what I'd do if I had to go to one of those SE&G evacuation centers. Have you seen them?"

They're parking lots with generators and Port-a-Potties. "You don't need to worry, Gina. The fire's not coming this way. Sit tight and think good thoughts. The Lord's got a plan."

I leave her smiling, rolling a rosary in her fingers.

Raising morale among my division isn't going to be as easy. Wildfire season gets harder every year. The deputies who haven't rolled out yet are clustered in the locker room for some girly-talk gossip, and we don't have the bodies for this kind of bullshit.

"Gentlemen," I say, approaching them. "At least half of you were meant to leave for Moundhouse twenty minutes ago."

It's enough to make most scatter, grabbing belts, hats, and service pistols heading out the door. Vasquez and Dresden linger. "Sir," says Vasquez. He's a short Black guy with a shaved head and dim eyes.

"You two don't look ready for your beat." I made their schedules; I know they're due on traffic patrol in twenty minutes.

"We're going." Vasquez lowers his voice. "Do you know anything about Wilkes?"

"It's so sudden." Dresden's as white as they come, the wholesome football-player type. He never swears. His world is so simple, I wouldn't be surprised to hear him say "aw shucks." Dresden is genuinely shaken by the news about Wilkes.

"Cuttino already took his office," Vasquez adds. "Dumped all of Wilkes's stuff in a box. He just put it out in the hall."

"This isn't like a divorce where you gotta wait a while before dating again, boys." I offer them a smile and jostle Dresden with an elbow. They laugh. It's not hard to make these two laugh. They're barely older than Bregan and probably shave twice a week, using washcloths. The new hires get younger every year. "Cuttino's gotta get everything under control, stat."

"What's this mean for Jobson?" asks Dresden.

"Hey," Vasquez mutters warningly.

I lift my hands in a calming gesture. "Jobson's one of us. I'll make sure he doesn't fall through the cracks."

"I'm not worried about the cracks," Dresden says. "I'm worried about Cuttino's claws."

"I'll handle Cuttino too." I tap my watch. "But we've got to keep things moving. It's fire season, after all. Fire isn't gonna wait for you girlies to get done gossiping."

"If you learn anything…" Dresden lets it trail off, an implicit question.

"I'll tell you about it at Jimmy G's tonight." It's the local bar where the deputies congregate after work. I don't always go. My guys need to unwind and talk without the sergeant listening. But stress is high, so I need to get hands-on. "Now get out there and do the job."

I skip the locker room to don my uniform in my office. I've got a door that locks, blinds for privacy, and a view of the parking lot. Not bad for a guy who only transferred five years ago. I put in hard work to become sergeant—work that would have been harder without Wilkes supporting me. The deputies aren't the only ones shaken. I can't imagine a day that doesn't start with coffee at Wilkes's desk.

A knock sounds at my door.

"A moment," I call, buttoning my shirt and straightening the line so it matches my fly.

Cuttino stands outside my door. His face reminds me of the coyotes that stroll through my yard first thing in the morning.

"Can I come in?" he asks.

He's already inside.

Cuttino looks around my office with interest, surveying my Master's in Criminal Justice hung on the wall, the Bible on my shelf, the photo of Eve. He's never been in here before. We haven't had many interactions. When Wilkes took me under his wing, he buffered me from middle management. *Too much bureaucracy is bad for you,* Wilkes liked to joke.

"I tried to visit earlier." Cuttino traces the crucifix stamped on my Bible's spine. "You weren't in."

"My brother-in-law's funeral was today."

I don't want the poison of Aaron's name on my lips, but I don't have to say it for Cuttino's glass-shard eyes to go sharper. He knows whose fault it is that Deputy Jobson isn't in the office this week.

"Ugly business," Cuttino says. "Wilkes, that is. Leaving like this."

"I understand you're acting sheriff. Thank you for stepping up, sir."

We exchange a handshake. Cuttino grips as hard as I do, then squeezes harder. "It was a shock, but I'm not a man to back down from a challenge," says the undersheriff. "I understand you're close to Wilkes. I thought you'd already know all about his retirement."

"It's a surprise to me as much as anyone."

He releases my hand and smiles broadly. "The deputies seem shaken to see me. I don't think I'm popular."

"A lot of them were here during the Peters case." That had been an internal investigation into the last sergeant of the patrol division. Cuttino had nailed Peters for stealing money out of evidence. And that had sealed the reputation that made Cuttino's name a swear word among the deputies. "It was before my time, and as far as I'm concerned, the past is the past."

"You must have heard about it, though."

It comes up at Jimmy G's constantly. Takes a few beers to get there. But once the older deputies start talking, I hear plenty. "Locker room talk," I say. "I heard he stole to pay medical debts."

Cuttino sits on the edge of my desk. "Sergeant Peters was embezzling. He spent the money in Moundhouse." He means hookers. Prostitution is legal on the other side of the county line. "I don't begrudge a man his vices, Everhardt. Boys are gonna be boys. You know how it is."

"Sure do," I say.

"The DA agreed not to prosecute the embezzlement if Peters left. If Peters had gone to court, more than petty theft and hookers would have popped up—the kind of stuff that gets a guy in jail a long time. So instead, I got him fired." He spreads his hands wide, a gesture of helplessness. "I can't clear my name with the deputies without tainting his." He keeps smiling while he says it. *I'm a good guy, Ever-*

*hardt,* that smile says. *Boys will be boys, and I'm just keeping the peace.*

"Sounds like Peters was lucky to have you on the investigation."

"I'm a lucky guy to have around." Cuttino's mouth looks empty, as if he should have a cigar butt crushed between his molars. "Do you understand the situation now?"

"It seems I do, sir," I say. At least, I've got a better understanding of Cuttino.

"Could I have done anything else?" he asks.

I know better than to criticize. "I'm not sure why you're seeking my advice on something that happened before I started working here."

"It's important that we get on the same page. I've followed your career, Everhardt. You keep the patrol division running like nobody else I've seen. Where you go, the other deputies follow. I'm running for sheriff, and your support would mean a lot to me."

In my experience, a man is on his best behavior the first time you meet him. They'll always show strangers the mask they've chosen instead of their inner self. This is the best Cuttino has. Moving through my office like it belongs to him. Talking about the secrets he kept for Peters. I don't have to guess why Wilkes kept this guy away from day-to-day operations, or why this kind of blunt glad-handing might be useful in the undersheriff's job.

The guy's a tool, but every tool has a use. Cuttino is now in charge of the investigation against Jobson. He holds the key to Aaron's case.

"You've got my support, sir," I say.

We shake hands again. Cuttino's hand isn't as tight this time.

He takes the photo from my desk. "This your wife? Sister to the guy Jobson tried to arrest?"

"Yes, sir."

"Beautiful girl. Doesn't look much like her brother. You ever heard that old Mother Goose rhyme? Jack Sprat could eat no fat, his wife could eat no lean..."

"And between the two of them, they licked the platter clean." My father used to read that one to me. It's the perfect description of Eve and Aaron. "Look, I just want to say how sorry I am for the way things fell out with my brother-in-law. Jobson doesn't deserve to catch flack for it. The arrest was by the books."

Cuttino's eyes cut right into me. "You saw the body camera footage?"

I wasn't supposed to. It hasn't been released to the public, but Wilkes let me copy the file. "Sir," I begin.

"I don't blame you. If something happened in my family, I'd be curious too." His thumb slides over Eve's face in the photo. He traces across her brow, down the bridge of her nose.

Something hot flops angrily in my gut. "My wife's having a hard time coming to terms. She's denying the fact Aaron was capable of any crime."

"Was he capable?"

"Oh yeah, but Eve won't hear it. I only wish she could see everything I've seen—maybe she'd stop treating her brother like the fucked-up saint of heroin, you know?"

Cuttino sets the picture frame down. "Death makes everyone a saint. A girl like that couldn't handle the truth. Most people can't. That's why we're here, Everhardt. Men like us fight the true darkness in the seedy underbelly of humanity so that our wives and daughters can stay naive." He pushes off my desk, straightening his jacket. "I'm gonna need a new undersheriff once I'm elected. Someone good with the patrol division. Someone who can build relationships with corrections and administration the way you have with your guys. Are you interested?"

"I'm interested."

"If your wife's too distracting, I can get someone else," he says playfully. He means it, though.

"I can handle the job and my wife."

"Glad to hear it." Cuttino slices back to my door, bumping my chair aside with his knee so he can walk a straight line. "I can promise you this. I've seen the police report filed against Ashe. I've talked with Don DeVos." He's the CEO of SE&G. "You won't have to wait long for your wife to see the truth about her brother. Plenty is going to come out. *Plenty.*"

# CHAPTER 4
# EVE

After Aaron's funeral, I'm on autopilot. I've done weekly grocery shopping at the same Smith's since I was eighteen years old. I can get our staples blindfolded. Single serving baggies of mozzarella cheese. A squash in a netted bag. Jugs of bone broth with necks linked by plastic ligatures. Only when I approach the registers do I realize there's too much. Neither Hank nor I eat Doritos, but I've placed five family-sized bags underneath the cart next to a case of Mountain Dew bottles that nobody will drink.

An employee helps me put the wrong items back on the shelf. His pimpled teenage face displays annoyance, so I tell him, "My brother liked to have this before he died. I forgot he doesn't need it anymore." After that, the employee looks alarmed. He finishes quickly and flees, afraid I'll start crying.

Without Aaron's shopping, there's room in the cart, room in my life, a gaping void in my belly. I fill it with konjac noodles, a carb-free pasta alternative, jars of pickles for the juice, and sugar-free energy drinks. Everything I love.

I even stop by the pharmacy to request ephedrine from the pharmacist, feigning a cough so I look asthmatic. They scan my driver's license to see how often I buy Bronk-Aid, my favorite source of ephedrine. The database shows I buy it monthly. I cough harder into my fist, giving the pharmacist calf-eyes.

"The smoke is terrible," he says sympathetically.

"So terrible," I agree.

Once I've put the groceries away at home, when I'm halfway through a can of white Monster, my phone chimes. I've received a Snapchat. There are only two contacts in it. The first is Aaron's, his icon a Bitmoji that fails to capture the radiance of his smile. The other contact is only named G, and he has no icon.

G has sent me a message. "I'm at the clinic."

I finish the energy drink, crush the can, and put it at the bottom of the trash bin before getting in my car. Self-care is the buzz of caffeine and ephedrine in my veins silencing the grinding of a hollow stomach. It's the jangling wash of dopamine that follows me onto the road. It's pulling my car's sun shade around so that I don't have to see the red-black wall of smoke on the northeast side of town.

I'm on my way to meet Aaron's psychiatrist, and my life feels briefly normal.

* * *

It's been difficult to maintain Aaron's consistency of care for the last decade. There are few psychiatrists in the region, and they're based an hour's drive north in Reno. Those who take Medicaid change yearly. My brother was a complicated case with frequent residential stays and constantly shifting medications. We were often "fired" by psychiatrists who didn't want the workload. Medicaid simply didn't pay enough to make it worthwhile.

One stalwart psychiatrist helped Aaron get his first job. My brother became an electrician for SE&G, and in return, was given health insurance superior to Medicaid. Without Medicaid, Aaron had to change care providers again. Replacing her was as difficult as always. Better insurance meant more options, but Nevada is filled with the crazy, the addicted, the suffering. Between rich and poor patients, an army of psychiatrists would still never have an empty office.

But I'm a white woman with money. I'm rarely refused when I'm insistent. People are charmed by the shine of my blond hair, my slender figure, the smile I've practiced. I gathered my binder of Aaron's medical history, put on a nice dress, and visited the offices of the top three psychiatrists in the region to plead my case.

The first two offered to take us, but only in six months, at which point Aaron's prescriptions would have long since lapsed.

Garrett Glass was the third.

Three years ago, Dr. Glass was newly out of his residency, young and smart. He was sympathetic to my brother's trouble. He took his fifteen-minute lunch to study Aaron's file as I sat before him, unwilling to leave without an answer.

Garrett fit Aaron in that night.

He fit Aaron in on a lot of nights, even on days off. He adjusted prescriptions at a moment's notice. He met us at every hospital where Aaron stayed. And because of that, Aaron's hospital stays were fewer. He invested hundreds of hours into my brother and accepted whatever pittance insurance would refund, plus our copays. Garrett told me over coffee one night that he found Aaron's challenges stimulating. This was the work that made psychiatry worthwhile, not the money.

Aaron got better day by day. After he repaid a credit card, he took me to dinner at Applebee's and gave me the diamond necklace with a bouquet of lilies and three mylar balloons. Aaron was proud of himself. Finally, he could treat me. It felt like happily ever after.

My life had always been closest to normal with Garrett Glass.

* * *

I peer through the window of a meeting room at the clinic to see him. Garrett's younger than Hank and has more hair, a thick wave that falls over his forehead. His eyes are a sympathetic brown. He talks using his hands, pacing as he lectures residents. Garrett's eyes light when he spots me watching through the door. His hands pause with his words. Then he's checking his watch, gathering his papers, and the residents stand. Garrett has ended the meeting. I stand aside so everyone can exit.

Garrett holds the door open for me when the last resident is gone. "Evangeline." He's the only one who calls me by my full first name. I don't hate it when he says it. "I'm so glad you made it. Come in?"

I step inside and Garrett locks the door. He closes the blinds. He doesn't have an office at the clinic, so we're borrowing a group therapy room filled with couches and potted plants. A white noise machine sighs by the door. It's a comfortable space, but I don't want to sit for fear that something inside of me will snap. "You weren't at his funeral," I say.

Garrett takes in my black dress, my dusty shoes, my hands tight on the strap of my purse. "I'm sorry. I didn't realize that was today."

"You didn't realize?"

"It's not as though I could go. Did you want Hank to see us together?"

I don't want Hank to see Garrett, period. My husband reads people as easily as I read nutrition labels. There's no doubt he'll see Garrett and know, immediately, that he's not just Aaron's doctor.

"I'm sorry," Garrett says again. His hands skim over my upper arms, grazing fine hairs that lift at his presence. My skin pebbles from the scent of his cologne. "How are you feeling?"

"How the fuck do you *think* I feel?" I don't have to hide my anger with Garrett. He absorbs it, lets it sink into the earth. The world doesn't shatter the way it does with Hank. "I buried my..." My fingers are cold on my feverish forehead. My voice has stopped working.

Aaron is in that hard, dry ground. I'm going to fall in after him.

"Let me drive you home," Garrett says.

I push him away. "No. I'm fine." I'm still not crying. What-ever emotion had clenched my brittle body is gone. "Why did you want me to come?"

"I've been thinking about you. I wanted to see you."

"I wanted to see you too," I say. "How was Aaron at your appointments in the last month? Was he acting erratic? Agitated?"

I'm not as adept at reading people as Hank, but I catch the disappointment in Garrett's eyes. This isn't why he wants to talk. "Aaron specifically asked me not to tell you anything."

"Yeah, well, he's dead." I want the words to land like a slap. He flinches. "They're going to announce that Aaron started the VC Fire before he died. SE&G claim he's the reason Virginia City Highlands is gone, along with half of Moundhouse."

Garrett blows a breath out of his lips. "Aaron? Starting a fire?"

"I know. It's ridiculous."

A fire had disabled Aaron while working for SE&G. Old power lines sparked in a remote region where it could take ages for emergency response. But my Aaron, dear sweet Aaron, hadn't followed SE&G dispatch's instructions to evacuate. He had grabbed a fire extinguisher and jumped in. The forest was dry. The fire spread quickly. His hands melted in it.

No longer capable of being an electrician, and suffering constant pain that could only be quieted by the same drug he abused, Aaron had done more than relapse. PTSD had consumed him. Any hint of fire sent him into a panic attack. One time, he cried when he walked into the kitchen to see the gas stove turned on. Of course he relapsed. But it had only taken one overdose to get Aaron back on track to recovery, and he'd been clean for months.

"I don't think Aaron was capable of arson," Garrett says carefully.

"Right." There's no question of that. "What was he talking about in therapy last month?"

Garrett steps back into a pool of hazy sunlight, away from me. "The search for more information is a search for control you can't have. If Aaron started the fire... The police will find out. Wait for justice."

"Justice killed my brother."

Garrett visibly debates with himself. He checks his watch again. Then he gestures for me to sit on the couch, but I get no comfort from the way my bones sink into fake leather. "His mood had been rapid-cycling. His behaviors deteriorated while his diagnostics got better. Aaron was masking symptoms."

"He was using. Wasn't he?" I ask.

Reluctantly, he nods.

It used to feel like betrayal every time Aaron got on heroin again. Even that can't shake me now. I'm hollower than a hole dug six feet deep.

"I threatened to tell you about his substance abuse if he didn't work with me," Garrett says. "Aaron didn't want that. He opened up, told me SE&G was starting fires deliberately. They knew he knew, so they were monitoring him, online and off-line. He saw black cars around the house all the time." Garrett's laugh is one of sympathetic disbelief, expecting that I will find the claims ridiculous too. "Those are common paranoid delusions."

"Are you paranoid if they're out to get you?" It's a common joke around psych wards, but I'm not kidding this time.

Garrett looks pained. "Aaron wouldn't have started a fire in his right mind, but he wasn't in his right mind. Maybe he was trying to frame SE&G. I know that sounds far-fetched, but Aaron kept telling me about making a treasure hunt so that the FBI could destroy Don DeVos."

"A treasure hunt? He used those words specifically?"

"Yeah, does that mean something to you?"

"No, it just seems odd. I saw Deputy Jobson's body camera footage from the arrest. Part of it, anyway. They say it shows Aaron attacking the deputy, but the clip—"

"Did Hank show you that?" I like the spark of emotion Garrett shows when my husband comes up. "No wonder you're struggling." He won't accuse Hank of being abusive again, not after the way I reacted last time, but the accusation is etched in his features.

"I wanted to see the video. I asked for it. I can't trust the police to find out what really happened, so I'm going to find the whole story."

Garrett's shoulders are knotted under his Oxford. "Obsessing can be about more than a search for control," he says. "It can be self-harm. How many times have you watched the video where Aaron dies?" He won't like the answer, so I keep it to myself. "God, you can't fall down this hole. Nothing at the bottom will give you peace."

I don't want peace. I lost every chance of peace when Ronnie died in my mom's laundry room. What I want is for people to see what I saw in Aaron. Not someone turned into a monster by addiction and poor brain chemistry. Someone with the kindest smile, the softest hugs, and the loudest laugh. "I'm going to leave. I have to be home before Hank."

When I stand, Garrett takes my wrist gently. He pulls me back to the couch. "I'm worried about you, Evangeline. I called you here to talk about what comes next for us."

The idea of an "us" makes my stomach ache harder.

Our affair hasn't lasted long. The closeness, the talking, the soft touches... That's been happening for a while. But we only had sex the night that Aaron died. While Aaron was being electrocuted and choked to death, I was riding Garrett on his kitchen floor, looking for ecstasy that wouldn't come.

"They approved my grants," Garrett says. "I'm going to be able to build my psychiatric hospital here in Carson City. So I'm moving to town. I've got a house up at the top of King Street. I know you love that canyon."

When I was small, Ronnie and I used to walk the long miles up King Street to the trail at the top. It overlooks a sweeping valley with a brook, perfect for making grass boats and sending them sailing. We took naps in the groves sometimes. Higher, there's a waterfall where it's always cool, even on the hottest days. I still jog on that trail sometimes. Hank often comes along. I can't slip away without getting caught.

"I can't hide an affair when you're in town," I say.

"I'm not asking for it to stay an affair," Garrett says. His gentle hands want to draw me near. He's asking me to fold against him, soft as my angles can manage.

I walk away, smoothing my dress over the ridges of my hips and my belly flab. I tug the hem to hide my jiggling thighs. "I've told you I won't leave Hank. The other night was a mistake."

"A real mistake would be spending another day with a man who hurts you." Garrett captures one hand in both of his. He's much warmer than I am, his skin more tanned, his palms soft. "You can have a life after this. Whatever you need, I can give it to you."

How can he know what I need? I don't know what I need.

I let Garrett kiss me. It's chaste. He's so respectful of my grief, but he takes his time with it. He uses the opportunity to brush my hair over my shoulders. His lips trace the lines of mine. I cringe when his hands find their way to my waist, knowing he will feel the meat underneath.

I don't look at him before walking out the door. I've put him out of my mind before I put the keys in my ignition. I drive an SUV, big and sturdy and insulated from the outside world, and I can barely smell the smoke with the vents closed. The windshield is dusted with ash. I flick the lever to wipe it off, clearing away the detritus, preparing for an evening with my husband.

# CHAPTER 5
# EVE

Hank never touches me gently. He never has. He is masculinity to his core, solid rock, and men like him only interface with the world with gestures which reinforce that strength. His lips are possessive, not exploring. His words of love are growled but never whispered. More than once, he's tattooed temporary handprints upon the fragile skin of my backside in the throes of passion, and he takes pride in them.

Before Hank, I had not seen the purpose in fucking men. But Hank made me aware of my body as nobody else had. He coveted me. Obsessed over me. He treated the possession of my flesh as a victory to be paraded in front of his friends, coworkers, and family.

Hank made me into something valuable.

There was other value to being desired by Hank. He wasn't like the people in my family, unable to maintain a job longer than six months. He had a career. Promotions. Benefits. *Health insurance,* for fuck's sake.

He proposed to me at a golf course. We were having champagne brunch, even though neither of us likes champagne. I ate a few pieces of melon and batted my eyes at him. He pulled a ring out of his pocket and kneeled.

"I'll always take care of you, Eve," Hank said. "If you'll want to take care of me too. Husband and wife. Marry me?" His nervousness turned his rehearsed speech choppy. Hank seemed afraid I would say no, and he didn't even fear losing at poker.

This big manly-man with the money was afraid of losing *me*. Aaron's sister. The dirty, feral child who spent half her childhood in the foothills. Someone ugly and poor and worthless until the moment I met Officer Everhardt outside the hospital.

Hank made me want to believe it was divine providence.

So I had said yes. We got married. Sometimes we even keep our promise to take care of each other.

* * *

I'm not just with Hank for the money.

There are plenty of ways to earn money. I'm not good at any of them. Try holding down a job when you run to your brother's care at every random hour. Try living off the money your mom's life insurance gave you after her death. Try paying for property taxes in West Carson City and groceries for a four-hundred-pound man using nothing more than that man's disability check.

Society doesn't make room for people who are always sick and the people who take care of them.

What I can do is look pretty and make dinner and say thank you to a man who takes care of me. That's all men like Hank want from a wife. They're willing to pay for it with half of their assets.

So yes, money is a factor. You might even call it the deciding factor that took me from a hesitant "maybe" to a firm "yes." But I wouldn't have considered it if I hadn't already loved the way Hank needed me and my body. His big hands make my waist look tiny. He sees me as a prize, and until Hank, nobody saw me as anything at all.

I love Hank. I just need to be clear about that.

The conversation with Garrett didn't take up as much time as the drive there and back. When I return, it's too late to prepare an elaborate dinner for Hank. I put ingredients into the Instant Pot, press the button, and pour a shot glass of pickle juice. A sip quiets the grumbling in my gut again. I nurse the remainder while sitting in our home office. The flash drive Hank used to transfer the footage is gone, but I copied the file to my documents.

I watch Aaron die again and again.

The entire video, from Jobson's arrival to Aaron's death, is only seventeen minutes long. Carson City Sheriff's Deputies are meant to leave their cameras recording for the entire patrol. It's a recent policy change. Wilkes pushed hard for it after Reno Police Department were accused of racialized violence last year, and all of Hank's deputies should comply. Yet by the time the video begins, Jobson is yelling at Aaron through a window on the trailer. He must have been there for several minutes.

Most of Jobson and Aaron's interactions happen through that window. Jobson says he's responding to a complaint and needs to talk to Aaron. Aaron replies with nonsense. He mentions a manifesto a couple of times, along with other paranoid ramblings that seem to align with Garrett's claims.

When he comes to the door, unresponsive to commands, Jobson shoots him with the Taser.

*Snap-sizzle.*

Aaron falls again.

He rises, he lunges, but there's no telling if he attacks Jobson. The footage during their struggle is too dark to tell. Obviously they were in close physical contact for that time. Long enough for Jobson to get the upper hand, hook his arm around Aaron's throat, and hold tight.

I skip back in the video.

*Ten twenty-seven. Mack. The manifesto.*

"A treasure hunt," I mused aloud. How strange it felt to hear those exact words from Garrett.

Aaron's hospitalizations hit me hard in my childhood. We shared a bedroom, and I relied on his presence to quiet my anxieties and fall asleep. I went crazy when Aaron left. Instead of sleeping, I crawled under the bed and punched myself in the face, crying until my mom found me. I'd go to school as a zombie, passing out on my desk.

So my brother started finding ways to keep my mind busy when he was hospitalized. Aaron loved numbers and codes, like in the Myst video games, so he concocted puzzles I could solve when my emotions got messy. My emotions were very messy, so Aaron's puzzles got elaborate. Sometimes it took an entire week to find the clues and piece them together.

He called them treasure hunts.

Obsessing about his puzzles meant I didn't see Ronnie's dead body whenever I closed my eyes. It felt like Aaron was sitting with me, keeping me safe, even on the longest nights.

I'm still not as good with numbers as Aaron, but I'm good at understanding his thought process. Those four digits he said, ten twenty-seven, might be part of a cipher. It's a short string, though. I never would have suspected they had meaning if Garrett hadn't also mentioned a treasure hunt.

*Has he left me one more?*

The last time I watch the video, I let it run to its frustrating conclusion. The final shot is a blurry frame of Jobson standing over Aaron. The camera is tilted, gone askew from the struggle. It points at the trailer.

I squint at the screen and lean in close. There's a figure in the doorway. Someone is standing on the steps where Aaron fell. "Who are you?" I mutter. I play the last couple seconds again, but the figure is only visible for the last three frames of video. The first of them is clearest. It looks like someone short and dark-haired.

Hank told me that Aaron had been alone at that trailer. There were no witnesses but Jobson.

Yet I seem to be looking at a witness right now.

*Ten twenty-seven. Mack. The manifesto.*

I take a picture of the last frame with my phone. Then I grab my purse and head downstairs.

I've been so enraptured by the video that I hadn't heard the Instant Pot beeping. I also didn't hear the front door open. But an hour has elapsed, and Hank is standing at the bottom of the stairs, hanging his hat on a hook, brushing ash off his shoulders. "I got you a present," he says. Hank's a tall man, though not as tall as Aaron, and he seems to block the stairs with his body.

I stop a few steps above him. "A present? Why?"

"Just thought you seemed like you needed a pick-me-up." He offers a blue-velvet box.

Inside, there's a necklace with a dainty bejeweled butterfly charm. It's lovely. It's silver. It won't match the necklace Aaron gave me. "Thank you," I say. "I made dinner. It's in the pot."

"Aren't you going to try the necklace on?" Hank asks.

My chilly fingertips are no good with tiny clasps. I slide the box shut. "Did you talk to Sheriff Wilkes about Aaron?"

Hank takes a step back, and that's just enough room for me to get downstairs. He is a full six inches taller than I am, and he outweighs me by a hundred pounds. "You're welcome for the necklace," he says with a caustic edge. "I try to do something nice for you—"

"Aaron," I interrupt.

"Wilkes retired."

"Suddenly? Just like that?"

"Nobody's more surprised than I am," Hank said.

"Then how will you find out about Aaron's cases?" I put the necklace in my purse. Hank's gaze tracks it, and his face screws up smaller once it's gone.

"I'm working on it," he says.

"So you don't have anything new," I say.

"I will."

"Dinner is in the pot," I say again. "It's your favorite. I used linguica." I slide my feet into ballet flats, worn well enough to conform to the shape of my toes. I'll have to throw them out when I come home. I have another five pairs like them.

"Where are you going?" Hank doesn't wait for an answer. He unbuttons his shirt as he says, "You can't go to Aaron's house yet. The police still haven't had time to search it for SE&G's property, and it's closed until we've got the manpower."

"When will that be?"

"Who knows? End of fire season?"

With the way Nevada has been burning lately, it could be months. "I'm not going to Aaron's house."

"Then where? What in the goddamn world could be worth going out now, in this smoke, when I just got home?" He follows me out the front door, leaving it hanging open behind us. The air is so thick that I can taste campfire. It's still easier for me to breathe there than standing close to Hank. "You've left me to eat enough dinners alone, Eve. Come sit with me. I've missed you."

His words prickle over me like brambles. I have no desire to eat linguica, and I'm not going to sit at our kitchen table thinking about Aaron's treasure hunt. "I need time to clear my head. I have to grieve."

When I reach for my car door, Hank puts his hand on the top to close it. "You're not grieving," he says too quietly for neighbors to overhear. "We both know that you don't have those kinds of feelings."

"What kind of monster do you think I am, that I wouldn't need time to cope with losing my brother?"

"You're the kind of monster who'd rather brood over a dead guy than thank her husband for spoiling her," Hank says. "You're spoiled, Eve, and you haven't even asked how my day was."

"It can't have been good." The outcome wasn't good for me.

"It was terrible. We have to move evacuees from Mound-house into an emergency shelter at the old K-Mart. We'll have to keep those people safe for God knows how long. My deputies hate the new boss. Wilkes isn't answering my calls. Do you even care?"

"Of course I care." But that's Hank's life, distant from mine. He never helped me care for Aaron. I never tangled with the sheriff's office.

"Then show it," Hank says. "You live in my house, sleep in my bed, eat my food... All I'm asking for is dinner."

"There will be dinners. So many dinners." I rest my hand upon Hank's wrist, offering a gesture of physical intimacy. It's enough that he softens. "Soon, we're going to have dinner together every night. We'll have every weekend together. Maybe we can take a vacation." I've never taken a vacation.

He looks mollified until I open the car door and slide behind the wheel. I start the engine. He has too much dignity to try to wrench the door open and pull me out, but he bends down to look in the window.

"You can't go to Aaron's house," he says. "This isn't something you can blast through by willpower. If you screw this up by going all *Eve* about it..."

"I won't mess anything up for Aaron's investigation. You can trust me about that."

He draws away. There's enough smoke in the air that my husband becomes a silhouette under the streetlight before I reach the end of the block. When I turn the corner, I can't even tell if he's still standing there.

I don't park outside Aaron's house. There's a GPS device in the car, and my phone's tracker is activated. Hank might check to see if I'm interfering with his idea of a proper investigation.

Instead, I leave my SUV three blocks away at Sunset Park where I used to play with Aaron and Wyatt. It's not much of a park. It only has a couple of swings, a bridge that wobbles when you walk on it, and a table under a tree. There used to be a merry-go-round, but they took it out when Ronnie flew off and broke her arm. Most of my memories are from my adolescence when Sunset Park was my favorite late night smoking spot.

Sitting at the park on a hazy night imparts a sense of surreality. This is a dream of my youth, painted in nightmarish hues of orange sodium lights and the pinpricks of lanterns.

The tree's shadows are deep, stretching fingers toward my car. Not for the first time, I wish I had a cigarette. I purse my lips, put my fingers against my mouth, inhale the campfire scent of the air. With all the caffeine I'm drinking, I almost feel the nicotine rush.

I disable my phone's Bluetooth and Wi-Fi, turn the device off, and lock it in my glovebox before setting out.

The nights are getting crisp. Smoke holds the cool air close to my skin as I circle the block to reach Aaron's house, passing a thousand memories on the loop. The gated house with the cannon in its front yard, the fence where a neighbor's dog used to stick his head out to greet us, the local middle school. There have been changes to the neighborhood since I was a child, but in the darkness, it all looks the same to me.

The Ashe house is at the end of Donne Avenue—a dead end where overgrown trees hide the "No Outlet" sign. It faces a half-acre lot with a garden and centuries-old tree. The quail are sleeping. Every house on the street has already gone lights-out.

I haven't taken care of the house in a month, so the foxtails have gone wild. What used to be Dad's prided grass lawn is now harsh yellow jags that reach for my knees when I slip through a rusted gate. Rose bushes have escaped the wires binding them to the fence. Ivy sprawls halfway across the yard, and widow webs stretched between the leaves shine in the streetlights.

My key enters the lock with familiar smoothness. I step on mail as soon as I enter. The mailman had been putting Aaron's bills through the slot, but Aaron hadn't been collecting them. The bills were paid automatically by direct deposit from the trust, so it was no real loss to leave them in a pile. Just one more display of how little connection Aaron had to reality.

The entryway smells like him.

He'd put a long folding table between the front door and the door to the living room. Computer parts are scattered across its surface, many broken, most deliberately. Aaron used to run a small server farm for fun. He'd mined bitcoin, hosted online games, ran websites. It brought him joy to tinker until the burns took his dexterity. Hence why Aaron destroyed so many motherboards. He smashed like a toddler when he got angry.

There's also trash. A lot of trash. Aaron was using a plank on cinder blocks as a work bench and it's become the peak of a fast food waste mountain.

"Ten twenty-seven," I say softly.

A four-digit string like that is likely a code. I try it on the stocky server rack with its combination lock, but it needs five digits.

"Ten twenty-seven," I say again. It's been years since Aaron left me a treasure hunt. I'm out of practice.

A piece of folded paper is stuck under the lock of the server rack. I tug it out, unfold it. It's a decades-old piece of construction paper with a crayon drawing on it. The proportions are wrong, but it's the layout of the Ashe house. There are numbers written on every room.

He drew that map for me when he went to first grade and began hiding messages on the bookshelves. He used four-digit codes in those days. The first two numbers were the room, and the other two were shelf and book. Room ten was the living room.

"Just like old times, brother," I say.

For a moment, it feels like he's standing behind me.

*Go look, Eve*, he would say. *Ten twenty-seven. The manifesto.*

I pass through the kitchen on my way to the living room. Aaron's sink is filled with discarded lancets on one side, moldy dishes on the other. The trash in the hall bathroom overflows. The living room isn't as foul because it's large; the lifted ceilings, exposed timbers, and tall single-paned windows leave it drafty enough to avoid accruing a stench. The skylight is mildewed around its edge. The fireplace has Burger King cups thrown in with the logs.

There are two towering bookshelves, built in from floor to ceiling. The second of them, nearer the back door, is less dusty than the first. I count seven spines down and pick out a slender picture book squeezed between titles by Mercedes Lackey and Anne McCaffrey. The book has friendly illustrations of forest animals on the cover. It's called *Badger's Parting Gift*. It doesn't belong among Aaron's science fiction favorites. It doesn't even belong to Aaron.

No note falls out of the picture book when I open it. I press my nose to the inside crease to smell the old paper and glue.

Immediately, I'm nine years old again.

And I know where Aaron has left my next clue.

*Go look, Eve.*

## CHAPTER 6
## EVE

The year Ronnie died I had a twelve-year-old tomcat named Felix. That scrappy little monster spent his days ranging around the neighborhood, picking fights and romancing the girl cats. He spent his nights curled at the foot of my bed. He was always close to the house. All I had to do was stand on the back step and call for him, and he'd come running.

He went missing a few months after Ronnie died.

Felix didn't show up one night, and then another. I assumed he'd just found an especially exciting lady-cat to cavort with. But on the third night, I called for him on the back step, and he called back.

A sad, pathetic yowl.

I found Felix dying in the ivy against the brick wall in the backyard.

Aaron was there, too. And a box cutter. And all the blood.

My brother was arrested with his hands still covered in tufts of Felix's bloody fur, but Mom had thrown away the box cutter before the police arrived. *They'll hurt him if they see a weapon*, Mom whispered to me.

*Badger's Parting Gift* was the book my mother gave me after that. It's meant to help kids handle the death of a pet. Mom made a point of reading it to me every night before bed for a week, and in my dreams, a badger took Felix into the ivy before slitting him open with a box cutter from chin to balls.

* * *

Standing out on the back step of my house, I breathe in the wildfire smoke and call out for my long-dead cat.

"Felix. It's bedtime."

A distant owl hoots.

The ivy crunches under my ballet flats as I wade in. The backyard is even more neglected than the front. It was a wet spring before this achingly hot summer, and every-thing has turned to jungle. I grab an abandoned rake to clear the spot where Felix died. Spiders and earwigs skitter into the night, stark black against orange-hued bricks hidden by crawling ivy. One brick is ajar, its end an inch higher than the rest. I wedge the rake's prongs under it and push it away.

There's a shoebox underneath, mummified in plastic wrap and painter's tape. The box is big enough for the body of a cat, but it was buried far more recently.

Aaron buried the box for me.

I sit at the kitchen table to open it.

There are two things inside: a note written on folded legal paper and a box cutter.

*The* box cutter.

The contoured blue plastic handle fits into my hand better now that I'm an adult. Felix's blood has long since been scrubbed off. The black switch slides easily when I press my thumb against it, and the razor that emerges from the end is brand-new, shiny, and sharp. I slide the razor in and out three times before setting it aside.

Aaron's note is no manifesto. He typed it out using Mom's IBM Selectric. Her typeball was never calibrated correctly, so the words print out of alignment. We used to kid that it made every letter written on it look like it had come from a serial killer. The content has never been so befitting the joke before.

"EV, if you find this, I'm already dead and I've been murdered. It won't look like it. You know how to mack this better. Follow the trail, EV, but don't look at the clues. Give it all to Wyatt."

At the bottom is another string: 46X-7EY, followed by 0724.

"Damn it, Aaron," I whisper.

His spelling, punctuation, and grammar was flawless. Spending much of his life bed-bound had given Aaron little to do except read. There's no way that *mack* is a typo, particularly considering his dying words.

This *is* a treasure hunt.

My brother was murdered, and I think Deputy Jobson did it on purpose.

I wonder if there's anything I can do about it if he did.

* * *

I purge in the hallway bathroom, shoving the middle two fingers of my right hand deep enough to bite my knuckles. All that comes up is energy drink and pickle juice. It's acid in my sinuses. The act is so violent that my body shakes, yet the responding adrenaline rush leaves me giddy, my head clear enough to stand. I'm high.

Like the kitchen, the bathroom sink is filled with tiny needles. They're all lancets or single-use insulin syringes. I left an old cooking spoon in the bathroom drawer so that I can scoop Aaron's needles into a cardboard box without getting stuck. Then I place the box under the vanity with three other boxes of sharps I haven't yet thrown away.

There are no spoons, cotton balls, or lighters. If Aaron had relapsed, as Garrett said, then he wasn't doing it here, or he took care to hide it. Both seem unlikely. He wasn't leaving the house enough to shoot up at his dealer's house. And Aaron was never cleanly enough to hide things.

With the sink clean, I can wash my smeared makeup off. I use a bottle of mouthwash from my purse to get the taste out. I reapply my lipstick. I've even got a tiny Band-Aid to cover the bite I left on my knuckle from purging too violently. The evidence is all gone. Nobody needs to know what I've done.

* * *

Aaron occupied the master suite after Mom died. The dark wood panels on the walls belong in the seventies, but the trash is all modern. Amazon Prime boxes, broken charging cables, discarded sleeves for video games. There's no clear carpet between the door and the bed. I have to flatten a pile of Funko Pop packaging and trading card wrappers to get inside.

His tangled bedsheets are stained. There are two TVs on the cabinet next to the bed, along with three different game systems. The dust on his consoles suggests he hasn't used them in weeks. Instead, Aaron's been fixating on some weird project that left Mom's bed covered in binders, folders, and stacks of paper. It looks more like the work of a serial killer than the typewritten letter. Especially when I find that Aaron has hung a corkboard at the foot of his bed, and it's covered in newspaper cuttings.

The police will be here tomorrow to search for SE&G's alleged stolen property. What will they think when they see this?

*Junkie loser.*

"What were you doing, Aaron?" I ask, climbing onto a pile of muddy work boots so I can look at the corkboard.

He's posted several articles about SE&G, ordered in rows to tell a linear narrative. His former employers were linked with wildfires in the Great Basin. An investigation had shown that they weren't maintaining power lines, which they claimed was a result of Nevada legislation capping rates. Aaron had defended them through that controversy. He'd told me that the amount of empty public land their power lines ran through were difficult to access for maintenance, but it was better than depriving rural customers of power.

I'm less familiar with the Nevada Appeal clippings about wildfire legislation. Assemblyman Frank had authored a bill to get SE&G to pay for damages. Frank's face is circled by red marker. The bill was A.B. 76. Those digits are also circled on the page.

But I'm most interested in the fact that Aaron wrote *TREA-SURE CHEST* above Assemblyman Frank in his sloppy, boyish handwriting.

"One more clue, huh?" I ask. "Every trail needs at least three…"

*Five or six,* Aaron corrects me. *It takes five or six clues to keep you busy, Evie.*

This clue points to a toy treasure chest we hid in the garage. We had to put it up high where Wyatt couldn't find it. I still have to stack boxes to reach a fire safe Aaron shoved in the back corner of the garage. Although the shelf is covered in cobwebs, the safe itself is clean. Its lock takes four digits, so I try the bill number twice, 7-6-7-6. It pops open.

There's no manifesto inside to my frustration. But I do find a folder marked as SE&G property. When I flip it open, I find accounting papers. The stolen property.

# CHAPTER 7
# HANK

Eve's soup is always good. She knows my taste preferences, from the level of spice to the thickness of the linguica's cut. I dump the entire pot down the sink without eating a bite. I flip the switch for the garbage disposal. It grinds her soup to nothing, leaving behind the aroma of a hollow gesture.

I check the tracker on my cell phone and find that Eve's GPS is at Sunset Park, near Aaron's house. Eve promised she wouldn't go to the crime scene, and I have to believe her. She never bluffs, whether her hand is good or bad. If she's sitting in her car at the park, then she must be grieving—finally. The beginning of the end.

I'm setting my phone on the counter when it chimes. I've gotten a text message from Undersheriff Cuttino. It says, "I'm at Jimmy G's. Want to join?"

Jimmy G's is where the deputies go to complain about men like Cuttino. "I'll be right there."

The bar is downtown, and I'm in the suburbs. For Carson City, that means I'm a five-minute drive and a one-block walk away from joining him. Even on such a smoky night, downtown is busy. The city narrowed the roads and widened the sidewalks and made space for live music. When it's warm, the whole town turns out. Adults cluster at the Fox while the lowlifes go to the Caterpillar. And then there's us—the cops at the cop bar, shepherds of the flock.

I don't see any of my patrol deputies at Jimmy G's. Only Cuttino sits aloof, a cigar smoldering on his table. As toxic as the air outside has gotten, it's thicker in here, and he's inviting the thickest of it into his lungs.

He waves me over. "Good to see you, Hank."

I order a beer from the waitress and sit. "I didn't see a speck of blue sky today. That wildfire's really something, isn't it?"

"A shit show, a real shit show. Not even five percent contained," Cuttino says. "And the forecast doesn't have me optimistic. Dry, windy."

"Moundhouse is evacuated now?"

"Mostly. Some folks're sitting tight."

"So long as we don't have to rescue their dumb asses when the trailer catches fire," I say. "Why don't they just get to the emergency shelters?"

"They'd rather take their odds with the fire than sleep in the community center's basketball court. What can you do? We don't have the resources or authority to pry them out of their homes." He leans back and takes a long draw on his cigar. "This one's good. Want to try it?"

I shake my head. I don't smoke. I only drink enough to fit in with the guys, to make myself seem approachable. It's easier to lead men who like you. Men who want to share weekend barbecues will tell me when they've got complaints, so I can get ahead of trouble before it arrives. "Why's it so empty? The guys said they'd get together."

"They were here a quarter hour ago," Cuttino said. "I sent them back out for search and rescue."

"Those men are tired. They need rest."

"Nothing calms people down like a busy mind." He sticks the cigar in the corner of his mouth and grins. "Is it a problem?"

The waitress brings my beer. I swallow a mouthful. "No, sir."

"Good. My undersheriff needs to start stepping back from the nitty-gritty of operations. Let someone else worry about the bullshit."

"What else can I do? You don't want me moving the pawns around the board, and I can't exactly help with the Jobson investigation…" Fuck it. "Unless you do want me to push that investigation a few steps forward."

"Is that all you've got on your plate?" Cuttino asks. "Pretty sure you don't bring down seventy-two big ones a year, plus benefits, just to babysit deputies."

There are times to hit and times to stand. "I'll handle meeting the fire chief tomorrow morning."

Cuttino takes an extra-large puff on his cigar and soothes his throat with a long drink. "Sure, sure. Half the investigative division is going to be at your brother-in-law's house tomorrow, so sure, you can be my man at the office." I'm salivating at the idea of detectives combing Aaron's house for evidence. Cuttino's watching me, reading me, clocking my pleasure. "You got any guesses about what they'll find?"

"Wouldn't surprise me if his house is a meth kitchen by now." Aaron hadn't allowed Eve to visit for a month. Anything could have happened to the house.

"You think SE&G's stolen property might be there?"

"I don't know where else it would be. Aaron barely got out of bed."

"Sounds like a real champ, that asshole," Cuttino says.

The beer's kicking in and my face is getting warm. Talking to Cuttino, I feel more grounded than I have for days. It's obvious what a stain Aaron was—*is*—on my life, but Eve's refusal to acknowledge it leaves me wondering if I'm the crazy one.

"Funny thing about Aaron," I say. The word "funny" comes out with an F so hard I just about bite my bottom lip. "He lost *every time* we played a game together. Lost every bet we made on football. Lost every arm wrestling match too." The last one's not a lie. Aaron would never take me up on the challenge, conceding defeat rather than face humiliation at my hands. "He had a loser attitude."

"Some people just come out like that. They're a waste of the toilet paper smeared over their shitty assholes."

I slam my hands on the table. "Thank you! At least *you* can see it. Eve still calls him an angel."

"Well, you don't marry a girl who looks like your wife for her brains." He winks and nudges me with an elbow. It wafts cigar smoke toward me. It smells a little like long nights at the hospital, watching the living ghost of my wife cursed to haunt her brother's Sisyphean recovery.

"I'd be less pissed off if Eve was stupid," I say. "There's a lot going on up there. She just wastes it. Didn't go to college, never had a job… It's like all she wants to do is clean up after her brother and cook dinners and paint her fucking toenails."

"You said yourself, some people have a loser mentality. How smart can she be if she's living like that?"

Cuttino's got a point, but I don't like it.

"Speaking of the Ashe case," Cuttino says, "maybe you should swing by your brother-in-law's house after your meeting with the fire department. Off the clock. You might have insight into whatever we pull out of that house, and if you happen to find something that makes your wife see sense…" He shrugs.

It's better than I expected. A thousand times better. All I have to do in return is swallow my dignity, let the man do whatever he wants with my deputies, and keep in step.

"I'm available for whatever you need. Anything at all," I say.

"Now I get why Wilkes kept you from me," Cuttino says. "The man was greedy up until the last minute at that desk. Now I'm the one feeling greedy." He sets the cigar on the edge of the ashtray, propped the wrong way. Embers fall from its tip to smolder on the table. "Real greedy. You like poker?"

"I used to compete. My first wife made me quit. Eve doesn't care, but money's tighter when you're taking care of a man-baby full-time. Still love the game. Just don't have the resources or time."

"I'm hearing a lot about Eve," Cuttino says. "Eve this, Eve that. Forget Eve. There's a poker game at Don DeVos's house tomorrow night. Officially, it's a fundraising event, but some of us are going to play in his den. No wives."

"No wives?" I give an easy laugh and empty my beer. "What kind of event is this?"

"One for gentlemen in the community like us. Good time to rub elbows with people who matter. Like the kind I'll need to support me in the special election for sheriff. You'd be doing me a favor saying a few good words on my behalf, and there's perks for you. DeVos is a good friend to make."

DeVos would be any would-be politician's best friend. He's a huge donor to the police union. He bought half the cars in our fleet. And now that my brother-in-law has been screwing with DeVos's power company SE&G, there are some scorched bridges that could use a mending.

"I'd be honored," I say, "as long as you've got a good sense of humor about your new undersheriff cleaning out your wallet."

Cuttino guffaws, slaps me on the shoulder, empties his drink. "We'll see about that, won't we? We'll see." He sets a manila envelope on the table. "I was taking work home on the Jobson investigation tonight. Tying up a few loose ends before packing it in. Jobson did everything by the book, and with the evidence against Ashe..." He waves at the folder like he's wiping it off his mind. "I've had a few too many drinks, Everhardt. Make sure that folder's on my desk in the morning. Be a shame if I lost it. I'm gonna walk home."

He drops a couple twenties on the table, pats me on the back, and heads out.

I down another beer before taking the folder to my car. I sit under a streetlight with the vents and windows shut. It's bright enough for me to read through Jobson's files. The "internal investigation" is a letter listing Jobson's documented actions and how they were all appropriate. The coroner's report underneath explains that Aaron died in an authorized chokehold because he was obese and asthmatic —unique health complications outside of Jobson's control.

The last page is the most interesting. It's Aaron's sealed juvenile record.

I'm halfway to sober by the time I reach that page. When I see the reason Aaron first got arrested, I wish I were a whole lot drunker. "Cruelty to animals. Ashe mutilated and killed family cat. Crime reported by parent."

Eve has always said that Aaron is innocent and couldn't hurt a single soul. It seems incredible to think she wouldn't know about Aaron killing their family cat.

Which means either my wife really is stupid or she's as crazy as Aaron.

And I don't think Eve is stupid.

**CHAPTER 8**
**EVE**

I fall asleep in Aaron's bed, entangled in sheets that smell like his T-shirts and hugging a pillow to my chest. The box cutter rests under my fingers. I drift away tracing the shape of the switch. When I slip into dreams, I fall back to my childhood, lying on the raised threshold outside Mom's bedroom door. I can hear my parents' voices inside.

"You have to do something to control your son," growls Dad.

"*My* son?" Mom asks in a thick voice. She's been crying. "Sean, I don't—"

"You're the one who wanted three. You skipped the pills."

"I told you, I never would have done that."

My parents were careful not to yell when we were awake, but I should have been asleep at midnight. They had no idea I had my cheek pressed to the carpet, my eye to the dim crack under the door, fingers tracing the wooden trim. I curled my legs to my chest so I could tuck my feet against the frame. When I inhaled, I smelled cigarette smoke and my father's cologne, a sticky-heavy combination.

"We can't afford any of the other daycares. You have to make this right with the director. I don't care what you have to do to keep Aaron in school. Just fucking do it, Mary."

"Sean," said my mother. "Keep your voice down."

"What, so you'll let your hellspawn of a son scream and kick people, but your husband must be silent? Am I a second-class citizen? Don't treat me like a goddamn child!"

When the years elapsed, the shouts on the other side of the door changed. The white carpet grew yellower, stained by years of Mom's smoking. Her voice grew hoarser as her throat grew more nodules. Dad stopped yelling, and instead, Grandma yelled.

"The insurance would cover his home!"

"You already sent Wyatt to the military academy. I'm not sending another baby to a group home," Mom said. "He hasn't done anything wrong. He's confused sometimes. When we find the right doctor, when we get the right medicine—"

"You can't control him, Mary. He's growing fast, and he's psychotic. As soon as that boy hits puberty, you're done for."

That argument I remember clearer than any other. It hadn't been at midnight. It must have been dinnertime. Grandma made a lot of dinners after Dad left. She answered Wyatt's phone calls home when Mom was too busy crying. But her favorite pastime was yelling. She made no secret of her opinions about Aaron.

Until Grandma came, Mom never thought about sending Aaron away forever.

The carpet outside my parents' bedroom slides away underneath me, turning to a carpet of brick and ivy. Thorny branches grow over my head. Roses uncoil to face moonlight, and they're the exact same color as cat blood spilled on the bricks. Felix has stopped whining underneath me. His paws no longer weakly scrape brick. I'm on my knees beside his body, which has unfolded like the blossoms. His skin flaps are pulled aside to expose lumps of viscera and blade-sheared ribs.

Aaron's sneakers are bloody. They're just a few inches from my right knee.

"I'm sorry, Evie," he says.

Police sirens echo through the air.

*I'm sorry.*

Mom threw away the box cutter, but I found it on the asphalt under her van after trash day. It had fallen out of the big green wheelie bin when the truck flipped it upside down. I picked up the box cutter with reverence. Pressed my thumb against the switch. Let the blade slide out.

It still had Felix's blood on it.

Just as I hadn't known how to safely handle a gun, I hadn't known how to safely handle a razor blade. But there are fewer consequences to a knife in child hands. I fumbled and it cut open my thumb. A thick line of blood tracked down the inside of my wrist. I stared at it, transfixed by the way that blood remained in the subtle crevices of my skin. The texture it displayed. The scent of it.

"Evie, where are you?" Wyatt shouted from inside the garage. He'd come home for the weekend. He was keeping a close eye on me, and I'd taken too long doing chores. He slammed doors behind him while seeking me out. *Bang, bang, bang.*

Wyatt would take the box cutter away. I had to hide it. I wanted to keep it forever.

*Bang, bang, bang.*

That sound comes from the waking world outside my dream.

It takes a moment to peel myself away from sleep. The first shock is that my body is adult-sized, which feels much frailer than my childhood frame. My arms are long in front of me in the darkness. My knees are so bony.

The second shock comes when I hear that sound again.

*Bang, bang, bang.*

That's a fist on the front door. Someone is here.

My eyes flick to Aaron's bedside clock. It's that hour between early morning and late night when everyone sleeps. There's no reason for anyone to come to Aaron's house, but someone is here, pounding on the door hard enough to make the wall shake.

Glass shatters.

My fingers curl shut around the box cutter. I slide out of bed to crouch behind it. The tall bed frame hides me when shadowy figures move through the hall outside the master bedroom. Someone must have broken out the window, unlocked the front door, and let themselves inside. Multiple *large* men.

The police won't break the window to get inside the crime scene. They have Aaron's keys.

I roll the file stolen from SE&G and tuck it into my purse before darting to the garage. Deep masculine voices make snide remarks about the trash in Aaron's house. Big feet crash through the mess.

My heart is stuck in the back of my mouth, and it tastes like regurgitated energy drinks. Purging didn't stop the caffeine from entering my system. My fingers tremble on the latch to the back door, and it jingles when I slip it open. The sound makes my heart pound even harder. I don't know how the intruders can't hear it.

I hide behind the air conditioning unit, a tiny space that few adults would be able to fit. It's as cobwebbed as when I used to hide here as a child. With the roar of the HVAC, my motions are no longer easily audible, but I also can't hear the men moving through Aaron's house. I don't know what they're doing.

Surely they're searching for the evidence I've taken.

The night's colder and smokier than when I arrived. I shiver too hard to dial 9-1-1. I don't think I want to call the cops anyway. If these men were sent by SE&G to retrieve the stolen property, then it's tempting to get them arrested. But what happens once they're in jail? Deputy Jobson killed my brother, not an SE&G employee. And I don't want Hank to find out I'm at Aaron's house.

I slip my shoes off and put those into my purse too. My bare feet make no sound against the side yard's bricks. The path to the back is overgrown with weeds, and I collect a few goat's head burrs in my heels crossing it. I bite the inside of my mouth to keep from crying out. Pausing, I yank the tiny thorns out of my soles. I'm bleeding. It looks black on my skin.

"Hey! Someone's here!"

They've spotted me.

I stop trying to wipe thorns off my soles and run. The dead grass and foxtails scrape my shins. It's muddy in the alley, where mint has grown bushy between brick wall and fence. I stomp over it and keep going.

"Stop her!"

There's a narrow-shouldered man at the alley gate behind me.

I throw myself over the fence into the neighbor's yard. A large SUV is parked crookedly in front of Aaron's house. It has flood lights on top, so I can't see who's inside, but they can definitely see me. The driver cranks the wheel to follow my escape.

I clutch my purse to my thrilling heart and run like I haven't run since middle school track team. My feet fly, slapping asphalt, and my hair streams behind me, and it feels like my heart will explode before I can get a block away. My childhood knowledge of the neighborhood helps me evade the SUV. I know whose fences are easiest to climb, which side streets will get me out of view. An engine roars behind me. I'm already jumping at the middle school fence to swing onto the property.

By the time I've gotten across their football field, I can see the SUV parked under the solar panels to the south, where the teachers park. Their headlights blaze bright. Two figures cross in front of them, pointing at the school building. They're not sure where I've gone. It won't take them long to realize.

I squeeze through a narrow gap in the gate to King's Canyon Road and keep going. I run through cold, smoky air even though my lungs are trying to explode. My heart is knifing at my gut. I'm leaving bloody smears in my footpath.

There's only a block of real civilization between the middle school and the foothills where town yields to pastures. The smoke is too thick to see anyone at my back. Half the streetlights aren't working.

I keep running. It's near-black in the smoke. My thighs burn from the incline, and I can hear Mr. Garber's chickens giving unsettled clucks from a nearby henhouse.

My body gives up once I reach the mouth of the trail at Kings Canyon's apex. I hit my knees on the trailhead. My ribs hurt. My thighs are shaking. Everything tastes like acid and campfire, and every inhalation feels like getting stabbed in the armpit. I'm suffocating.

But I escaped.

I crawl to the nearest rabbit brush and slide in, with apologies to whatever rabbits I scare out of their nighttime dens. The wilderness feels restless, but the SUVs never find me. I'm alone in the unsettled predawn, but I don't feel lonely. Aaron's presence looms. Like I'll solve his last, most deadly treasure hunt, and he'll come home.

* * *

The sun has risen before I crawl out of the bush and jog downhill to my car, still waiting at Sunset Park. I peer at myself in the driver's side mirror and grimace. "Filthy," I mutter, stretching a blanket from the trunk over my seat so I won't get it dirty. "Filthy, filthy." I swish mouthwash on the drive home and spit it into a gutter at a stoplight.

My house is stick-built, sided with stucco, and indistinguishable from the hundreds of other thirty-year-old homes in the development. It has none of the character of the Ashe home. Hank would never allow the weeds to grow wild. It's a blessing that I don't have to walk through more foxtails to get to my front door, but the bushes are trimmed back so tightly as to seem artificial.

I slip in noiselessly. Hank's keys are on the hook. His shoes are by the front door. His jacket hangs on the rack with my autumn duster. He hasn't gone to work.

My purse and shoes come upstairs with me. I peer into the master bedroom—Hank is sleeping—before continuing to the office. I can't let him see my filthy shoes. Those go under the desk to be cleaned later. My dress stinks of wildfire smoke, so I take that off too. I'm wiggling out of my underwear to take a shower when I catch sight of a file on the desk.

It has Aaron's name on it. It also has Deputy Jobson's name on the tab.

I keep my ears perked for movement as I flip the folder open. It's a report that Kaleb Cuttino wrote in response to the investigation into Jobson's conduct. In the conclusion, Cuttino absolves Jobson of wrongdoing and recommends the DA not press charges.

My heart sinks further when I see the medical examiner's report. After Aaron died, they performed an autopsy. They're blaming my brother's death on him…for being fat.

The world turns red. I don't even remember grabbing Aaron's box cutter. I'm just holding it suddenly, gripping it so tight in my fist that the switch digs into my thumb.

Aaron didn't die because he was *fat*.

And yet even that isn't as terrible as finding Aaron's sealed juvenile arrest record in the back. It's several pages long. His earliest incident when he was arrested for animal cruelty is on a page of its own. Whoever gave Hank this report has given him a record of Aaron's violence.

With a press of my thumb, the razor blade slips out of the cutter. I slice it through that last page, fold them together, and slice again, and again. I let the shards snow into the trash can. Then I put the remaining papers back together, close the folder, and leave it on the desk so that I can shower the blood off my feet.

# CHAPTER 9
# HANK

The news about the wildfires is bad. "Containment is still impossible," says Ferguson, the fire chief. He's just come in from Virginia City Highlands. His shirt is white with ash. His gray hair's turning white from stress. Gravity drags deep lines down either side of his mouth. "There's all this overgrowth around the power lines, old trees that grew close—"

"I thought they fixed those," Dresden says. "What was that court case, the one where the little town got wiped out? They were supposed to do maintenance after." He came to the meeting to represent the department at my side.

We've also got a representative from SE&G with us, and he doesn't look happy. "Maintenance has been progressing according to plan." Mallek speaks so smoothly it's like he's rehearsed lines. "The State of Nevada capped the rates for selling power, and the fund we were supplied for mainte-nance isn't enough to cover the region we service. Also, I'll remind you that the court determined the county was liable for their emergency unpreparedness, and allegations toward Sierra Energy—"

I interrupt him. "Right." We've gotten his hackles up in that cosmopolitan, political way. He'll talk until someone makes him stop. "There's no time to point fingers. Ferguson sent his bulldozers out there, but the terrain is impossible. They can't clear new defensible space. We've got the whole county under mandatory evacuation, and it's not lifting anytime soon. We've gotta pull together. Dresden, can you see if Gina's got an update from NHP?" The deputy leaves, and Mallek's tension eases.

"Sierra Energy and Gas is erecting more shelters to help the influx of evacuees," Mallek says. "The entire parking lot in front of the former K-Mart has been fenced in securely, with charging stations, bathrooms, and water available. We'll have another at the Target in Douglas by tonight."

"Pulling together already," I say. "I love it. Ferguson, what about you?"

The fire chief ticks a brief smile at one corner of his mouth. "I know the CCSO is strapped for overtime, but we need more help evacuating. Is there any way you can send more men out to check houses, Everhardt?"

"I'll have a group by tomorrow morning."

"Great." Ferguson toys with the papers on his desk. He ticks another smile. "You gotta tell me, Deputy. Is it true that the guy who started this is your brother-in-law?"

I'm hot and cold all at once. My blood roars. "No time to point fingers. Remember?"

Ferguson lifts his hands in surrender and stands. "Just trying to wrap my mind around how it's possible for things to get this bad this fast."

"Everything is in His hands, and it's not ours to reason why," I said.

"Amen," says Ferguson. We shake hands and exchange brief promises. Then the fire chief is shuffling out, hustling back to the emergency at all the speed of my grandpa with his cane.

Mallek shakes my hand at the door too. "I hear that you're going to join us at DeVos's dinner. I look forward to seeing you."

It's gray outside, our cars brushed in white, the mountains invisible through the smoke. "The party is still on through this?"

He misunderstands my question. "Don's house is on the southwest side of Washoe Valley, far from Virginia City Highlands. The area's safe." Mallek dons sunglasses. "God only knows I'm ready to relax, right?" Somehow he's slipped a business card to me. I've got his phone number.

Mallek leaves.

Vasquez is outside the door. He watches Mallek's departing back with open loathing. "I heard what he said in there about too little money to trim some fucking trees. Did you know that Don DeVos has a base salary of a cool million a year? And he's getting another ten million in bonuses over the next three? That information's online, we all know it, and he still tries to pull that garbage."

"You okay, Vasquez?" I ask.

He shakes his head. "My friend Trent lost his house in the foothills. It's gone. His dogs, too."

"God bless him," I say gruffly. Vasquez looks like he's going to cry. I wish I could tell him to take time off, send him home. But he's one of my fittest men when he's not wimping out like this. "You can make a difference for people who haven't been hit yet. I want you to spearhead a volunteer drive to get up there in the morning. Can you handle that?"

Vasquez doesn't respond until Mallek's out of view. "I'll do what I can."

* * *

I hurry to the Ashe house before the investigation shuts down. Cuttino's had the entire end of Donne Avenue taped off, but I'm welcomed in by one of my deputies, who doesn't make eye contact when he greets me. He knows I shouldn't be here. He won't talk. I don't think anyone will talk.

Cuttino meets me when I park right next to his car. "Glad you made it in time. We're packing up."

Selfish disappointment streaks the inside of my ribs. "Tell me you guys found something."

"We're taking boxes back to the office to search them. But we were expecting some security discs, and we're pretty sure those aren't in there. Hard to tell when it's such a dump." It's the right word for what I see in Aaron's front yard. It'll be worse inside.

"Hey, you forgot this last night," I say casually, quietly. I hand the folder about Aaron to Cuttino.

"Thanks for watching my back." Cuttino flips through the folder. "Hey, it's missing page seventeen."

"What?"

"The last page isn't there. Did you take it?"

I shake my head. "It must have fallen out." But I'd been careful with the file. I'm not the kind of person who drops things.

"I'll print another one." He tosses it into his front seat. "Come on, let's go in for a minute."

I'm unpleasantly surprised at the mess in the entryway. There are bags of trash piled on top of boxes of trash that are crammed behind mountains of laundry. This mess hadn't accrued over a month. Eve had been letting her brother live in these conditions for at least a year.

If I'd come to the house in the last year, I might have realized Eve was slipping. She let Aaron wreck the place. Needles everywhere. Moldy plates on his kitchen floor. His shelves cleared off so that the books are scattered across the carpet. Notebooks burned in his fireplace. The whole place smells like rot.

"Got any insights into where Ashe might have hidden things?" Cuttino asks. "We've been through his bedroom."

"How about his old bedroom?" I nod to the room behind the kitchen.

Cuttino exchanges words with a deputy, who goes to check it out. "You look even more disgusted than I feel," Cuttino remarks. We're standing in the living room under the skylight, covered in such a fine layer of ash that it looks like snow. The edges of the glass are mildewed. It streaks green-brown down the wood like tears.

"I keep thinking about how Eve calls her brother an angel, but if you just walk in here…" I gesture broadly to include every wretched detail that I don't want to name. "Honestly, it makes me worry about my wife. You got one? A wife?"

"Not anymore. I like women with less control over my life." Cuttino nudges me with an elbow. "Bit of advice from me to you—no matter how bad your spouse gets, don't let her divorce you. My ex empties my bank account every month to buy shoes. At least I had some control over the money when we were together. Now she's like a goddamn child."

Someone calls to Cuttino from outside.

"I'll be right back," he says.

I'm left watching crime scene techs box up the scene. The house doesn't look anything like I remember, and I remember it well. There used to be a card table in the living room, close to the back door. Occasionally, we played Texas Hold'em at that table. It was big enough for all three of us to spread out our cards and near enough the kitchen that Aaron never had to stop eating snacks. Motive enough to move the Great White Whale sometimes.

Getting Aaron to walk out to the living room had also meant Eve could keep an eye on the two of us while she was cooking, cleaning, and dispensing medication. Once I got engaged to Eve, Aaron had gotten more hostile.

It's been a long minute since I visited him, but his stench is all over me.

* * *

It was at the card table where Aaron and I finally came to blows.

Eve had left her purse behind when she left to get dinner out of the oven. I'd gone to the bathroom at the same time. Aaron had gone nowhere, as usual, staying comfortable in the stained green recliner with the broken footrest that he always used. When I came back from the bathroom, I found Aaron with his arm inside Eve's purse.

"What the hell do you think you're doing?" I asked.

"I was looking for my inhaler," Aaron said.

"You mean your pills."

"I wasn't d-doing anything wrong. I'm allowed t-to g-get my inhaler." He was lying. Aaron was *always* lying. It made me madder to see how bold he was. How stupid he must have thought I was.

Eve had come out at the sound of raised voices.

"Your brother was trying to help himself to the Vicodin," I said quickly before Aaron could establish his story first.

"He's lying," Aaron said just as fast. "I wasn't anywhere near your purse. I wasn't doing anything."

Eve checked her purse. Nothing was missing because I'd stopped the theft. "I wish you guys would just get along," she'd said as if Aaron hadn't been stuttering, as if I hadn't just helped keep her junkie brother out of the pills. The oven timer beeped, and she rushed back to the kitchen, purse swinging at her side.

"You're a rotten liar, Ashe," I said once she was gone, keeping my voice low.

"You're a piece of shit for trying to make my sister hate me," he said.

"She's going to be my wife. You've got to respect me and our relationship. I'm not going anywhere, no matter what her spoiled 'tard brother says."

Aaron didn't get angry at the insult. He never got mad at insults, a sign of a man without dignity as much as a loser. "You don't even know Evie."

"You think I don't know her? You think I don't love her?"

"Everyone loves the idea of her. Nobody knows her well enough to love her. Be careful of Eve."

He had such a fucking punchable face.

I still don't know exactly which part set me off. It might have been getting treated like an idiot. It could have just as easily been the fact I'd glimpsed Aaron's hand and knew he was sitting on a full house. But he'd barely gotten those last words out before I was hauling him out of his chair so I could punch him where he stood.

When he got up, I thought for a second I'd made a mistake. Aaron did so little moving that I often forgot he wasn't just fat—he was *big*. It was like having a mountain rise in front of me. Not a lot of people have made me feel small since I was a child in my dad's lap. I felt small then, looking up at him.

I didn't need to worry. My fists were enough to bring him down.

They shouldn't have been. Aaron was a beast, a human tower. One blow from that guy would have sent me to the floor.

In a way, I wish he had.

Instead, Eve came back into the room to find me punching at her brother, who'd dropped to his knees. I was the one who got screamed at. "What do you think you're doing?" Eve shrieked. "Hitting a defenseless man?"

"He's not defenseless," I said. "Aaron folded so I'd look bad!"

I swear to God that asshole had been smirking at me while I walked out the front door, shouting at them for being a family of fuck-ups.

Later, I apologized to Eve, and only Eve.

I stopped playing poker with her brother.

* * *

This is the first time I've seen the house in years, but the rage that drove me to beat Aaron is fresh and new. Frustration is a living animal inside of me. I'm gasping to let it out somehow. The house reeks like Aaron's body odor, that unwashed stench he'd left everywhere that his body slugged around, and I'd rather be outside gagging on wildfire smoke than inside another minute.

"Hey, Everhardt?" Cuttino calls to me from the side yard.

I go outside to find more activity. A group of techs is pulling up bricks between two trees.

"What's this?" I ask. "Did you find the stolen property?"

"We don't know what we've found yet. These bricks are newer than the other ones around here, which were placed in the fifties. These are only about twenty years old. But they were pulled up in the last year. Thinking a secret compartment of some kind."

"Sir, over here," says a deputy.

Cuttino heads over. He crouches down and looks inside a plastic bag dredged from the dirt underneath the bricks. He shakes his head. I can see the swears on his lips, though he keeps it quiet.

He comes back and grabs my arm.

"You've gotta get out of here," he mutters. "This case is going to get more scrutiny than I realized."

"Why? What was under there?"

"Bags of human remains," Cuttino says. "Bones now. And there was an ID in there too." He glances over his shoulder at the hole they've dug, his features tight. "Hank, that's Sean Ashe. Who's Sean Ashe?"

My throat's dry, and not just because of the smoke. "My father-in-law."

## CHAPTER 10
## EVE

I don't get any sleep after arriving at home. The fitful
hours spent in Aaron's bed will have to get me through the
day. I'm dizzy in the shower, so I choke down a bowl of
oatmeal before chugging an energy drink. Putting food
into my stomach stops the dizziness. I can drive to the
trailer park where Aaron died.

Hank said he died in Crest View Mobile Home Park, but
the exact trailer is unknown to me. I cruise through lap-
sided mobile homes looking for the one from the video.
White, with missing windows covered in particleboard, a
weedy yard, and rickety stairs leading to the front door. I
locate it in the back of the lot. The trailers around it are
well-tended. This is a young neighborhood filled with
families, so most yards, while not grassy, are scattered with
toys and baby swings. A dog barks at me from next door.

I enter the squealing gate to the place of Aaron's death.

The weeds aren't flattened where Aaron crushed them.
We've had several windy days and the weeds waved away
the imprint of his undignified death. It feels like being in

this place should allow me to somehow wrest the events away from history, reaching back to change one little thing. Like answering Aaron's phone calls instead of ignoring him so that I could screw Garrett in his kitchen. Or having him institutionalized again the instant I realized he was acting erratically. Or...

There's nowhere to go but forward, up the wobbling steps, to knock on the door of the trailer my husband described as a "known drug house."

For a few seconds, I only hear shuffling and cursing inside. The twitching, picking scarecrow from Aaron's funeral answers. I knew Johnny was an addict, but I didn't realize he was also a dealer. The single wide is also new to me. When Aaron used to hang out with Johnny, he lived on the reservation. "Evangeline, right?" Johnny asks.

"Eve." Only Garrett calls me Evangeline. "I need to talk about Aaron."

"Fuck, I told the cops about it, I don't wanna talk about it again. You're not supposed to be here." He glances around the street.

"I'm not here for trouble. Just information."

"Fuck." He wipes a hand over his lip, steps outside, shuts the door behind him. It doesn't fit in the jamb and squeaks back open an inch. He glances me over. "I didn't invite Aaron over that night. I didn't invite him over any nights lately. I didn't think he'd come."

"Were you fighting?" *Did you call the cops on him?*

"No way. He was a good guy. Wouldn't hurt nobody, the big bear. A real sweetheart."

An addict is the last person I expected to show kindness toward Aaron. But it's the glint I need to see. The civilized world of law and medicine had decided Aaron was a lost cause before he hit puberty, but crack dealer Johnny thought he was good, just like I did. "Nobody you know called 9-1-1 on Aaron that night, then?"

"We don't call the cops," he says. "The fuck are you smoking?"

"I just don't know how they would have known he was here if one of you didn't. Like, does your house have a security system?" I ask.

He glances at the cracked door and laughs. "Yeah, right."

The wind kicks up and changes direction. We're pelted by sand. Both of us turn to face away from it. It puts us next to each other instead of face to face, looking at the patch of ground where Aaron died.

"There's nosy fucks in every trailer around us. Any of them could have called the cops," Johnny says. He hacks a dry cough into his sleeve. "Sorry. Hang on." He reaches inside for a box of Kleenex. "This smoke, man. I can't rip a dab without having to get my inhaler, and my nose, it's always running. Want a tissue?" He offers the box to me. I shake my head and he blows his nose loudly, which turns to another bout of coughing. "Fuck!"

"So where were you when he died?" I ask.

"We'd all gone to Denny's. House was empty."

"That's not true," says a nasally female voice. A young woman appears behind Johnny. She's wearing low-rise jeans and a cropped Misfits T-shirt, its collar cut into a vee to expose fresh dermal piercings on her breasts. They're red and inflamed. "Mack was here."

My heart jumps. "Mack?"

"Mackenzie," says the girl.

Johnny tries to push her away. "Go back, Kit. This isn't about you."

"No, wait." I reach out to grab Kit, but my hand stops in the doorway. I don't want in there. That dark place that smells like skunk and cat piss. "Who's Mackenzie? Why was she here?"

"She was trying to score addies off Johnny," she says. A common street term for Adderall, a stimulant. Aaron used to sell his prescription and buy heroin.

I show her the picture from the security footage on my phone. "Could this be Mack?"

"Could be Bigfoot," Johnny mutters.

Kit shrugs. "I guess. I don't know."

"Can I have Mack's phone number? Snapchat?"

"I guess," she says again, "but she's not going to answer you. She's not going to school, neither. She's going to lose her scholarship."

"No school, no phone?" I ask, and Kit shrugs once more. "Is she okay?" Another shrug.

Whoever Mackenzie is, she's the only witness to my brother's murder.

And she's missing.

"Speaking of losing scholarships," Johnny says, giving Kit a deadly look. "You're supposed to be getting to class." Either Johnny was ambitious and had a daughter young, or the drug dealer's trying to get his kid sister through college. Kit rolls her eyes and grabs a backpack off the floor. It's cheap pink plastic, probably ten dollars from the Walmart down the street. One of its straps is broken.

"College is open today?" I ask. It looks like Hell is creeping over Carson from the east.

"Going for my GED online," says Kit. "Gotta do shit at the library. Deadlines are deadlines."

"Give me Mack's number first."

The girl gives me both a Snapchat and phone number. "You can try WhatsApp, but seriously, Mack's not around," she says. "She never talks to anyone when she's run off with her rich boyfriend."

"Rich boyfriend?"

"Mallek," Johnny says. "Fucking Mallek."

"He's got a fancy job as assistant to the SE&G guy," the girl says. "I don't blame her for running off with him. I'd probably quit college if some rich guy wanted to be my sugar daddy."

"Don't do anything fucking stupid like that, Kit," Johnny says. "You hear me? You're not marrying your way up. You're getting your welding cert. You're starting a business. You're not having babies and—"

"Fuck off!" She flips her middle finger at him and gets on a bike. "See you tonight, asshole!"

He's grinning toothlessly at her back. "Kids," he says to me apologetically, scratching his skinny neck.

"Hey! Johnny!" A neighbor steps out of her trailer. She's old and fat, wearing pajama pants with Cookie Monster patterned on them. Her hair beats around her head in the wind as she squints against the blowing dust. "Did you see what Nevada Appeal just posted on Twitter? They're going to cut off the power tomorrow!"

"What, who? Where?" Johnny asks, sauntering over to look at his neighbor's phone. "Cutting off power to Carson… bullshit! The fire's still up the highway!"

"The utility says it's so dry and windy something could spark," says the neighbor. "How's my dialysis gonna work without power?"

"Big deal. I don't have power half the time," Johnny says.

"You don't pay your bills," the woman says.

I turn from them as they spark into an argument. There are only two days before it goes dark. Hank will insist that I evacuate. He takes care of me like that. But it will mean distancing myself from Aaron's clues, putting miles between myself and Mack. It could be days more before I can return. The power lines swing in the wind like jump ropes. A shingle on Johnny's roof rips free and cartwheels over the fence.

* * *

I can't get home to use my computer. Traffic's a mess and roads are closed. After two detours leave me in traffic for thirty minutes, I grudgingly pull out to park behind Comma Coffee and head into the shop. It's a café filled with mismatched vintage furniture, wallpapered by local artists and a TV behind the bar showing wildfire coverage. There's a huge warning at the bottom of the screen. *BREAKING: SE&G announces planned blackout for Carson City.*

There are only a handful of patrons in Comma Coffee. They are served by a single teenage barista leaning on the counter next to her laptop. I order coffee, then send two messages on Snapchat, one to Garrett Glass, and one to Mackenzie.

"Hey, could I borrow your laptop?" I ask the barista. "I need to look stuff up and I can't get home right now."

"Sure." She turns it around to face me. "Don't get coffee on it."

I pretend to smile.

I'm as much a private detective on social media as anyone else who stalks their high school graduating class, but it's a lot faster on a laptop than a cell phone, even with the slow coffee shop Wi-Fi. I go searching for Mackenzie, friend to Kit—and maybe my brother, too. Aside from the deliberate misspelling of "make" as "mack" in his note to me—"mack this right"—and saying her name before he died, he never told me that there was a girl in his life in any context.

But it seems like there were a lot of things he wasn't telling me about in his last weeks.

If he'd left clues about Mack, then he wanted me to find her. And if he died shouting her name, it must have been urgent.

"But who is Mack?" I mutter to myself.

Finding Kit's Facebook profile leads me to Mackenzie's. Her profile picture is familiar. It's the girl from the cemetery. Pale-skinned, dark-haired, and dressed in a modest T-shirt and jeans, Mack looks too young for college. Her average posting rate is two Buzzfeed quizzes and one photo cross-posted from Instagram every day. Her friends list is an array of young strangers, aside from Kit. We have no acquaintances in common. Mack was important to Aaron, and Aaron is important to me, yet we never intersected.

She hasn't posted since the night Aaron died.

A dead end.

I can't find anyone named Mallek, so I turn my searches toward the cop who killed my brother. Deputy Jobson's internet presence is minimal. He has no Facebook, no arrest record. A background check website offers a partial address and phone number. I order the full report while perusing his wife's Facebook account. Mrs. Jobson runs three different public wine club groups, and their daughter is attending the University of Reno. She runs with a different crowd than Mackenzie. There's no connection to SE&G.

Another dead end.

Don DeVos is easy to search. The results are numerous but disinteresting. Articles describe him as a philanthropist associated with the police union and local hospitals. He appears in photos at big events like the Nevada Day Parade. But Nevada is a very large state with very few people in it. Even our regional celebrities don't have Wikipedia pages. And DeVos is too smart to have social media.

"Do you think you're gonna be long?" the barista asks, leaning her elbows on the bar in front of me. "Unless this fire burns down Carson High, I've got to produce a proposal for my senior project." She picks at acne on her chin. "Do you think the fire's gonna reach the school?"

I'm saved from having to answer when a man enters the coffee shop. Garrett Glass unwraps a scarf from around his face. His eyes brighten at the sight of me. "Evangeline."

I push the second cappuccino at him. It's still steaming. "Let's sit somewhere quieter." Somewhere without a teenage barista picking at her skin, which makes me want to dump my drink into the bathroom sink.

Garrett and I take a mismatched pair of chairs in the back room, distant from listening ears. "It's good you got here," I say. "I was sure you'd be stuck at one of the hospitals in Reno."

"I couldn't even leave town."

"Did you hear about the power outage?"

"God, yes," Garrett says. "I've got a generator, but I'll only have a fridge and laptop for three days. It's ridiculous. I can't believe SE&G is cutting us off."

I can believe it. I spent hours listening to Aaron rant about SE&G cutting hours and benefits. Every penny they saved was pocketed by the big guys, meaning they skimped on operations. *With new electricians every month, nobody has expertise*, Aaron told me once. *When there is maintenance, it's sloppy. Nevada is their cash cow, and we're just living in it.*

"I could have picked a better time to move into King's Canyon." Garrett gazes woefully into his coffee. "At this rate, the house is going to burn down before my new TV gets delivered."

"Why did you move up there in the first place?" This might be our biggest fire, but it's not our first, and the hill burns more years than it doesn't.

Garret's cheeks tint red. "The perfect house became available. You know the one right at the top of the road, looking over the valley." I'd run past it in the dark while escaping those thugs. "You always told me what a great neighborhood West Carson was for a family, so I just thought..." He elects to take a sip of his coffee rather than finishing the sentence. "I wasn't entirely stupid. I had the last owners finance a fire abatement system—sprinklers, some heat shielding in the outer walls, that kind of thing."

He lost my interest with the word "family." His words slide right over me, and I switch subjects. "Have you ever treated a young woman from Carson City named Mackenzie?"

Garrett blinks. "Why?"

"She was there when Aaron died. She's a witness."

"Evangeline," he says softly, brow knitting, face falling into his hands. He needs to let out a long breath before he responds to me. "No, I don't have any patients named Mackenzie. How did you...?"

"The video. There's three frames at the end that show someone there, so I went to the trailer and asked around. Aaron was with a girl named Mackenzie." I show Garrett my phone.

He won't look at it. He pushes my hand down. "No, I've never treated a Mackenzie. I'm sorry." His brow crimps. "You...went to the trailer. Evangeline..."

"Police murdered Aaron. I won't wait for their sham investigation," I say quietly, savagely. "They opened his juvenile record, Garrett. They saw that Aaron killed our childhood cat. Did he ever tell you about that? They're pointing to that as proof of his violence, like he was criminally crazy."

"Animal abuse in childhood *is* a worrying symptom." Garrett takes a slow drink of his coffee, which I recognize as a stalling tactic. He's arranging his thoughts. He's going to tell me something I don't want to hear. "It's often an early sign of antisocial personality disorder. ASPD."

I'm shaking my head before he even finishes the sentence. ASPD is a fancy term for sociopaths, and Aaron was no sociopath. He was one of the most moral people I knew.

"He fit a lot of the criteria," Garrett says. "His stories started changing in the last few months when we talked about his history in session. There were inconsistencies. Emotional outbursts. It's possible that he had been masking his behavior previously. I don't think he was, but I also can't rule it out."

"It doesn't matter. Either way, Aaron wasn't delusional. He was preparing a case against SE&G, and he had evidence. That's why he was talking about a treasure hunt. He left his findings for me so that I can finish his work, but I need to connect Jobson to SE&G if I'm going to prove Aaron was murdered."

I appreciate Garrett's quiet consideration of what I've said. He's surprised, but not disbelieving. He sips his coffee again. Sets it down. Looks at me through his steepled hands. "What if there's no connection?"

"There's a connection."

"Police always represented a danger to Aaron," Garrett says. "It's just a matter of statistics. Cops aren't trained as first responders to psychiatric interventions, so the mentally ill are sixteen times likelier to face police violence. Half of people who die in fatal police shootings are mentally ill. Aaron had the police called on him so many times…"

"I avoid reading statistics," I say. "Crazy people die more often from everything. Higher rates of cardiac disease, higher risk of stroke."

Diabetes is more common among the mentally ill too, a complication my brother suffered, which statistics would rule as normal. It wasn't normal. It wasn't a number. It was an ugly daily battle of math versus the practice of eating, calculating insulin for the food my brother claimed to eat, then trying to dose him for the food he'd hidden too.

From the moment my brother was born sick, he was a ticking time bomb.

"Aaron's not a statistic. He didn't die because of a spread-sheet," I continue. "Aaron died because Jobson choked him out, and I think Jobson did it because SE&G wanted Aaron's evidence to disappear. I know how that sounds. I can't prove it yet. But Aaron spent the month before he died setting up a treasure hunt for a reason."

Garrett's done with his cup. He sets it aside so there's more room for him to curve his hands around mine, warming my fingers. "You should consider Occam's Razor here."

"What's the simplest explanation I'm missing?"

"Paranoia, or manipulation if he did have ASPD," Garrett says. He brushes my cheek and the hair touching my temple. It's too much contact. Too intimate for a public space. My skin wants to flay itself off my muscles.

"Are you saying I'm paranoid too?" I ask.

"I think you're stressed, and for good reason. You're right to mistrust the police. You would never forgive yourself if you didn't look into this. But I can see how you're tearing yourself apart, and it scares me." His hand drops to mine—my right, where I've got a little bandage over my knuckle.

I jerk my fingers away.

He gives a small nod, understanding. "You haven't touched your coffee. When's the last time you ate?"

"I had breakfast." And my gut is grumbling its protest. I need to stay close to a toilet.

"Did you sleep last night?"

"Stop. I'm not one of your patients, Garrett."

He sighs, nods. "I don't have any resources to help with Aaron's treasure hunt. But I'm here for you, Evangeline. Tell me what you need to have done, and I'll do it."

I open my mouth to reply, but nothing comes out. My head drops into my hands, so heavy, and I don't like the view. My dress has gotten tucked under my belly roll so I can see the fat lying on my lap. I can't believe I ate breakfast and already feel hungry again. What a waste of calories.

"Here..." Garrett glances at the barista, then reaches into his briefcase. "You're not my patient, but I can still give you samples."

"Samples?"

"I know I can't tell you to stop doing the treasure hunt, but I'm not going to watch you tear yourself to shambles while you do it." He folds a palmful of pills into my hand. They're long white bars crossed by lines to make them easy to quarter. "One at a time. No more than one every six hours. They'll neutralize your stress. You might focus better."

"What are they?"

"Alprazolam. Xanax. They're anti-anxiolytics."

Xanax was in Aaron's medication cocktail, included in the substances I had to protect against abuse. They're meant to produce mild euphoria. It makes them an appealing addition to an addict's self-medication. "I don't know, Garrett."

"I'll write a prescription if it makes you feel better," he says. "I can't do much to help you, but I can do this. I can keep you going."

I never take pills. I'm not like Aaron, you see. I saw therapists as a child, but I'm otherwise well-adjusted. Aside from the occasional dose of ephedrine, caffeine, and aspirin—a mix ideal for energy—I don't mess with the curses that plagued Aaron's half-life.

Yet this is why I called Garrett, isn't it? Because I need help and there's nobody else I can ask. He's the last person I trust. The only person who cared for my brother half as much as I did.

I wait until I get back to my car so I can take a tablet with another sip of white Monster. I won't purge this afternoon. I don't want to bring the pills up. I've got control, I've got more information, and I'm still going to find justice for Aaron.

## CHAPTER 11
## HANK

I call Eve after I leave her family's house.

She picks up and says, "Did you find something?"

I almost tell her about her dad's bones right then. But I want to see her face when she finds out. I want to know if there's going to be emotion in her eyes when she learns he's dead, not just "moved away." And if there's emotion, I want to know which one.

So what I say is, "I'm missing you, baby. Rough day at work."

"I'm sorry, Hank."

"I sure could use some of your tender loving care right now," I say.

"Yeah," she says.

"You sound distracted. Are you with someone right now?"

"I just don't have anything to say. Do you need something from me? I'm getting in the car, and I don't like talking when I drive." Eve's voice is too soft for any of that to sound as cruel as it feels.

I can't wait to tell her that her dad is dead.

"We can talk tonight after work," I say. "Love you."

"Love you," she says.

"Do you want to—?"

The line's already dead. She hung up on me.

* * *

There aren't many people at the office when I return, but the parking lot is full. The city is building a temporary shelter for evacuees on our property. Gina's at her desk, like she's always at her desk, but she's doing a sudoku puzzle. "Trying to keep my mind off things," she explains.

"Don't keep your mind too far off," I say. "You're at work. You've got a job. Are those flashing lights people on hold?"

"Oh, no. They're just people calling constantly. So many calls right now! One line clears up and another call comes in." She squints at the phone. "That one's for IT, two for the sheriff, one for active cases. Nobody is in to answer, so…"

"You silenced the calls?"

"I'm one of the only people here," Gina said. "Folks should have set their phones to forward, shouldn't they?"

This is the kind of town where a murder can go unnoticed for twenty years because someone put a couple bricks on top of the bones. I'm surrounded by people like Gina, sweet but slow herd animals. They don't notice the wolves coming after the flock. They're too busy chewing cud.

My head's throbbing when I say, "You might as well go home. Everything's starting to close anyway."

"They're not really going to black out the city, are they?" she asks, spasmodically clicking her pencil's eraser. "I can't go without power. My oxygen has a battery for outings, but it needs to be charged every six hours."

"You don't have a generator?"

"Oh, those are so expensive. Insurance doesn't cover that."

She might be a sheep, but that's why we've got shepherds. "Call the church's help line before the power outage, Gina. Pastor Johns will have something."

"But—"

"I have to go," I say, striding past her desk. "Trust in God." If God wanted me to help Gina, he wouldn't have thrown so much at me simultaneously. The community will envelop her. Fifty years going to church in the same town, she'll be fine.

I'm not sure I'm fine. I'm tense, carrying bad news knotted at my back. I can't stop thinking about those shopping bags piled on top of displaced bricks. I think about Sean Ashe's old driver's license, faded over the years, and printed in a style I haven't seen since the nineties. I think about Eve insisting to me that her brother would never set a fire, never hurt a fly, never do a damn thing wrong.

I'm scowling when I head into the bullpen, where only Vasquez is working. He stops typing frantically at my approach. "Hear about the blackout?" he asks. "We're going to get a lot of calls about that, right?" These men have come to rely on me for their cues. I'm not just their boss; I'm a rock, stable in the embattled seas of Nevada justice. I should offer him a smile, words of encouragement. All I've got is a stare. It's hard to even focus on the man. His expression shifts. "Are you all right, sir?"

"Fine," I say gruffly. "I'm in a hurry."

When I pass, I see another reason for the tension in the air. Deputy Jobson is collecting his belongings.

An impulse seizes me.

"Jobson," I say, stopping beside him. "You got a minute?"

Jobson shakes his head and grabs his box. He won't meet my eyes. "Not right now, sorry. The road's down to one lane out to Dayton. I'll be lucky to get home before dinner."

"You've got a minute." This time, it's not a question. "There's an incongruity in the internal investigation."

His face turns the same color as the walls.

Jobson sets his box down and follows me into the office, where I lock the door. "Cuttino's recommending I return to full service," Jobson says anxiously, taking the chair in front of my desk. "But I'm quitting. I'm not coming back to the office. I'm done with Carson City, you hear me? The office in Dayton said they'll have me."

"They won't want you when they hear you messed with the body camera footage," I say. "It's cut short. That's the incongruity."

Jobson isn't a small man. He'd seem a bear next to anyone except Aaron. But he's trying to disappear into my chair, make himself tiny, and there's nowhere to go. "Camera malfunction."

"Was it really a camera malfunction? I have to ask. Not because I don't believe you—I do. But the time stamp on the footage shows it started earlier, even though there's nothing else on the servers. I know there's a good reason for it. I just need something to put on the paperwork that will withstand scrutiny."

Jobson looks up at me slowly. Thoughtfully. I don't like the sight of a hippo thinking. "You shouldn't have seen that. You're not supposed to be involved in this case."

He's right. I'm already pushing my team's goodwill by showing up at Aaron's house. Questioning Jobson is another level of trouble, and he knows it. I roll my tongue against my teeth, fold my arms. I don't think it'll be hard to get Cuttino on my side. "Where's the footage, Jobson? How did it get deleted?"

Jobson should have a tidy resolution for me. *I accidentally deleted it while trying to get a copy for my lawyer.* Or maybe, *I deleted it on-camera because I have fat fingers.* Instead, the deputy says, "I already promised Wilkes I wouldn't tell anyone."

"Are you telling me that Wilkes knows you deleted the footage?" I ask.

"He's the one who deleted it." Jobson stands up. "I can't talk about this."

I shove him back into the chair.

The energy in the room gets electric. It's that weight that comes before lightning strikes, the bass line of thunder hitting the earth before it hits your ears. I feel it any time I get to the last table in a poker tournament. It's the feeling of knowing your real opponents at last.

Jobson is shiny with sweat. His skin's so thin, I can see right through him. His adrenaline response has kicked in. This man killed Aaron when he grew afraid, so he's as likely to punch me as he is to talk.

I reduce my profile by sitting on the edge of the desk, unfolding my arms. I imagine myself as Cuttino, friendly and sharp. "I'm not trying to get you into trouble. I'm not looking for revenge."

"I heard you hated Ashe," Jobson said.

"You did what you needed to do. But here's the thing..." I weigh my next words. Jobson isn't a softie; I can't appeal to him with an emotional connection. "There's going to be a new murder investigation. They found a body at the Ashe house—his father's body. The first case needs to be tidy. You understand?"

"Look, the missing video doesn't show anything because I didn't do anything!" He swings freely between fear and anger, clenching his fists and sweating hard. "I kicked him, all right? Just a couple good kicks. Wilkes thought it would make the case too complicated."

"That's it?" He's not the first law enforcement officer to kick a man while he's down. That kind of thing can fall under the umbrella of self-defense with the right judge. "So you didn't record anything else?"

"Well, the witness too," Jobson says. "She had her camera going, so I took her phone and deleted the file."

Nobody has mentioned a witness. It's another thread, messier than the last. "Who was she?"

"I don't know, Sarge." And there's the rest of his anxiety. He knows that someone out there saw him kicking a dead man, some agent he can't control. I'm surprised he hasn't atomized in my chair.

"Don't tell anyone what Wilkes did," I say. "He retired a hero. Don't tarnish that."

"I would never," Jobson says. "But you, on the other hand… This is completely out of line. Dragging me in here. Sticking your nose where it doesn't belong. Who the hell do you think you are?"

I open my door. I make him pass me to get out. And when he's close, I lean in to say, "Test me."

Former Sheriff Pete Wilkes lives south of Carson City in Minden. Like my father, Wilkes thinks neighbors within a mile are too close. His daily commute is nearly an hour on normal days, but I haven't even gotten out of town after an hour of driving on the shoulder with sirens. I make up for lost time gunning it on a couple side-roads through the farms as a shortcut. Afternoon sun flashes in a narrow band between smoke and the mountains on the horizon. There's no fire out this way. Lucky thing too. The fields lie yellow after summer heat, and the cows graze on kindling.

I pull up to Wilkes's house for what must be the hundredth time, after so many barbecues, and I take my last first steps onto his driveway. I've got the practiced knock of law enforcement. Wilkes knows it's one of us and answers without checking the curtains. "Hank." Wilkes shakes my hand and pulls me in for a pat on the back. "How are you doing?"

"My boss vanished during a disaster and threw my job into upheaval," I say. "How do you think I'm doing?"

He doesn't make excuses. He nods, accepting the blame. "Come on in. Have a drink."

Wilkes's house has the same brown shag carpet in every room, from living room to bathrooms. His easy chair is molded to the shape of his body. That's where he reads the newspaper every morning after chores, before coming into work. It's what he's done for years. Nothing changes here.

It doesn't smell like wildfire in Wilkes's house because it smells so strongly of cigarettes instead. I lift my eyebrows at him. "You're not smoking inside, are you?"

"The ball and chain is on a girls' cruise," he says. "Have to have a little fun while she's having fun. You won't tell her, will you?"

"I'm not going anywhere near your wife. Once she finds out you walked off your job— Wait, does she know?"

"Not yet. I won't ruin her fun." Wilkes grabs his ashtray, lighter, and cigarette off the side table, where it looks like he's been camped for days. Empty beer bottles are scattered on the floor beside the recliner. A rumpled blanket pools in his easy chair. "I know how you feel about smoke. Let's go out on the patio. Got a brand-new dining set there."

The table is shaded by Karen's garden, where her three neat rows of corn grow tall. His stream isn't running. The statue of Mary praying has gone green in the stagnant water, growing mold and mosquitoes.

Wilkes lights a citronella candle before relighting his cigarette. "How's the wife?" he asks.

"Emotional. What do you expect?"

"It's hard losing a brother. Even if that brother was Aaron Ashe." Wilkes knows Aaron well because he got called into the courthouse next door every other month. "I'm gonna ask Karen to send flowers when she gets back from the trip. What does your lady like?"

"I'm sure she'll love whatever you send along. Means a lot."

"Don't start thinking I'm sentimental, now," said Wilkes. "I don't have much else to do these days except be thoughtful. What have I missed at the station?"

"We searched the Ashe home. Found twenty-year-old human remains in the backyard." I hold the identity inside of myself, waiting to see Wilkes's reaction. He doesn't give me the satisfaction. He just brings the cigarette to his lips again, inhales, exhales. Looks at me. "It's Aaron Ashe's father."

He flicks ash into the tray. "Huh. Twenty years. Aaron must have had help since he was so young."

"I assume it was the mother. She's been dead half as long, so I can't ask."

Wilkes shakes his head and puckers his lips around the cigarette butt. "Does Eve know?"

"Not yet. Is it better to think your dad didn't want you, instead of knowing your brother killed him?"

"Secrets aren't a kindness to anyone," Wilkes says.

"I'd sure as hell agree with that. That's why I've got whiplash with this stunt you've pulled, retiring out of the blue." I make myself smile. My tone is light when I say,

"The rumor is that you got caught partying with hookers and blow and had to get out before the news caught on."

He scowls. "Did Cuttino say that?"

"Is that something Cuttino would have reason to say?" I laugh at Wilkes's expression, reaching over to gently push his shoulder. "I'm just messing."

"Well, I didn't leave for fun," Wilkes says. "The worst part is thinking that asshole's sitting at my desk."

"But there are no hookers, right?" It seems like I shouldn't have to ask.

He blows the smoke out the corner of his mouth, away from me. "I'm not that kind of man. I'm not like Peters."

I didn't think so. "You don't need to worry about Cuttino. He keeps everything moving, just how I like it." Cuttino doesn't question pages missing from files he shouldn't have given me. Cuttino doesn't care what the deputies do on their own time. Cuttino accepts Aaron as guilty because he looks guilty.

"He's already started trying to make nice with you, hasn't he?" Wilkes snorts. "Cuttino's like that. He makes nice up until the minute he thinks you're not on his side, and then wham, whatever you thought was loyalty goes out the window."

"I'm the patrol sergeant. It's important for me to have a good relationship with the sheriff."

"Sheriff Cuttino." He mutters it like a curse.

"Not elected yet."

"But he will be. Cuttino's made nice with all the right people, and I'm not one of them. Not anymore."

"I don't know if he's making nice. He told me that he made nice with Peters by firing him to protect him from investigation. That makes me wonder if Cuttino might be protecting you, too." I don't like the next question I have to ask. "For instance, did Cuttino catch you deleting footage from the Ashe case?"

Wilkes is too thoughtful to be as transparent as most people. My question makes him retreat into the shadowy corners of his cop mind, where even I can't tell the paths he's walking. "I wish you didn't know about that."

"I'm not going to tell anyone."

"I don't care if you do. I'm worried about what example that sets for you." Wilkes's wrinkled eyes crease deep. He's smiling at me in his way. "How much do you know?"

"Everything Jobson does."

"That little shit," Wilkes mutters. "Well, there was a witness. Couldn't have anyone looking too close at her. Because, you know, Jobson broke the law deleting the file from her phone. Cuttino called in an old favor and told me to delete the file. But it's not why I retired." He takes another drag. When his lips pucker around the filter, the lines get deeper still, like his skin is made of rubber without any stretch left. "Whatever happens under the sheriff is his responsibility. I didn't want to lay claim to what was going on underneath me anymore."

Wilkes isn't done with the cigarette, but he stubs it viciously in the ashtray.

"None of us is a perfect lawman because the law isn't perfect. Sometimes we make choices that close the gaps in the law because we're good men, and we want to see good happen. But you also know now that sometimes the choices don't happen for moral reasons."

"Sometimes you've got zero rage control like Jobson," I say.

Wilkes shakes his head. I'm missing his point. This isn't about Jobson. "There are two other ways that men like us end up coloring outside the lines. Call us grass feeders versus meat eaters. Some of us graze on the grass if it looks good—take free coffee from 7-Eleven, skip writing a ticket for the judge's son, search a guy's car without probable cause. But then there's the other kind, the meat eaters. The one who sees the herd and start chowing down." He pins me to my patio chair with a hard look. "Cuttino's a meat eater, and he's been in charge of internal investigations for years."

"What do you know about him?"

He lights another cigarette. The sunset's bloody from smoke and his hair's the color of the clouds. I almost think he'll blow away the next time the wind kicks up. "Nothing. What he does is his business now. I'm not the sheriff anymore."

For the first time, it strikes me that Wilkes is gone. Really gone.

No more lunches at Wilkes's desk. No more shadowing him at work. He won't be there when I've got questions, and he won't be able to buffer me from whatever happens. Now he's just an old man who drinks and smokes too much and watches TV, so he doesn't have to think about responsibilities shirked.

Now he's more than useless to me. Instead of giving closure to Aaron's case, he's made it more convoluted than the yarn knotted at the bottom of Gina's knitting bag. It feels like I've got yarn wrapped around my throat, a braid tightening slowly.

When I stand, Wilkes just takes another inhale. "Mind showing yourself out?" he asks. "These creaky hips are just getting comfortable."

"No problem, sir."

He doesn't seem inclined to stop me, but there's a wistful twist to his bushy eyebrows. "You're gonna come visit me again soon, right? Keep me in the loop?"

I shake his hand. "Thanks for all your service, sir."

"Come see me," he says.

"I will," I lie.

## CHAPTER 12
## HANK

The drive back is faster than the drive out. It's still a half hour of silence behind the wheel, wondering what Wilkes knows about Cuttino, which is only interrupted when Cuttino himself calls my cell phone. "Everhardt," I answer, sticking one of my earbuds in so I can talk hands-free.

"Thought you'd want an update on the Ashe case." Cuttino's voice is tinny over the speaker.

There it is, right in front of me. A pasture filled with juicy grass. "Did you find something?"

"The ME pulled a rush job for me and took a look at Sean Ashe's remains. The vic died by a gunshot wound to the chest. It wasn't self-inflicted."

I hadn't expected it would be.

"You ready for the weird part?" Cuttino asks. "Someone cut into Ashe's ribs with a knife. Looks like it was a small blade, done postmortem. Like somebody was poking around his insides."

It's not weird when I consider that Aaron Ashe was first arrested for killing his family's cat. He was worse than I realized, and I'd thought he was terrible. "Are we launching an investigation into Sean Ashe's death?" I ask.

"Sure, but it won't be a long one," he says. "There's not much justice to be served when the primary suspect is as dead as the victim. If only we'd found the body last week."

"If only." If we'd found the body, then Aaron could have been arrested before he was martyred.

I consider asking Cuttino why he wanted the body camera footage deleted. It was easy to ask that same question of Wilkes. But they're not the same men and can't be handled using the same methods.

"Mallek tells me you're on for the party tonight," Cuttino says, filling my thoughtful silence. "It's a decent drive. Want me to swing by and get you on the way? Half an hour?"

"Sure. See you." I hang up.

I'm almost home. I'm about to tell my wife that her father is dead. I won't tell her about the witness. And then I'm going to do what she's always done to me, and I'm going to leave her to eat dinner alone.

* * *

Eve's on the computer in the office again. As soon as I'm inside, I hear her rocking in the chair upstairs, rhythmically thudding her heels against the floor. I halfway expect to round the doorway and find her watching Aaron's death again. Instead, she's on a teenage girl's Facebook profile, and she clicks away when she hears me coming. She turns in the chair so she can rest her shadowed gaze on me.

"Hey baby," I say.

She's popped a blood vessel in one of her eyes, and she's got dark rings. "Did you bring news for me?"

"That's it? No hello, no kiss? Not much of a welcome."

"Sorry, Hank." Eve gets up to kiss me, a light brush of lips against lips. I press against her harder when she tries to pull back. I try to inject passion into the kiss by holding her against me. I give it everything I have, but she returns nothing.

"You look beautiful today," I say, and I'm not lying. Eve's beautiful the way that most women aren't. She doesn't need makeup, a fancy dress, or her hair done to be beautiful. It's in the way she moves. Her ghostly presence haunting every room she enters. She's wisps of smoke swirling through sunlight, and sometimes I think I could catch her if I moved fast enough. But the burst vessel isn't a good look, and I don't think she's been sleeping. Eve doesn't respond. "Did you hear me? I said you look beautiful."

Her smile's as ghostly as the rest of her. "Thank you, Hank."

That's better. "I do have news. You might want to sit down for this." She takes the couch under the window, and I sit on the coffee table in front of her. "I found the rest of the footage. It doesn't show anything that changes the arithmetic. Aaron went down, but he got up again and attacked Jobson, so he had to be put down again. It confirms everything Jobson put into his report."

Eve drops her face into her hands, massaging faint blond eyebrows. "That can't be right."

"It is right. Aaron was violent enough for it. We both know that." I'm watching for something to shift in her posture. A hint that she might be crumbling, accepting my explanation. Nothing. "The cat proves it."

Eve just drags her eyes to mine and says, "What cat?"

"Your childhood cat," I say. "The family pet."

Her brow wrinkles. "Felix?"

"Aaron killed him."

For an endless moment, Eve looks past me into nothingness. Where Wilkes retreats into his mind to think, Eve seems to fold outward, her soul leaving her body. I can't tell if she's surprised or sad or in such complete denial that she's shut down. Then she starts rubbing her brows again. "No. Aaron didn't hurt Felix."

"It's in his juvenile record. Are you telling me you didn't know why he was arrested as a literal child?"

"Just because he was arrested for something doesn't mean he did it," she says. "And I'm not judging Aaron for fighting Jobson until I get context from the witness."

I've been controlling my anger well, but it swells up inside me when I realize what she's just said. "How the hell did you find out about that?"

"I watched the video again. There's a couple frames at the end where you can see a girl. Her name is Mackenzie Reese. She's eighteen years old, a nursing student at Western Nevada College, and she's missing." Eve says this matter-of-factly, listing off details like she's a deputy relating a traffic stop. "I talked to one of her friends. Mack is known for disappearing with boyfriends for weeks at a time. Sometimes she uses drugs. I don't think she's been reported missing yet."

"God, Eve, I can't believe you've been digging around like this. What the fuck do you think you're doing? Where'd you go to find some junkie's friend—that crack den?"

Her quiet is answer enough.

Eve's been playing cop while I've been trying to bring her closure.

Everything I've done has been for her. Threatening Jobson. Getting friendly with Cuttino so I can access information. Going to crime scenes where I'm not permitted. For her. And how does she repay me?

"Think about it," Eve says. "Why was Aaron 'trespassing' at that house? Why would he meet a girl there?"

"He was probably fucking her."

She blanches. Finally, a reaction. "Aaron wouldn't be involved with a teenager."

"You also think he wouldn't kill your cat or attack the deputy, but guess what, princess? There's a little thing called reality out there, and you're not dealing with it." I had planned to be so much more careful telling her about her father, but there's no point. Nothing's going to pop her bubble if I don't jab hard. "They found your father's remains at Aaron's house today."

"My father is living on the other side of the country," Eve says.

"Those are his bones. They were with his driver's license. He was buried under the bricks in the side yard. Looks like Aaron killed him twenty years ago and covered it up."

She only reacts a second time when I say Aaron's name. A shiver in her spine, like someone's walked over her grave. "My brother was a child twenty years ago. Even a big kid couldn't hide a body alone."

"Then your mom was complicit," I say. "Both of them lied to you. They said your father left to hide the truth—that Aaron's a monster." Eve just stares at me, and I say, "Don't you care at all that your father is dead?"

"Should I? I barely remember him." Eve's head tips back against the couch. She stares at the ceiling. "I don't feel…anything."

It's not easy to hurt Eve. She's not exactly an ice queen, but so many years spent taking care of an impulsive, tantrum-throwing adult child has left her with a hard shell. Even when I've jabbed at her over Aaron—always out of love—she's bounced it right back to me. But now I've jabbed too hard. Instead of popping, she's gone into shock.

I slide onto the couch beside her and grasp her hand. "I'm sorry you have to find out like this. I know how hard it is, losing a father."

There are no tears glistening in her glassy eyes.

"Look on the bright side," I say. "You know he must have loved you. Aaron let you think he didn't. You've gone years thinking he just started a family somewhere else when I bet he would have loved to be with his little girl." Her fingers twitch in mine. I brush the hair off her face, tuck it behind her ear, stroke her forehead. "Did I ever tell you about how my dad died?"

"Cancer." Eve's voice breaks between the syllables.

"It was a horrible way to go. Long and slow. When he was at the end, he told my mom to take care of me, to give me all the love she'd given him through months of hospice," I say. "She didn't. God put her on Earth for one man, and she never got over Dad dying. I had to deal with all that pain alone. But I don't blame her, Eve. And I'm going to make sure you're not alone while coping with this, all right? I'm right here for you while you work through all this hurt."

Her head lifts, and she pulls her hand out of mine. "My dad didn't love any of us. He beat my mom. It happened when he got drunk. He'd start wailing on her because, I don't know, she hadn't done the dishes. He hated a sink full of dirty dishes when he got home from work. So he'd beat her. And if we made too much noise, he'd beat us too."

"You never told me that. Baby…" I move to put my arm around her, but she pulls back. Having her shrink back from me every time I try to offer comfort feels like thorns over my flesh.

"Aaron didn't kill my dad," she says. "Someone must have, if his bones are in my brother's yard. Is it that bad? Killing a man who beat his wife?"

I grab her wrist tight, feeling the frail bones inside. "Listen to yourself! You think that your *brother* murdering your *father* could be any kind of justice?"

"Why not?" Eve yanks but can't pull out of my grip. "Would it be justice if a cop killed my dad instead?"

I don't intend to yank Eve to her feet. I don't remember doing it.

But suddenly we're standing, and her back is against the wall as my elbow's digging into her chest. Her hair's gone wild around her face, clinging to slender cheeks, framing muddy eyes gone wide. "My dad is gone," she said in a small voice through labored breaths. "I can't do anything about it. But Aaron found skeletons in SE&G's closet, so they ordered his death, and Jobson was the assassin."

The accusation doesn't sound wild to me after the day I've had. But I get angrier anyway.

"I'll tell you this, you ungrateful bitch." I breathe fire into her face. Let her feel as awful as I do, take some of my pain and put it into her blood. "Jobson wasn't a great cop, but he was good. He lost his job. He's paying the price for your shit-sack brother getting exactly what he deserved. There's no conspiracy!"

On the last word, I shake her hard, trying to make her *feel* it.

Eve looks like a frail little mouse, pinned between me and the wall. Her skin's translucent. Paper-thin. She smells like mouthwash and home. Eve's lost her crazy brother, and now she's breaking down, just like he did.

It feels a little bit like I'm breaking down too. Because what I haven't told Eve is that Cuttino is the one who demanded that footage deleted, leveraging his weight against Wilkes to conceal something that has little to do with Jobson. Her talk about conspiracy hits the right notes.

"Tell me," I say. "Did you know that Aaron killed your father?"

"No," she says immediately, genuinely, her eyes so huge. "Of course not, Hank."

My hand hurts when I uncurl it from her arm, one finger at a time. She remains shrunken back. Her shoulders are lifted all the way to her ears.

I don't care if she's right. This ends now. "I'll see about filing a missing person report, if it makes you feel better," I say. "For this witness. What's her name again?"

"Mackenzie Reese," Eve says.

"We'll find her. *We* will—the sheriff's department. But it's not going to change anything. You know that, right?" I rub her shoulders, trying to loosen her up. "You need to take care of yourself, baby. Get some sleep. Forget this stuff."

She doesn't relax, but she nods. That's the assent I want to see.

"I can start dinner," she says.

"Don't bother. I'm going to dinner with Cuttino tonight. I got invited to meet Don DeVos himself."

Eve's eyes spark with interest. "Can I come?"

"No wives." Thank God. "Besides, what if DeVos remembers you?"

"Then I can talk to him again," she said.

I haven't heard many worse ideas. Eve kept showing up at DeVos's office during the battle for Aaron's workers' compensation, and we'd be lucky to escape the night without a restraining order. "You can just, I don't know, go for a jog. I can tell you haven't jogged in a while." I head into the bedroom and leave the door open, expecting Eve to follow. Everything's fine between us now. She's not going to keep investigating Aaron, I'm going to file a missing person report on some teenager, and we're fine. Just fine. It's over.

She doesn't come.

Once I'm dressed in my best polo and slacks, I stick my head into the office. Eve is still standing against the wall. She's lost in thought, isolated by the yellow circle of light from our standing lamp.

The doorbell rings. "My ride's here," I say. "I'm leaving. Love you." She nods. "Love you," I say again, louder, prompting her to act like a normal wife just one fucking time.

"Love you," Eve says.

## CHAPTER 13
## HANK

Cuttino greets me with a bob of his head. I get into his pickup. It's a shiny black dually with a gun rack where he's mounted a Remington. "Evening," he says. He's wearing a collared shirt with the top button undone. His sports jacket has a camouflage liner. His belt's got a buckle the size of my head pressed against the roll of his stomach with a longhorn's head staring from his crotch.

"Evening," I say. I *think* that's what I say. I'm humming, my skin packed with bees.

We get stuck at Carson Street, caught by the same traffic that slowed my visit to Wilkes. They've put another evacuation station outside of PetSmart, with tents and a couple generators. It looks like Moundhouse has shipped the worst of their trash to us. Cuttino barely glances that way. "Sorry if the truck smells like blood," he says. "I pulled a tag for a buck and found a big one, but he made a mess, and I haven't been able to get it out."

I hadn't noticed the scent under the smoke. "How was the rack?"

He barks a laugh. "The rack. Let me tell you about that rack. The main beam is only seventeen inches, not a big guy, even fully grown. His body was big but the rack, it was a shame. I'm putting it in my basement," Cuttino says. "Gonna look nice mounted over my TV."

"Seems like a shame to put something like that where nobody will see it."

"I know I killed him," he says. "The stag knows who killed him. God knows." He grins. He's got gold teeth in the back, like he's hiding those too, and for a heartbeat I wonder if they're sharpened. "I hunted all day, sunup to sundown. I sat in a blind for twelve hours, Everhardt. That bastard was teasing me. Walking around just where I couldn't reach him. I spent four hours around lunch on foot trying to sneak up, but nothing. When the sun started going down, I thought I was only going to get to pop off a few tweety birds."

"Tweety birds?"

"You know, those little brown things, the sparrows. I pass the time using them for target practice. I use double-aught buckshot, so they just kind of poof." He makes a hand gesture—a fist to spread-out fingers, like a blossom—and he laughs. "Anyway, I was heading back around sunset, and I caught him during a rut. I'd seen him enough by then to know his rack was too small to be worth it, but I wasn't going to let that fucker get away after wasting my time." Cuttino's grin glimmers in the dashboard lights. "It's a matter of pride."

Traffic moves. We get across Carson Street. He turns up the radio while we pass a family holding up signs asking for money, and he slaps his hands rhythmically on the wheel.

"What happened to the doe?" I ask. "The one he was rutting with?"

"Nothing, nothing," he says, though his eyes haze with nostalgia. "None of us had a tag. She ran away. Sure was a pretty one, though—nice hide, tasty meat." He winks at me. "Don't you hate it when you have to let the pretty ones go?"

Cuttino knows all the back roads to get us to the south end of Washoe Valley without hitting more traffic. His dually has no trouble with elevation. I can't see the lake, the farms, or the four-lane highway through the trees on such a smoky night. Once the forest closes around us, I can see even less.

"Can't believe how windy it is," I remark. When the trees gap, it feels like the wind's going to yank Cuttino's truck off the road.

"The weather's supposed to quiet down at midnight," he says. "We'll just have to stick around and party until then."

I'm about to ask *where* we're meant to stick around when the house appears. Civilization is hiding in the form of timber-built houses with pyramidal windows, which begin dotting the right side of the road. We turn past those and drive longer. Our elevation climbs, and the wind roars. We pass two layers of gates to reach where Don DeVos lives, and even through the smoke, I can tell he's in a mansion.

"Nice, isn't it?" Cuttino asks. He parks his truck behind a Tesla Model 3. "Looks like Chuck is already here." I assume

Chuck is Charles Frank, a state assemblyman. He's got a sticker for his campaign on the bumper. He's also got a police union sticker in his window.

Once I get out of the pickup, I realize the air feels fresher despite the smoke. Cuttino's cab does smell like blood.

Robert Mallek is waiting to greet us at the door, tall and young. "Mallek," Cuttino greets, shaking his hand. "Good to see you again."

"Glad you made it up." Mallek offers his hand to me. "Hello again, Hank." I see a glint of metal under his jacket when he moves. This man isn't here for social purposes, but as personal security to DeVos. "Help yourself to the bar. It's hosted. Veronica's still setting up for the game, but you can buy in any time before seven."

Entering DeVos's house reminds me of the kids entering Willy Wonka's Chocolate Factory. I've got a nice a house for a sergeant's salary, and Eve's got ample budget to keep our furnishings updated, but DeVos is a powerhouse. His entryway has polished wood floors, the walls are decorated in fine paintings from local artists, and everything's got the open feeling of an especially nice museum. The floral arrangement in the giant vase is fresh and alive. I can smell its perfume instead of smoke or deer blood.

I'm surprised by how many people are in the house. I recognize the faces of a couple guys from the courthouse, though I don't know their names. Other white men stand around the bar, none of them younger than Cuttino. Mallek is the only one around my age. Conversations are quiet. Seventies oldies play from speakers I can't see.

We pick up drinks from the bar.

"Did you tell the wife about her father?" Cuttino asks. "How'd she take it?"

I just shake my head. "No wives tonight."

"Hear, hear!" He raises his glass so I can clink it with my beer bottle. "Come on, Veronica's waiting for us."

"Veronica, huh?"

"Veronica, and Candy, and Suzie Q." Cuttino draws me to a nearby lounge where a fireplace roars in open defiance of the wildfires.

Veronica stands at a table blocking the door. She's a buxom woman with platinum hair and an easy smile. "Hello again, Kaleb. It's so nice to see you." She scans a card that he hands to her. "And who's this?"

"My sergeant, Hank Everhardt," Cuttino says. "I'm sponsoring him."

She scans his card again. "Welcome to the game, Hank. We're playing no limit Texas Hold'em tonight. The small blind starts at a hundred, and the minimum buy-in is a thousand." Cuttino places a cool grand down. He counts the hundreds one at a time so I can see.

I had suspected poker at DeVos's house was going to be pricey. Redoing the kitchen hasn't left me with much liquid capital, and that's a little steep, even for me. I've got enough to get in. I won't be able to get more chips if I bust, but when I hand a thousand bucks to Veronica, I do it with the casualness of a man who's got thousands more to spare.

"Got room for another?" A man in a suit sidles in beside us. His thick neck is barely constrained by a collared shirt. His blocky shoulders strain inside his sport coat, sized just a hair too small for him. Either he's gained weight recently, or he's in denial. I'm thinking he's in denial because I've seen this face on a thousand billboards over the last couple decades, and he's always looked like a spray-tanned Santa Claus.

It's Bernard Batley. *The* Batley, who owns all the car dealerships in the area, not to mention a few restaurants and a massive share in one of the biggest Reno casinos. "Sir, it's an honor to meet you." I shake his hand. I squeeze hard, but he squeezes harder, if only because his fist is a slab of steak with the crushing weight of a car behind it.

He slaps my shoulder, grips me, gives a solid shake. "I see that my reputation precedes me."

"More like that ugly mug," Cuttino says, feigning a punch at Batley's jiggling brick of a jaw.

They boom with laughter.

"We do have room for you, Bernie," Veronica says with a chortle that makes her breasts ripple. She leans forward to show them off. She wants people to notice. Women like her always do.

Batley puts cash down. His bankroll is fatter than he is. Money must be good in cars, and he wants us to know it. "I'll get that back as soon as I knock you chumps off the table." He winks at us.

"Don't be too sure about that." Cuttino slings a wiry arm around my shoulders. "Hank is a real card shark. You can't beat him."

"I don't know about that," I say. I might not win the first hand or two. But then I'll know Batley's tell, and he'll watch me walk away with his money. I think beating

Batley will impress him. He's affable, laughing at the jokes that Cuttino slings, and he smells like he's on his second drink.

"So Bernie, this is my guy that I was telling you about," Cuttino continues. "The wonder sergeant everyone loves."

"Hank Everhardt, right?" Batley asks, and I think I'm supposed to be flattered that he remembers my name. Men like him always retain names and faces. That knowledge is money.

"That's right, sir," I say. "You should already know it because I've given half my earnings to you, getting my cars over the years."

He laughs again. His laugh smells of good scotch, which isn't what he's holding. That looks like a highball. Maybe he's more than two drinks in. "Let's see if you can get some of that Ford money back!"

We each take a rack of chips and collect at the purple-felt tabletop to play. Cuttino and Batley go to my left. There's a man to my right I don't know and one empty chair beyond him. "Don's the last player," Batley says.

I set my beer on a coaster engraved with a big horn sheep. "Where is he?"

"Getting his massage, I bet," Cuttino says with a chuckle, jostling me in the ribs. "The guy loves his massages."

"I'm up next." Batley pats his belly and stretches his back. "Good thing, too. I'm feeling real sore."

Veronica comes along to play dealer, and she bends forward while she flicks the cards to glide to each of our seats. It gives a full view of her bolt-ons, straight down the center to the soft skin at the top of her belly. She's got a freckle in the middle. Her eye contact is methodical, her smile seemingly private every time she looks at the next man. Sluts like her are always fishing for their next daddy, but she's not getting it from me. I'm not rich, but I still don't do cheap.

Batley likes Veronica's act. He takes his cards and returns her smile, sending his apple cheeks to his ears. "I hope you dealt me the good ones."

"The best ones," she says.

Batley gets the dealer chip. That makes the man to my right the small blind, and I'm the big blind, out two hundred bucks instantly. "Ouch," says the small blind, sounding tired. "I'm Charles, by the way. Better known as Chuck Frank on those big blue billboards."

"The assemblyman." I shake his hand.

"And you're the sergeant," Frank says. "Can I call you Sarge?"

"You wouldn't be the first," I say.

The flop comes up. Ten of hearts, ace of spades, and king of diamonds. My pocket cards are a two of clubs and seven of diamonds—a terrible start. But I paid the big blind so there's no point folding now. I'll see what comes up in the turn when Veronica deals one more card to the table.

"Massages, huh?" I ask. "This a spa day or something?" I punctuate it with a barking laugh, masculine and deep. They laugh with me.

"Get our little toesies done," Batley says. "*Someone's* getting a facial!" That starts another round of laughter. I join in.

"Massages are a perk of being friends with Don DeVos," Cuttino says.

They all say his name with an emotion I can only describe as awe, somewhere caught between admiration and fear. "What's he like?" I ask. "Don himself, that is. We haven't met." My wife has. Eve once humiliated me by going into DeVos's office to argue about Aaron. I wasn't sure if DeVos would walk into the room and shake my hand, like the others, or punch me in the gut for the trouble Aaron and Eve had given him.

"Don is relaxed, I'd say," Batley says. He puts down the chips to match the big blind.

My eyebrows lift. "Relaxed?"

Cuttino puts down chips too. "Confident, more like. Nothing to worry about when you're the big man in charge."

"Aren't we waiting for him?" I ask.

"He'll buy in later. No limit, remember? You don't have to stop throwing in more cash until you run out," Cuttino says.

"Or beyond." Assemblyman Frank rests his chin on his hand, glowering at the flop. His toupee doesn't look like human hair. His polo is faded from being worn a couple of summers.

We've all met the big blind. Veronica puts the turn on the table, which is a two of diamonds. I've got a pair of twos now. As soon as it gets around to me, I fold. I'm not a Batley or a DeVos. Their no-limit isn't the same as my no-limit, and I need to survive long enough to figure them out.

"Don's going to like you, Hank," Cuttino says. "He collects people. Interesting people, in his words."

"He's funny," adds Batley. He checks his cards and sniffles. "I'm going to raise by five hundred."

It's good I folded. A pair of twos wouldn't be worth raising to five hundred, but I'd be tempted to do it, because I think I've already spotted Batley's tell. He's got nothing. Bluffing. I might be able to beat him with a pair.

The others, I'm not sure. Cuttino folds but Frank meets. Neither twitch when Veronica places the river—the final card from the dealer—leaving her with five faceup on the table. I'd have been stuck with nothing better than a pair of twos. Cuttino's mouth twists, and I think maybe he wishes he hadn't folded. The last card was good for him.

"Let's see what you've got," Veronica says.

Batley's got nothing, as I suspected. The assemblyman has a straight. I'll have to watch him closer in the next hand.

"Well played," Batley says. "Very well played, Chuck."

Frank lifts his glass to him and drinks it down. Mallek replaces it with a fresh beverage the moment he swallows the last drop. It seems that DeVos likes having his players drunk, maybe because he loves to win. Houses like these don't belong to losers.

"How did you get to know Don?" I ask Cuttino.

"I fell in with these genius bastards when Don and Bernie donated those patrol cars," he says. Cuttino's teeth look sharper when he laughs, cast in harsh contrast by the single overhead light. The play of shadows that makes Veronica's breasts look like pool balls turns him leering and clownish.

"We got drinks after the first meeting to arrange the dona-tion," Batley says. "Turned out we had common interests and goals." He pulls a face. "Back then, we thought Wilkes did, too."

"Wilkes and Hank are close. Don't talk bad about his friend around him," Cuttino says. There's a hint of taunt to the tone. A deliberate schoolyard jab.

"He was the sheriff and my colleague," I say. "Now he's neither. Don't act like the PC police around me."

"Then I'll say it. He's a cowardly piece of trash." Batley drains his drink.

Victoria places another card for the turn. Cuttino raises. The bet's up to three hundred.

I've got three of a kind, all jacks, with a king in the pocket. I meet. "Did you guys play poker with Wilkes, too?"

"He wasn't one of us like that," Frank says, forehead resting on the heel of his palm. His eyes seem to be sinking deeper into his skull with every drink.

Another deal, another flop. I'm the small blind and I've got an ace in the pocket, so I check. Cuttino raises. I meet. Batley shakes his head and folds with a laugh.

*One of us.* Who are they?

Right now, all I see is a cluster of important people hanging around Don DeVos like a fan club. They're less like meat eaters and more like sucker fish. If they're not hoovering up his waste, then they've got his hook in their lip. It's normal. Weaker men cling to others' power. But it's enough to have me mulling Eve's conspiracy theory, and I don't like any of it. "So you guys met getting the new cars," I say. "And now you've got this weekly poker thing?"

"Not always weekly, and not always just us. Some of our other regulars got outta dodge as soon as Don announced the blackout," Cuttino says. "Headed to Cancun, Florida, the Riviera…"

"I'm going to my house in Truckee tomorrow," Batley says.

Frank is quiet, watching the cards, watching the other players. When we get to the river, the corner of his mouth twitches before he raises, and I think he's bluffing. I've got his number now.

I win this hand with three kings.

Veronica's dealing the next hand when DeVos enters. I can feel him coming before I notice him in the doorway. There's a shift in the house, literally, a change in the music. Oldies turn to upbeat tunes. The fireplace flares. It's a smart home programmed to herald its owner, and I'm halfway expecting DeVos to come swanning out with rose petals dropped before his holy feet.

But the guy who walks through the hallway is casual in jeans, Henley, and white Nikes. He's matched it with hair too dark for his age, but it's as convincing as his affable smile. He shakes Mallek's hand and bumps elbows, like a secret handshake at a fraternity.

"The man arrives!" Batley cheers.

DeVos does the rounds, greeting and shaking. Batley first, then Cuttino, and then me. "Hank Everhardt, right?" DeVos asks. His hands are soft with massage oil, and I pick up a whiff of coconut on him. "You're Wilkes's chosen one."

"Cuttino's, actually," I say.

"Is that drink sitting good for you? I can get you another one," DeVos says.

"It's good, thanks." I'm a few sips into my Bud and won't go faster unless I must.

He greets Frank next, then swings a leg over the empty chair and settles with an arm draped over its back. "Who's next up with the girl?"

"I could use a good rub." Batley gets up and stretches out. It's a miracle the button on his jacket doesn't pop.

"Oh, you'll love her," says Don. "It's Suzy Q again."

Knowing groans emanate around the table, and a lot of men bob their heads appreciatively. Cuttino himself says, "Suzy Q with the magic hands."

"She's a local, you know," says Don. "You'd never believe it. So much talent out of the Carson Valley?"

Batley is squirming with anticipation. Mallek guides him into the hallway, and the bulk of his form recedes into shadow.

Once he's gone, Mallek tidies Batley's chips and takes the rack off the table. He's expecting Batley to be gone for a while.

"You've got a beautiful home, Mr. DeVos," I say.

"Call me Don. We're friends here," he says. "And thanks. I've put my best into everything. I scooped this house off the last guy for a cool twenty million and did a gut renovation. Couldn't stand to think about living in another man's house. So this is all me."

Mallek brings new chips to DeVos, who's also holding the dealer chip. That makes Frank and Cuttino the blinds. With a ten and a nine in the pocket, I don't feel good about meeting the big blind, but I'd feel worse folding as soon as DeVos arrives.

"I heard you got a generator put in that can power everything here for two days, no break," Frank says. "That's a lot of power for a property this size."

"I can go a week with only essentials," says DeVos.

"So you won't have to see any blackout if SE&G pulls the plug." Cuttino accepts a fresh drink from Mallek, even though he already can't pry his bleary gaze from Veronica's tits. "I can't stand the thought of being in the dark for, what, two days? Three days?"

"Up to five," Frank says.

"Come on, public safety is always my first concern." DeVos's smile is so easy. This isn't a man who even considers losing a possibility. He's got the resources to reshape his world and he knows it.

"Come on, man. Don't do this to me. I just got a whole deer in my freezer. If I lose power, that stag's going to waste. Think about the animals!" Cuttino laughs at his own cleverness.

"You know what? I can have Mallek run a generator to your house." DeVos raises. Two hundred up. I haven't caught him looking at his pocket yet, so he's bidding blind. If he were any more relaxed, he'd be melting through the grout in the floors.

Frank raises the bids too. He must have good cards.

"You're a generous friend," I remark. "Loaning out whole generators. Got any extras for a sick old lady I work with?"

DeVos waves his cigar so the smoke draws ladders in the air, mouth twisting. "We have programs for that. There's a website. Isn't there, Robert?" Mallek nods without speaking. "Maybe you can get him the website. We've got great people to figure out where resources go."

The conversation turns to great vacations. Cuttino and Frank are transparently jealous of the missing poker players, who went to beautiful warm places without fire or power outages. At least one of them went on DeVos's dime.

"Mind sending me to Cancun, too?" asks Cuttino.

"I owed him a favor," DeVos says with a shrug. "Right now, you and I have drawn equal, so maybe next time. Next time you do something real good for me." To me, the man explains, "I have a house in Mexico, you know. And the girls who give massages there are out of this world. Real cuties. You should come on our next big weekend trip. Check it out. I'd love to get to know the future undersheriff on a more personal level."

I've never had the extra cash for such trips. I don't care for the massages. But the access—the casual hangouts with people of DeVos's caliber—my mind starts spinning. "That sounds wonderful," I say.

The lights flicker and then dim. The sprinklers outside the windows stop. Everyone quiets and looks around. Mallek checks his phone.

"Everything's okay," says Mallek. "There's nothing to worry about."

A moment later, the lights come back full power.

"Fire must be getting close," Cuttino says.

"Mind telling me what kind of filtration system you've got on your A/C, Don?" I ask. "I can't smell any smoke."

"It's proprietary. I've also got sprinklers out there." DeVos gestures to the towering windows with a cigar. The forest is opaque beyond. "Everything's fire-resistant. This house could stand through the apocalypse. It's unburnable."

"A lot like how the Titanic was unsinkable," I say.

Everyone laughs, even DeVos.

"You should be grateful we're not gonna sink," he says. "After all, every last one of us is on the same ship. Even you now, Hank."

## CHAPTER 14
## EVE

Maybe Garrett's pills make me reckless.

Maybe I took too much ephedrine.

Maybe Hank knocked something loose in my head when he shoved me.

But I decide to do something wild.

I watch Hank get into Kaleb Cuttino's pickup from the front window. By the time they drive away, I have a scarf over my face, shoes on my feet, and keys in my hand. I leave my cell phone at home and pull the GPS out of the car, just in case Hank checks. I'm two cars behind them when they pass Carson Street, tracking the double exhaust pipes jutting past Cuttino's rear windshield. I'm still behind them when they take a turnoff into the foothills.

I have to stop when they enter a gated property. Only the road and a few yards in either direction is walled off. They're depending on obscurity to keep folks from entering. I drive past the entrance and park out of sight in a weed-riddled field.

The wind rattles and roars over the foothill's ridges. I can't hear my own footsteps crashing over pine needles and through rabbit brush, so there's no way I'll be heard by someone else. It's lucky because I'm not prepared for subterfuge. My little flats rub my toes raw and I stumble frequently. Every stick seems at the perfect angle to scrape my shins. I take my purse off to clutch it against my chest, triple-checking the zipper to make sure nothing will fall out in a place I can't find it.

Hank isn't just meeting Don DeVos. He's gone to his house.

I've seen the floodlit timber exterior before. It's the most expensive house in the area, so DeVos gave a tour to the Reno Gazette-Journal to show off, right around the same time he was refusing to pay Aaron's workers' compensation. Aaron and I once spent a night throwing darts at pictures from the article.

It's even more beautiful in person. The haze tints everything amber, and the forest vanishes outside the reach of the floodlights. The house seems to float in space. There are dozens of cars. Most are nicer than Cuttino's truck, and all are more tasteful. I watch my husband duck his head against the wind as he climbs the stairs into the house, exchanging brief words with the doorman before stepping inside. The doorman turns. With a startle, I realize it's Mallek, Mackenzie's so-called boyfriend. His Facebook profile showed that chiseled nose and long ponytail. It's easy to imagine falling for a face like that.

I won't be getting in past Mallek. I hang back among the tree line and watch my husband move through the party. The windows are big enough that I can see everything, but only the mansion's front rooms are lit. The wings in the rear stand dark. Anything could be back there.

I'm hazier than the woods, like Garrett's medication laid a blanket over my face, and I can feel my brother's presence hovering over me like a guardian angel. It's like he's standing over me again. I can almost hear his voice.

*Mack. Ten twenty-seven. The manifesto.*

"I'm working on it," I whisper.

I slip through the garden, looking for an unlocked door. Everything feels distant. It's unreal to walk past DeVos's house. My life is as insulated as a hamster in a Habitrail, scampering from my house to Aaron's house to hospitals to the courthouse and then back again. This luxury doesn't exist in my tiny bubble. His wealth is a physical weight pressing on my lungs, reminding me that he had no pennies for Aaron's accident, but he can spend them all on cherub statues.

I can see a lot of equipment on the darker side of the house. DeVos has water tanks and a huge backup generator, though I've never seen one that big. He also has a garage back there. It's two stories tall. It's bigger than my house.

The curtains on one of the furthest windows gaps open, a narrow slit that allows candlelight to shine through. I risk a step across the grass. It's as neat as a golf course, a thin layer that crunches under the balls of my feet.

Through the slit, I can see a small room with a massage table and bench. A woman sits on the bench. She hugs her knees to her chest, body swathed in a bathrobe. She's short and has a curvy figure. Her hair has been done in pigtails.

I have to step to the left to see an adult man buttoning his shirt on the other side of the massage table. He's speaking to the woman. Even if I can't make out words, his expression tells all. He's angry.

It's Don DeVos. He looks like he would have been a fun college boy thirty years ago. Now he's aging and fighting it, with Botox as much as his boot-cut jeans, and he seethes with frightening energy when he speaks to the girl.

He leaves and slams the door hard enough that I can feel it outside.

She stays on the bench.

I slip toward the window and rap my nails on it. Her head snaps up. It's Mackenzie. She's wearing a lot more makeup than she did when she was at Aaron's funeral, and the makeup doesn't suit her. With the heavy eyeshadow and bright lips, I can only assume she was done up by a middle-aged woman who learned to do lipliner from an undertaker.

Recognition flares and Mackenzie does a double take—to me, to the door, then back.

"Open the latch," I say quietly, pointing.

Mack opens it, but she's shaking her head while I climb in. "What are you doing here? You can't be here." She smells like coconut oil, and her hands shine with it.

"Aaron sent me to find you," I say.

Emotion shifts from fear to grief. "How? He's—he's gone." It comes out of her in a sob. She's already on the brink of crying, and now I've shocked her over the edge.

"That doesn't matter." I evaluate this girl for the ability to escape. No shoes. Probably no clothes under the robe. "Are you here with Mallek?"

"You *have* to get out of here," she says. "If they find you—"

"You're not here with Mallek." I don't have to be a genius to understand why DeVos would have been in the room with a teenage girl, getting dressed, while she looks shattered. And I'm not surprised. "Come with me."

I grab her arm. She jerks it to her chest.

Her wrist is bruised.

Mack catches herself, stops crying, and takes a breath. "I can't," she says. "If I leave early, they'll send my pictures to everyone I know. And my parents will owe them a lot of money."

Something like panic swells inside of me, but it quickly fades. Garrett's medicine is strong. Even when Hank had me pressed against the wall, anger etching every line of his face, I'd only felt the space where fear should have been. "But you witnessed Aaron's death," I say. "I need your help. He's being accused of things. Terrible things. They say he started this fire, that he stole property from SE&G—"

"He did," she says. "Steal from them, I mean. That's how we met. He broke into Robert's office here—that's Mallek; his name is Robert—and he grabbed some things. I was waiting in the office at the time, so I caught him, but I didn't tell anyone. Aaron tracked me down the next time Robert and Don let me leave. Sometimes I go home for a couple weeks, until they—"

"They're using you," I say.

Her eyes flood, but her tears don't escape. "Aaron found me. He was nice, so I told him everything. He was going to make sure I didn't have to come back. But my parents… They get the money I earn, so it's not like they care what

I'm doing. They told Robert where to pick me up when he came looking. Aaron tried to hide me. And he…"

*He got killed.*

I've watched the video so many times I can relive it in my mind. Those horrible noises. The mass of Aaron's body on the ground.

"Did Aaron give you his journal? Is that how you know about me?" Mack asks.

There's a journal to find. That's good to know. "I'm going to finish what Aaron started. He thinks I can nail DeVos. But I can't do it without you. You're the only one who saw him get killed, and you're the only one who can say it was murder."

"I recorded it on my phone, but I don't think the video's going to help you," Mack says.

"Let me be the judge. Let's go."

She doesn't follow me toward the window. "Don't go that way. They've got cameras. They'll have already seen you. Go out before they come back, because they *will* be back."

"I'm not leaving without you," I say.

"Look… My phone, you can find it without me." She clings to my arm, dragging me to the door. "I took it to Aaron's house. He had his journal in this box under the washing machine, so I put it in there. The cop made me delete the video. But it's in the trash folder for, like, a month."

"Mack," I begin.

"If they catch me helping you, they'll fucking kill me," she says.

Something in her eyes convinces me. At this point, in the belly of the beast, I'll be lucky if I get out safely. Mack pushes me into the hall and shuts the door.

The hallway is dark and long, but I can hear voices echoing from the den where the men are gathered. No wonder Mack was afraid. Any of them could be waiting to hurt her.

*Including Hank?*

It's darker deeper into the house, but lamps shine out of some of the rooms. I spot an office. There are Bankers Boxes piled in front of a small desk. One of the computer monitors is tilted so I can see security footage. The cameras are recording like Mackenzie said. But nobody is watching now.

I veer into the office. There's a photograph of Mallek with his parents, so this must be his desk. These are his belongings.

Except those boxes look familiar.

The first lid is rotten and falls apart when I open it. The papers inside are Aaron's. I saw them at his house right before those men chased me away, and now I know the identity of at least one of those men. I quickly shuffle through the pages and take photos so I can have copies. Even with the Xanax, my heart's beating fast, and every pulse feels like footsteps coming up the hallway.

A few layers into the box, I find insurance paperwork. It's from the time when Aaron still worked for SE&G. This is an insurance agreement he signed to use his personal pickup during work trips.

The license plate number catches my eye. *46X-7EY.*

That's the string of characters that Aaron had written on the bottom of his letter to me. His next clue is in his pickup truck. The one that the police seized because it was found parked near the VC Fire. "Damn it," I whisper.

And then the door creaks behind me.

I shoot to my feet, but it's too late. I've been found by Robert Mallek.

* * *

I'm held in Mallek's office for a quiet hour, left to wonder what will happen to me next. I consider screaming. I consider running. I note that Mallek has a gun and decide against doing either. After an eternity, Mallek's phone rings. He answers, listens briefly, and hangs up. "Come with me," he says.

Mallek leads me through the shadowed splendor of DeVos's mansion. We don't go into the solarium or back toward the party, but take a right to go behind the kitchen.

Don DeVos waits in a trophy room lit by a single fireplace. He's gazing at a class picture on the wall, hands folded behind his back, and he grins when he sees me. "I see we've got a party crasher." He looks at my chest, hidden by a modest neckline, and at my hips, which are fat enough that few dresses can hide it. His gaze is a physical force on my body. "I know you, don't I? You're that lady," he says, snapping his fingers. "You came to my office last year. Something about health benefits?"

Somehow, I manage to speak. "Workers' compensation."

I'm tensed with the expectation of violence, but he laughs and nods. "Right, right. I remember that now."

I'd dressed provocatively when I went to his office. Men are hard to predict, but squeezing the mosquito bites of my breasts into cleavage usually gets *some* reaction. Most think they can fuck me, which can be useful, or they think less of me, which makes it easier to catch them off guard. DeVos fell in both camps. He wasn't secretive about either. I still wonder if he'd have given Aaron money if I'd fucked him.

"Come look at this," he says, beckoning me over. "Mallek, can you get our guest a drink?"

I'm no safer at a distance than I am beside DeVos. I make my way over, clutching my purse in both hands.

"You're Hank's wife." He takes a hearty drink and sets the glass on the mantel. DeVos props an elbow against the wall, looking me up and down again. "Is that why you're here? Worried that Hank's gonna cheat on you during a boys' night?"

Getting massages with happy endings from a teenager doesn't qualify as cheating. It's some other kind of blacker evil, and for all Hank's failings, that's not one of them. "It's stupid," I say, which isn't exactly an answer, but it sounds like a confession. I am a petty jealous wife. I don't like my husband going out without me.

Mallek returns. "Sir," he says.

"Just a moment," DeVos says to me with saccharine hospitality.

He confers with Mallek by the door. I'm left to look at DeVos's memorabilia. He has sports jerseys with others' names on them. He's posted degrees from different colleges and accolades from governments for public service. There's an entire wall dedicated to pictures of

DeVos shaking hands with important people. The last governor. A couple of senators. A dozen different models and actors.

The class photo looks like it belongs to a fraternity. All the men in it are standing with their fists lifted, grinning at the camera. A much-younger DeVos is front and center with his arm around a classmate.

Mallek leaves the room, shutting the door behind him, and I can't hear the party anymore.

DeVos approaches me with a fresh drink. "Right, I remember everything now," he says again. "You're Aaron Ashe's sister. That was an ugly situation, wasn't it? I hate how everything has turned out."

"Me too," I say. "He's dead now."

DeVos puts on a sympathetic face. "The police told me he died. Was it all the pills?"

"No." It comes out of me sharply. "What makes you think he was on pills?"

"I've got a mind like a steel trap." He laughs. The cliché is a witticism from this guy. "The lawyers found everything about Aaron Ashe, including his love of oxys. I might know things about him that you don't. But you, I don't know quite as much. I'd love to have a drink and get to know you." DeVos offers the drink that Mallek brought. "Here you go. I hope you like rum and coke."

I don't, but the smoke has left me parched, so I drink. The alcohol doesn't taste too strong. I drink deeper.

"What do you do for a living, Mrs. Everhardt?" he asks.

"I'm a housewife."

"No wonder you're so worried your husband might run off and cheat on you. You don't have much going on for yourself outside of your husband, your sergeant, your…daddy? No employment record, no educational history, no criminal background…"

"Have you been researching me?" I asked.

"You sneaked onto my property, Mrs. Everhardt. Let's be honest with each other," DeVos says. "Are you here because you're suspicious of your husband or because you're up to something with your brother?"

"I told you, he's dead. I'm just a jealous, fearful woman who can't stand her husband having fun with the boys." I seem to have forgotten how to simper. I take another drink to hide the anger twisting my face. I'm calmer when I set the glass down again.

"Dead or not, he started a terrible fire that's going to kill a lot of people. I can't think it's coincidence that you showed up at my house at a time like this." His smile looks genuinely relaxed. DeVos isn't afraid of me. He isn't afraid of anything.

"I heard that you guys, Sierra Energy and Gas… I heard that Aaron stole something from you guys. Ever since he died, I've just been… I don't know." I can't think of a plausible excuse for breaking into the house. I make myself look distraught. "It's all so stupid. It doesn't make any sense."

"Calm down. Like I said, you're not in trouble. If I'd known you wanted to talk, I'd have passed word to Hank to bring you along. I've been wanting to clear the air too." He starts on his next drink. "I can't help but feel like Aaron's breakdown started because he lost his job. We couldn't pay him workers' comp, you know. We told him to get away from that fire, but he tried to fight it, which is explicitly against company policy. His injury was self-inflicted. But maybe if I'd just paid him..." He sighs. "Maybe things wouldn't have ended so badly."

My fingers are digging hard enough into my purse strap that I can feel the seam under the nails. "There's no changing the past. We can't undo what we've already done." DeVos can't take away what I know about him now —any of it.

He watches me lift the drink to my mouth again and just keeps smiling. "We can be friends. I'd like to make a gift to you in Aaron's memory." He goes to one of the chairs in front of the fire, and as I watch, he writes out a check for nine thousand dollars. "Under ten grand is a gift. You won't get taxed on this. It's all yours, free and clear."

My legs feel weaker still. I have to sit down. "A gift because...you want to be friends."

"So you can move on," DeVos says. "You might have heard some confusing things from your brother. He was obviously *so* disturbed, especially in the end. He was making wild claims. Nothing true. But I can see how it'd make it hard for you to move on, why you'd be skulking around looking for answers that don't exist."

He signs the check with a flourish, tears it out, and hands it to me. I have a hard time focusing on the numbers. There must have been more alcohol in the drink than I realized.

Nine thousand dollars.

It's more money than I've ever held in my life, and I want to throw it into the fireplace.

But I slip it into my purse, where Aaron's blue-handled box cutter sits. I wrap my fingers around it. It feels smoother than it should, sort of slippery, so I clutch it hard enough to make my knuckles ache.

"Let's drink to our friendship." Don lifts his drink.

I lift mine too, and we drain them together.

"So tell me," DeVos says casually, leaning back with his empty glass. "Why'd you come through that window?"

My fist trembles on the box cutter. "I don't..." *Where are my words? Where is my voice?*

"You and Aaron are apples from the same tree," he says. "Both of you so confused. Probably drugs. Shameful. I think I should have Hank drive you home."

The floor is skewing. The fireplace is above me, a fire in the treetops climbing down branch by branch to reach for me. "Hank," I say. He can't tell Hank I'm here. If Don is going to rape me, kill me, silence me... I don't want Hank to know. I'd rather die than have him discover me.

The world is so distant.

DeVos swirls in front of me, taking the glass from my hand.

"It was nice talking with you, Mrs. Everhardt," he says as I slip away to oblivion.

# CHAPTER 15
# HANK

I've doubled my buy-in by the time I finish my beer. The dregs taste like victory. Without Batley or DeVos at the table, the latter drawn away by Mallek for business, I've only got Frank and Cuttino to contend with. Both are trashed. It's laughably easy to goad them into higher bets. If I can get them past the flop, they'll keep going, no matter how bad their cards, and it makes it easy to rake their chips toward me one hand at a time.

I'm feeling good by the time DeVos returns.

Until I see that he's got Eve at his side.

My Eve, my wife, a wisp who looks like she wouldn't be standing if DeVos wasn't helping. She's unfocused. Her head bobbing. "What the hell?" I shoot up from the table fast enough to bump my chair back. Cuttino's hand shoots out to catch it before it hits the floor.

I grab Eve, cupping her face between my hands. She's not there. She can't seem to see me and doesn't react to my presence.

"Someone invited herself to the party and hit the bar a little too hard," DeVos says. He doesn't sound angry. If anything, he's amused.

Eve's not a hard drinker. Watching her brother go thirty rounds against addiction has kept Eve on the straight and narrow, and she's a lady who likes to keep her wits sharp. But hell, what do I know about Eve after Aaron? She doesn't have to be responsible anymore. She sure as hell doesn't have to listen to me, obey me, just do *one fucking thing* to make my life any easier.

After everything I've done for her.

"Jesus Christ." I take her from DeVos and everyone's laughing at the way that she wobbles before collapsing against my shoulder. Only my arm locked around her waist keeps her upright.

I should muster an apology to my host, but I can't. I've never been so humiliated.

"I'll let Cuttino cash you out and get the winnings into your wallet tomorrow," DeVos says. He's so friendly, so understanding. Still so *relaxed*. DeVos could have taken every penny I owned playing cards and he wouldn't have beat me so thoroughly. My dumb bitch of a wife has trespassed and gotten drunk, and what would my deputies think if they found out? How will anyone respect me as a man when my woman acts like this?

DeVos walks us to the door. Cuttino comes too.

"Don't worry, seriously," Don murmurs. He pats me on the shoulder. "She's harmless. And I've warmed her up for you a little, so the party's not really over, is it?" Another chuckle.

I just leave. I can't meet his eyes.

"She had to get here somehow," Cuttino growls. "Bet she parked down the drive. I'll walk you."

It's harder to make Eve walk than to carry her, so I pull her into my arms. She's a feather against my chest. Such a tiny thing to be such a huge thorn. Her purse, settled in her lap, must weigh more than she does. "The fuck were you doing?" I hiss under my breath, although she's not getting any more responsive. Her head falls back against my arm. "I don't buy the idea you'd crash a party. I know you were doing something. Talk to me, Eve!"

She mumbles. "The drink."

"It smells like she cleared out his bar," Cuttino says.

Eve's SUV is a half mile down. I pour her into the passenger's seat. She attempts to buckle herself four times before succeeding. Even now, she's not wearing the necklace I got her. Aaron's fine gold chain disappears down her dress.

I shove her leg into the car and slam the door.

Cuttino waits for me on the other side, his hand braced so that I can't get behind the wheel. "Hell of a way to end the night. I vouched for you, got you around Don's friends. You've had my total trust despite being Wilkes's ass-kiss. And now this," Cuttino says. "Keep your bitch in check."

He looks like he has a glass jaw. I'm tempted to find out, but I swallow down my misplaced anger.

Because this is *Eve's* fault.

Cuttino's not done. "You don't even know what you're fucking with here, Everhardt. You seemed smarter than

Wilkes. I thought you were the kind of guy I want to work with."

"Hey," I say sharply. "My wife's having an embarrassing moment, but we don't have to make a big deal out of it."

"Oh, it's a big deal all right. Don't you get it? DeVos throws parties so we can relax, let loose, be ourselves. So we don't have to worry about loose lips. Keeping a tight hold on what information gets out of this house is a matter of life and fucking death, Sergeant." He slams his hand against Eve's car so hard that I'm surprised it doesn't dent. "If you look bad, *I* look bad. If we look bad… We get cut loose."

Slowly, I nod. "I'm going to take care of this. I'll fix it."

"You better." He knocks his fist on top of my car. "We need each other, Everhardt."

* * *

The drive home is a surreal slipstream through Carson City. The roads are packed with too many cars from evacuees we don't have the space to hold. They emerge from the smoke one at a time, then vanish, specters in the darkness. Visibility has shrunken to a tiny gray bubble. The wind isn't blowing any of it away. There's no limit to the smoke.

Eve's unconscious, and I realize I'm going to have to carry her upstairs. Her head bumps the car when I pull her out, but she doesn't wake.

Our house is quiet. Even with the air conditioner running, inside is as smoky as outside. I hate DeVos in that first breath of trapped air. I hate his wealth, his filtration system, his reputation. And I especially hate him for being so *relaxed*.

I toss Eve onto our bed and she sprawls with an arm under her. She mewls, twists, gets it out. I turn on the bedside lamp to light up her skin. Her chin's wet. She must have spewed in the car and I missed it.

"What did you think you'd accomplish tonight?" I demand. "Did you really think you'd do anything besides piss me off? Do you have any idea how angry you make me, especially when you just don't *listen*?"

I'm ready for a fight that she's not capable of rising to meet, and that makes me angrier. She's the one who fucked me over with DeVos and Cuttino. Yet I'm the one who has to be awake to think of it, stewing in it, looking at Aaron's necklace around her scrawny little throat while she snores. "You bitch," I say. "You goddamn bitch."

Her dress came up when I dropped her on the bed. It's rucked around her waist, exposing plain white underwear. She probably bought it in a five-pack at Walmart. She never wears sexy underwear for me. That's Eve. Always thinking about her life; never thinking about what I might need.

I yank them down to find the bruised ridges of her hip bones.

She groans, face compressing.

"What's that?" I ask. "That better be an apology."

I rip her neckline down. She's got old white scars on the undersides of her breasts, high on her arms near the pits, in the crevices of her thighs. There are even a few on her lower belly. They're parallel lines, some of them overlapping. I haven't seen them in such good lighting before. Eve insists on keeping it dark when we make love. In the past I believed her story, that she had a hostile cat as a child, but now I see Aaron in those marks. I see damage all over her body where some psycho who murdered his dad and sliced at his bones must have been torturing his sister.

Even as I hate her, I pity her. I love her.

Looking at her naked body gets me hard. Sure, she's scraped up from running outside. Sure, she's scarred. But her skin's got the tissue paper look of white roses at a wedding—or a funeral. Blue veins grip her body. There's a thick one that runs under her belly to her ribs. I can see every single bone.

I want Eve.

More than that, I wish she'd want me back half as much. She's halfway into the ghost world, and Aaron's death has only dragged her further. What makes her so evasive makes her beautiful too.

God, I fucking love those tiny tits.

I fumble with my belt. I can't even wait to get my pants off all the way. I shove her legs apart, and Eve looks at me through the slits of her eyes, like she does when she's in ecstasy, and I put myself in her. It's like screwing a photograph that I can touch. I press one of her thighs flat with the heel of my palm, my hips jerking against hers. Pressure and pleasure build in my gut. My belt jingles until it gets trapped against the soft skin of her leg when I start losing rhythm. My nuts get tight.

I bury my face in her neck. I bite, I suck, I take what I need that she so seldom gives. My teeth come up against the gold chain.

She's still wearing the necklace Aaron gave her. Not mine.

"Fuck," I snarl.

My fist grips the little diamond. I wrench it hard enough that the chain snaps. It hits the wall and I fill my fingers with her hair instead, wrenching her head to the side so I can bite her ear.

"Is it that hard, Eve? Is it that hard?" I'm not even sure why I'm speaking or what I'm asking. She's wetter now. I move easier.

Orgasm hits me out of nowhere. I squeeze her within the cage of my arms, the weight of my head on her shoulder, my guttural roar in her ear. I pull the specter of my wife against my chest, and it feels like I've really got her. There's nobody here but us, in this white light of ecstasy. And I've finally got what I need. For just a moment, I've got everything.

* * *

I don't sleep in bed that night. I pray for Eve from the other side of the wall, lying on the couch in the office, wishing for the light of God's love to find her. The couch is comfortable enough, but I'm not comfortable in my skin. I've been turned to fire by shame.

Once or twice, when I beat Aaron at poker, he'd gotten angry because, as he said, "You're a shitty winner, Everhardt." He told me I gloated. He said that I was smug.

He only thought I was bad at winning because he'd never seen how bad I am at losing.

*DeVos beat me.*

I hadn't even known we were playing a game, and I had lost.

Suddenly, I want Eve to be right.

I *want* Jobson to have killed Aaron at DeVos's orders.

My phone rings. I grab it off the coffee table, and my gut lurches when I see Cuttino's name on the screen. "Everhardt here," I say. "Did you cash out for me?" Light tone. As far as Cuttino knows, I've taken care of my wife and everything is fine.

"Yeah, but forget that. We've got a problem. Turn on the news."

I head to the downstairs TV, which is always turned to KOLO-8. This late at night, it should be playing infomercials. Instead, a reporter stands in front of a dark hillside pocked by fires, squinting into the floodlight above the camera. "…started just an hour ago, when local residents reported seeing a power line spark," she says. "Earlier, Sierra Energy and Gas announced a planned blackout to prevent this kind of fire, but it wasn't scheduled to begin until tomorrow at 7:00 a.m."

The camera cuts to show a hillside consumed by fire. I can't tell where it is—it's too dark. The screen says it's in West Carson, near C Hill. Wind is blowing hard north.

When the reporter's gone, the TV returns to a news studio in Reno, a safe distance from the wildfires here. I mute it.

"We have to get out there," Cuttino says. "We're evacuating houses on the west side of town."

I swear under my breath. "I'll be right out."

# CHAPTER 16
# EVE

I wake up and everything hurts. I feel like I slept hanging upside down, letting all the blood rush behind my eyeballs and punch the top of my skull. My head is the worst of it, but when I try to move, I find a lot of other pains too. My arms are bruised. I've pulled a muscle in my back. I'm in my normal bed, with a pressure-adjustable mattress that cost as much as a car, but it feels like I'm resting on nails.

Sitting up is a necessary evil. I find myself mostly naked. My clothes are a mess, as bad as my skin. My questioning fingers seek between my legs. I find dried blood on the friction burned skin of my vulva. I'm shaking while I stare at my fingers. The Xanax has lost its hold, and I have the worst hangover of my life, which is compounding into something like terror.

I don't remember having sex.

Obviously it happened here, right here, in the safety of my bed at home, and that means it could only have been one person.

I can't stop shaking, but I manage to stand up and remove what remains of my clothing. That dress is one of my favorites. Now it's in the trash. I turn the shower on as hot as it can go and wait for steam to collect before stepping into the stall. The water sluicing down my skin is brown. I press my hands to the tiles to keep myself standing, and I try to remember the night before.

Everything feels like an emotional abstract rather than a linear series of events. Some of the bruises on my back are from when Hank and I argued, which I recall as a few red-hued sensations. His elbow digging into me. The heat of his breath.

Then he left to go…where?

I shut my eyes and press my forehead to the tiles hard, but memory doesn't come.

God, my head hurts.

A gentle wash from head to toe leaves my body clean and my wounds easier to inventory. My vulva isn't too bad. Just tender. No worse than when Hank demands a quickie and won't wait for me to grab the lube. It only looked so bad at first because I had slept in it, wallowed in it. I've got new bruises elsewhere, mostly on my shins and knees. I remember a forest. I was stabbed and scraped and dirtied by branches. *Because…why?*

The memories slip away with another pulse of migraine. I'll remember once everything stops hurting so much. I count out the pills I need to take this morning. Two Bayers. An ephedrine pill. Another bar of the Xanax given to me by Garrett so I can stay sane.

My phone rings before I can find new clothes. It's Garrett again. "Evangeline," he says.

"Hi," I say hoarsely.

That's all it takes for Garrett to know. A single word. "What's wrong?"

I don't want to tell him anything. I don't even know *what* I'd tell him if I wanted to. "Did you see me last night?" I ask. "Do you... Did we talk? Do you know anything at all?"

A moment of silence, and then he says, "Are you at home?"

"Yes."

"I'll be there in ten minutes," Garrett says.

My phone closes out of the conversation and the camera roll appears in its place. That must have been the last app open before locking my device, but there are a hundred shots I don't recognize, and I took them all during the hours I can't recall. I've photographed papers packed inside boxes. Aaron's papers, Aaron's boxes. The last picture is a close-up on a string of figures I recognize—a license plate number.

A connection sizzles to life between two half-dead neurons, and I remember I need to find my brother's pickup.

The rest of the night is black.

I put on a fresh pair of underwear and a crewneck dress from Zulily. I've always liked the way that Aaron's diamond necklace looks against the solid lavender.

The necklace. Where's the necklace?

It hadn't even occurred to me that I didn't have to take it off to shower. I look in the mirror and find a cruel red stripe across the side of my throat. Aaron's necklace was ripped off me. I don't know if that was Hank or the person who drugged me. I can't even be sure that those two aren't the same people.

A knock thunders from my front door, and I jump. I hadn't expected Garrett to arrive this quickly. There's little pause before the person at my door knocks again, louder, so I comb my purse for the necklace while I go downstairs. The jewelry box that Hank gave me is in there. My favorite necklace isn't.

Another knock.

"I'm coming," I say right before pulling the door open.

It's not Garrett on the other side.

Deputy Jobson is taller than me, wider than me, and he fills the doorway. I've seen those hairy hands gripping a Taser. I heard his shaking voice when he threatened Aaron. And now he's here. My brother's killer is here.

At least the box cutter is still in my purse. I curl my fingers around it.

"What do you want?" I ask.

"I just want to talk," says Jobson.

I peer around the intimidating bulk of his body to see a sky smokier than the night before, both darker and redder, and I have to double-check my phone to be sure it's after sunrise. It's almost nine. Everyone on the block is awake. Several neighbors are waiting for an opportunity to turn at the stop sign, trapped by a line of cars on the cross street. Others are still loading.

There must be another fire.

"Hank's not home," I say automatically, trying to shut the door.

He puts his foot in the jamb. "I'm here to talk to you."

"I have to evacuate."

"I'm sorry," Jobson says quickly. The words are meaningless. Hank apologizes every time he wins against me or embarrasses me, but only because he knows his win can't be taken back. Aaron can't be brought back to life by a simple sorry. Jobson seems to think it gives him permission to stay in my doorway. He glances around the street. "Can I come in to talk?"

It hasn't occurred to me that I might get Jobson alone, even in my wildest fantasies when I've imagined him behind bars waiting on death row in the shackles of the incontrovertible evidence Aaron left behind.

But like I said, I'm feeling unhinged.

This is the man who killed my brother. What would I do to him if I got him alone?

"Can I come in?" he asks again, uneasy. It's taken me a long time to answer.

The box cutter's weight is perfect.

"I'm not apologizing for doing my job with your brother," Jobson goes on, realizing he'll get no real response. "I'm apologizing because I'm going to keep making your life worse. Your husband threatened me at work, the last sheriff did something illegal, and I'm about to report all of it. It seemed like I should give you fair warning before I leave this hellhole."

He's leaving all this behind. If I find proof that he murdered Aaron for DeVos, Jobson will be gone before I can take action.

*DeVos.*

My head throbs sharply, and I press the heel of my hand to my temple, pushing back against the pain. My ears are ringing.

"Are you okay?" Jobson asks.

I double over from the headache. I'm not okay, but not in the ways that he thinks. "I'm feeling dizzy. Can you help me get a glass of water?"

He helps me into the kitchen, gets a glass, and pours water into it. He leaves the front door open. I wonder if he's afraid. Not afraid of a tiny girl like me, but afraid that Hank is in the house, afraid that he'll get caught.

"Thank you," I say and take a drink. I really was thirsty.

Jobson stands at the edge of the kitchen. "As I said, your husband threatened me at work. He's going to face consequences."

Hank's always gotten along with his deputies. They love him. When he had his appendix removed two years ago, we were drowning in flowers and casseroles. I cover the broken skin on my neck with a hand and try to look pathetic, which isn't difficult. "Why would Hank do that to you?"

"Because he's a corrupt asshole protecting corrupt assholes," Jobson snarls.

I miscalculated. I thought that looking vulnerable might invoke protective instincts. Instead, I've prodded the button that throws him into instant rage. I bet Jobson has a lot of those buttons.

"But it's insane. It's like I'm the only one who sees it. People are whispering. I'm hearing weird shit. Talk of SE&G buying cops, things your brother did, things he didn't do… But nobody will say a damn thing out loud."

"I've heard about SE&G too. I heard that you're one of the people who took bribes from them." I've found nothing that supports it, but I don't mind fishing for a reaction.

Jobson puffs up with anger, his hands balled into fists at his sides. "Who told you that? Who?" He takes a step toward me.

*Well, there's the reaction.*

"Do you mean it's not true?" I ask.

Jobson slams a fist into my counter. "Fuck! I don't have anything to do with bullshit like that. Fifteen fucking *years* of service and I make one mistake—*one mistake*—and now everyone's looking at me like I'm the criminal!"

"Your one mistake killed my brother," I say through my teeth.

Emotions scrabble like rodents across his face. "He attacked me. I already told you I'm sorry."

"If you're really sorry, you won't run," I say. "You'll help me. I want to know why Aaron died."

"I just told you—"

"His truck," I interrupt. "There's something in his pickup I need to see. I know it's impounded at the sheriff's office. Get me the keys."

"You're not going to find anything that changes the facts," Jobson says. "I was working overtime that night. Dispatch sent me to a trespassing call. The subject became violent when I attempted to arrest him, and because of his asthma, he died in an authorized chokehold."

Someone's been rehearsing with his lawyer.

I almost believe him. I can see the simplicity in this man. He veers between anger and fear like a drunk driver behind the wheel of a police cruiser. I could armchair diagnose him with generalized anxiety disorder, and I'd put money on PTSD as well. Police work is traumatizing. Mental health is a moving target, and cops don't take time to heal. They're too busy chasing down the next trauma.

Right now my brother's murder weapon, that fleshy elbow, is folded across Jobson's heaving chest. Blood pounds through the veins cording his arms because his heart still beats, while Aaron rests as ash in shadow.

Jobson denies killing Aaron on purpose, but there's no denying that he did kill him. It doesn't matter if he knows that it was somehow ordered by Don DeVos.

*DeVos.*

My head still hurts, but when I squeeze my eyes shut, Mack's face comes to mind. Not the blurry shot of the girl from the body camera, but the girl at Aaron's funeral. That sad little scrap of a thing.

DeVos is trying to hide her.

"Whatever you're hearing about SE&G is true," I say.

"But…" Jobson flounders. "Then that means they got Wilkes. Cuttino. Everhardt. Everyone on top."

"I'll prove it. Get me the keys to the truck. I'll come to your house and get them from you this afternoon, and then you can leave."

He looks so angry that I expect him to refuse me. But Jobson eventually nods. "All right. After everything I've done to you, the least I can do is get you the keys. I have to go in to file my report anyway. I swear to God, if you tell anyone that I got those keys—"

"I can blame it on Hank," I say. "He's given me evidence before. He does whatever I want."

Jobson is nearly purple. "Your whole family is fucked up. You're all insane."

"I'll pick the keys up from your house after lunch. What's your address?" I ask.

He writes it down and the slip goes into my purse, wedged between box cutter and jewelry box, where I know it will be safe.

I walk him to the door.

The cars that were on the road before are gone. Traffic has sped up. I can't see the houses further down the street. The smoke is much too thick. Everything nearer than the corner is tinted red.

Garrett is parking on the street, and the sight of his familiar blue car slowing in front of my picket fence is wrong. A long body emerges from the driver's seat. Then Aaron's psychiatrist is forging a path up my windy drive with a sleeve shielding his eyes, and all parts of my life are colliding.

Jobson slams past him, shoulder against shoulder, and Garrett spins to watch him go. He's confused until he sees me in the doorway, bruised and pale. Then he's angry. "Did that man just hurt you?"

"No, this is…something else. Get in." I slam the door behind Garrett and lock it, peering outside. Everyone still seems distracted by attempts to evacuate. Who would tell Hank that two strange men visited my door this morning? There won't be anybody on our street in an hour, assuming the line of cars ever breaks.

"I'm sorry I took so long getting across town. I had to make some illegal maneuvers to get around the deputies guiding people north, then swing around the back of the neighbor-hood, but…" Garrett trails off. His fingertips hover over my shoulders and neck. Close enough to brush the fine hairs on my skin. "What happened?"

I open my mouth to tell him the whole truth—that something happened with DeVos, and then Hank hurt me. But I can feel Hank's hands around my throat, squeezing the words. "I don't remember." That much is true. "I woke up in bed this morning and… I don't remember last night. I think I left the house, but…"

"Jesus, Evangeline. Can I hold you?"

I nod and he accepts me into his arms. It's convenient because I no longer have to support my weight. I'm so tired I'm shaking.

"Sit down," he says. "I'm going to make you something to eat."

"I don't want to. I'm not hungry."

But Garrett puts me in a dining chair and opens my refrigerator. It feels like looking into an alternate life where I made different choices. Met different men at different times. Garrett's too soft for the stark black-and-gray kitchen that Hank wanted. In Garrett's house, he took off all the cupboard doors and put plants on the shelves. I might be softer in Garrett's life too.

He makes me toast with an egg and sits across from me, watching as I eat. "Have you been taking your medication?" he asks.

I nod.

"You didn't drink alcohol with it, did you?"

"I don't usually drink," I say, but it feels like a lie. "Would Xanax and alcohol make me black out?"

"They're both central nervous system suppressants. It can kill you."

I know that, but I also know that there are no circumstances under which I'd drink enough to have a deadly reaction. I've spent more time combing medical papers than most doctors, I bet, and I've certainly spent more time on addiction forums. A half a Xanax and a few sips of alcohol, my absolute maximum, wouldn't take away my entire night.

"Why would I drink?" I ask.

Garrett's cool fingers brush the edge of the stripe on my neck. "I can guess."

"Why is everyone evacuating?"

"Haven't you heard? There's another fire above King's Canyon," he says. "It's spreading fast. The wind never stopped."

"And SE&G hasn't been maintaining their power lines," I say. My words are punctuated by sudden darkness. My refrigerator is no longer running. Every light blinked out. The microwave screen doesn't show the time.

It's not a surprise, but we still stop talking and stare at the windows.

"What caused this fire? Do they know if it's SE&G's fault yet?"

"Does it matter? I have no idea," Garrett says. "Come on, Eve, eat so we can leave. We're bracketed by fire. Evacuation orders are mandatory."

"Leave…with you?" I ask.

"Hank's hurting you," he says slowly, clearly. "I've always seen it in your eyes. Now I can see it on your skin."

I slide my hand over the mark on my neck. The absence of the chain hurts more than the actual wound. "You don't understand. Hank's so strong, and I bruise very easily. Accidents happen. Yes, he could be more careful, but it's hard sometimes. I make him angry."

"Why do you always make excuses for him?" Garrett asks. "You can't tell me you still love him. Hank wants to control you. He uses you."

"He's predictable," I say. I always know exactly what he will do. I frequently invoke his wrath, but I see it coming, like a punch swung in slow motion. Not everyone is so transparent.

Garrett cups one of my hands in his. "Do you know what Aaron and I talked about in our last sessions? You. All he wanted was to make sure you'd be okay, whatever happened. So just come with me, Evangeline, please. We'll get out of this together. I'll take care of you." His eyes have grown wide with compassion, earnestness in every line of his body. The last time someone looked at me this intently, it was a girl. I can almost remember her. She took my arm. She tried to get me to leave without her.

A memory rises to the murky surface.

*Mack. I found Mack.*

And while the surrounding details remain a fog, some things stick out.

Mack told me that she put evidence in Aaron's laundry room, where Ronnie died. Nothing can take it away from me now that I've got it back. Once I have that cell phone and Aaron's pickup, I'll have the whole picture.

"Okay," I say. "I'll leave with you." Garrett looks relieved. I hate to keep talking and ruin it. "But I'm going to my parents' house first. I've almost finished Aaron's treasure hunt. I'll collect these last clues and give them to Wyatt, my other brother, the one in the FBI."

I can tell that Garrett wants to argue, but he doesn't. He urges me to eat a little more instead. "My house isn't far from the fire," he says. "I've got protective measures in place, but I should put a couple of things in my car. I'll meet you at Comma Coffee again at noon."

"Two," I say. I need time to visit Jobson and the sheriff's office.

"One o'clock," he says, "at the latest. And then I'm going to come looking. I'm not leaving this town without you, Evangeline."

He kisses me gently before leaving. I wonder what it means to him, leaving together. Does he think it's that easy? That I'll get in his car, drive through this smoke to Reno, and we'll suddenly be safe and happy?

I wonder if there's a minute chance he isn't wrong.

Garrett gets in his car and goes opposite the people trying to evacuate. The line has moved, but from the honking, it sounds like it's still congested near the freeway. The wind hasn't abated. I don't think SE&G turned the power off deliberately. I watch Garrett's lights retreat into smoke, and it feels like waiting at the mouth of Hell.

I take a shot of pickle juice for electrolytes. I crack open a white Monster. I dump the rest of my eggs and toast into the trash.

Then I go to Aaron's house one last time.

# CHAPTER 17
# HANK

I'm sitting outside my house when a man I don't know leaves through the front door.

At least, I don't know him personally. But I've seen his picture on the website of a psychiatric practice. Garrett Glass is a clean-cut man who looks like he's never thrown a punch in his life. His hair touches his ears. He doesn't stand up quite straight, like his back hurts. And he's coming out of *my house*.

I've been with Cuttino at the sheriff's office since oh dark thirty, responding to the King's Canyon Fire. I've been neck-deep interfacing with the state's disaster management team while slamming Folger's, and I deserve to come home for a shower, a nap, and maybe an apology from my wife.

But it seems like Eve hasn't been missing me.

She sure as hell hasn't been coming up with an apology while pretty-boy Garrett Glass is holding her hand.

There are two options.

I could go into the house right now. I could confront Eve. But with the way she's behaving, I can't trust she'll tell me anything coherent. She's probably still hungover from the night before. If I get angry again, I'll do something I'll regret, and for which only God can forgive me.

Which leads me to the second option.

I follow the other man to his house.

* * *

Garrett Glass lives in the foothills near King's Canyon, and we pass homes that are actively burning on the route to his property. I didn't get to this side of town while immersed in logistics overnight, but I'd heard about every one of these houses, and how the high winds were carrying embers to unexpected places.

This is the first time I've seen the nightmarish hellscape of West Carson, where wind blasts embers off C Hill to shower brimstone on the rooftops. Carson Middle School has already lost its outbuildings. Cars are abandoned on the side streets while people hurry to the overflowing emergency shelters on foot.

After the school, King Street is barricaded by the fire department. Glass talks his way through. I follow him, waving at the firefighters. Most are wearing respirators.

Glass's house isn't as big as DeVos's, but it's big enough, like a modernized cabin on steroids. He's got sprinklers firing on all sides to keep his lawn damp. Probably the only reason he isn't already smoldering. The porch light turns on when he goes up the front walk, so he's got power too. A generator somewhere. Being a quack must pay well.

I call to him before he can shut the door. "Garrett Glass!"

He turns. He's lanky, but more athletic than he'd looked in his professional photograph. A filtration mask covers the bottom half of his face. His eyes are bright, intelligent, and friendly. "I won't be here long, sir," he says. "I'm just grabbing a few last things." He's got a serene podcast voice.

"I'm not working the fire right now." I push into his house with him. "I'm Deputy Sergeant Hank Everhardt. You know my wife."

To his credit, Glass barely pauses before saying, "Yes, I treated her brother for the last couple of years."

"That's why I'm here." I can't get close enough to him to tell if he smells like Eve's perfume. "To talk about Aaron."

Glass takes off his jacket and tries to edge past me to the coat rack. "I don't have time to talk right now. I can't think that you do either."

"I've got plenty of time," I say. "Do what you've gotta do. Don't let me slow you down. We can talk while you evacuate."

His eyes flick to the badge on my belt. Glass beckons to me before heading into his den. "I'll answer your questions, but I can't tell you much. I don't discuss my patients with outsiders."

"Doctor-patient confidentiality doesn't apply when the patient is dead."

"There's more to ethics than what the law states," Glass says.

"Aaron Ashe might be responsible for multiple murders. Any information you can give me about that—where he might have hidden more bodies—now, that would be real ethical. Bringing peace to the families and all."

"*More* bodies?" he asks, straightening from a table where he's gathering papers.

"The remains of an adult male deceased were located at the family's home. Forensics will do a DNA test to confirm, but evidence suggests it's Sean Ashe. I like Aaron Ashe for that murder. Did he confess to anything in therapy sessions?"

"Of course not. I'd have to report that."

"Do you think he was capable?"

Glass waffles. "Aaron had layers. Some that I don't think we reached before he was killed. In situations with violent childhood trauma, it's common to have a dramatic reaction. Some hide from it. Many cope. Others…embrace it." Glass adds his briefcase to a stack with a backpack and weekend bag. "Yes, I think he was capable."

"Sounds like you knew him well." I've got my arms folded so that I don't start swinging. "You must have gotten to know Eve during all those appointments, too. I imagine Aaron told you everything you'd want to know."

"I probably understand the two of them better than anyone else," Glass says.

*Including you, Hank,* he doesn't have to say.

I have to rise to the challenge. "So what do you think? Was it Ronnie's death that fucked over the whole family or the cat's?"

"Ronnie's," Glass says promptly.

"Did you ever get the impression that maybe Ronnie's death wasn't an accident?" I ask, stepping nearer the table. Garrett takes a quick step to the side to put a folder into his bag. "I looked at the old reports. Two kids playing with a gun, nobody supervising… It's a tidy story that doesn't ask why Eve was unsupervised when both parents and Aaron were home."

"Evangeline's been clear about what happened that day," Glass says. "I believe her when she says it's an accident."

*Evangeline.* I could think that her full first name is formality, the way he talks to any professional contact. But his voice changes when he says it. If I was playing poker with Glass, I'd think he had a good pocket. A real good pocket.

Glass takes everything to the front door. "If you're questioning events surrounding Ronnie, then I'm assuming you've got reason to suspect Aaron's involvement in her death. Is there another? The Ashe mother, maybe?"

"I haven't looked into it."

"Between you and me, I could believe Aaron killed his father," Glass says. He's talking even quieter now, without meeting my eyes, as if confessing a patient's sins before a priest. "Sean Ashe beat and berated his wife. Aaron was a frequent witness. He shared fantasies of violence against his father in therapy."

"Other people think Aaron was too young to kill Sean," I say.

"Aaron's medical records show him reaching six feet tall and two hundred pounds before middle school. He was a *big* kid. And when you consider how many bodies there are in the Ashe family's past, including Ronnie…" Glass cuts off before finishing the thought.

"What?" I ask.

He shakes his head. "Never mind." He presses a button to shutter his windows against the smoke then waits by the front door again, implicitly urging me out of his house. "I hope I've been helpful."

"I've only got one question left. Why were you just with my wife at my house?"

Garrett blanches, and I'd love it if I weren't so fucking angry. There's no keeping it packed under the surface anymore. I advance on him, closing the space in the entry-way, letting him see the shine of the gun in my belt holster.

"It's not what you think." He's sweating. He noticed the gun. "I'm treating Evangeline for symptoms of psychosis. I've been trying to get her to accept psychiatric care since Aaron died." He backs up and bumps the door. "She came to my office raving about the same conspiracy as Aaron. She was trying to get my help in solving some mystery that doesn't exist." Garrett holds up his hands, a soothing gesture. "I think she needs help, Sergeant Everhardt. I know that can be hard to hear."

It was exactly what I'd been thinking the night before. *Eve's sliding.*

Walls slam down around my anger, sucking away the fuel. "I've noticed it too," I say.

He nods. "This isn't the time for it, I know. But I couldn't help worrying. Evangeline can obsess to the point that she might not care about external factors like the wildfire. I needed to check her mental state."

"And?"

"Her mental state is bad," Garrett says. An idea strikes him. "Look, I need to be out of here before the fire crosses the street. I can give you recordings of my last sessions with Aaron, though. He told me something about Ronnie's death I always dismissed as impossible, but maybe you'll find it helpful."

"What about doctor-patient confidentiality?" I ask.

"You said it yourself. Aaron's gone. Do you think those tapes could help with the investigation?"

"Yeah. I'll take them."

I want to hear everything.

* * *

Glass gives me an MP3 audio recorder along with the data card he used to save the last few sessions with Aaron. There's a process to collecting evidence, and it's likely this qualifies. I should do paperwork, establish chain of custody, whatever. I don't do any of it. I stick the device on my dashboard when I get into the patrol car. My radio's a cacophony of chatter. I turn it off.

I've used my shower-and-nap break following Dr. Glass, so I have to get back to work. Dispatch has left me a notice. Cuttino needs to be relieved from duty running the mobile response unit, which is stationed at an SE&G emergency shelter.

I hit play on the recorder and start driving on autopilot. I'm a sergeant following disaster protocol. I need to be at work, so I'm going to work. But my mind is a roar of white-hot anticipation, and I don't care about justice, my job, or public service.

Aaron's session is long, but Glass digitally bookmarked several segments of conversation. "Those times correlate to notes, but I'll have to find the notebook for you later," Glass had explained apologetically.

The first bookmark jumps me right into the middle of the conversation. "I always kept an eye on Evie when we were kids." Aaron's voice grates the way it did when he was alive. He's got a faint lisp, his words overly precise, like a fucking girl. "So that afternoon, I realized I hadn't heard her in a while. I went out back. Instead of my sister, I found the cat, Felix. He was already sick. I j-just wanted to m-make him stop hurting."

That stutter. He's lying.

I have to stop at an intersection. The lanes are still packed down Carson Street. I'm getting a dozen emails, alerts, and text messages every few minutes, and I'm ignoring all of them.

"Aaron," says another voice, reassuring and friendly. That's Garrett Glass. "About that story…"

"I loved that cat," Aaron says. "Seeing Felix in pain was hard-d, even h-harder because Ronnie just died. I was confused. I had too many f-feelings without any way to cope."

"That's what you've told me before. You've given that story to every therapist in the last twenty years, I'd suspect. Word-for-word, you use the same explanation every time we go over it again."

"N-no, I d-don't," Aaron says. The tic has gone wild.

Eve has told me about their childhood trauma, but I never talked to Aaron long enough to hear his take. The details are identical to Eve's—except he was stutters through it.

"You've been struggling more lately," Glass says. "I wonder if your inability to externalize and process the truth of these events has been getting to you. I could help you if you're honest with me. I want you to be able to heal, Aaron. Until you want to heal, I can't help you reach that goal."

Another long silence follows. I skip ahead to the next bookmark.

"You're the victim, and it's not your fault." Ten minutes later on the tape, Glass is still babying his client's ego. He did know Aaron well. Babying him was the only way to get through that thick skull.

"You won't tell Eve, will you?" Aaron asks.

Garrett says, "Everything here is private, even from her, unless you ask me to do otherwise."

The cross-traffic moves, so I flash my lights and cut across Carson Street. There are so many people on foot that I have to creep along at two miles per hour.

On the tape, Aaron says, "Eve told me that she found Felix dying, injured, and that she was just… I mean, she just saw Ronnie die."

"You're telling me that Eve killed your cat?"

"Adults freak out about killing pets. They don't see it happen and think, 'This here's a kid who needs help.' They'd think, 'This here's a budding serial killer.' I was already labeled as a troubled kid. I *was* a troubled kid. I could handle going to jail and whatever, but Eve… She didn't deserve to go. I protect her. I've always protected her."

"Fucking lies!" I snarl aloud. Eve doesn't even kill spiders in the house, much less a childhood cat.

I have never once seen her kill a thing.

*She cannot be a killer.*

Therapy continues unbroken by my outburst. "You don't get labeled a budding serial killer after one cat dies," Glass says.

"Not after one death, no."

Another pause.

I think the words almost at the same time as Glass says it. "Did Eve kill Ronnie?"

"It was an accident," says Aaron. "She didn't mean to do it. She was just curious about that gun."

This time the pause is long enough for me to pull into the parking lot in front of the North Carson Save-Mart. It's right against the freeway where the congestion bottle-necks. The Department of Transportation started tearing apart the overpass for maintenance last week but didn't finish before the evacuations. Half the people trying to get out of Carson City are escaping here, and half of them seem to end up trapped in the emergency shelter, which is a series of white tents.

I park behind the mobile response unit but don't get out of the car. I skip ahead to the next bookmarked spot in the audio file, but when the conversation resumes, the topic has changed.

"Are you in love with Evie?" Aaron asks.

I grip the steering wheel harder, leather creaking under my fingers. Blood rushes through my head.

"This isn't about me," Glass says.

"Come on. I've seen you guys. Are you in love with her?"

"I've come to care about your sister," he says. "She's really something special. When it's just the two of us, she lets down her walls, and she's a lovely human on the inside. Really lovely."

Glass wanted me to hear this. He bookmarked it.

I'd have to get all the way back across traffic to kill him. There's no time. I can't retaliate, and he *knows* it.

"Then you've got to help Evie," Aaron says on the recording. "It's about to get worse for me. I'm getting into some real shit, and I need you to protect her."

"What are you talking about?" Glass asks.

"I was just trying to get paid. I thought if I blackmailed them… When I went looking, I found something bad. And then bad got worse. It's in the manifesto. Look at it or you won't see it. Nobody wants to see it. Just take the money and turn your backs." Aaron is rambling the way he was on the body camera footage. "I need you to make sure that Eve doesn't get into it too deep, you know? They're watching me. Take this." Paper rustles.

"Aaron, you're worrying me," Glass says. "I don't understand."

"Just put it away, and when they kill me—"

"Aaron."

"—give it to Eve. Can you do that? Tell her to pass it on to Wyatt."

"I can do that. Okay? I promise to do that," Glass says. "I think we need to have a talk about your current mental state, though."

"No. Not right now. I don't have time." Metal shifts. "If you love Eve, be careful."

"I know she's married. I would never—"

"Forget that. Don't worry about that. Be careful of Eve."

Heat prickles over my scalp, down my spine, into my knuckles. I kick the door open and take the audio recorder with me across the parking lot. I hold the tiny speaker to my ear so I can hear it over the wind.

"What do you mean, be careful *of* her?" Garrett asks.

"Evie's not bad," Aaron says. "But she's not interested in anyone else's rules. She knows what she's doing. She does what she wants, how she wants to. She's always in control."

That doesn't sound like my wife at all.

But I can't help but notice that Aaron doesn't stutter when he talks.

# CHAPTER 18
# EVE

When I think of West Carson, I think of long summer strolls in the shade under hundred-year-old trees. I think about following the Blue Line Trail to see historical buildings while Aaron sulks beside me, bored by the same history I found so interesting. I think about sneaking past lavender bushes buzzing with bees. I think of stumbling across the last governor, who waved at me when I was across the street from his mansion. These locations have been the backdrop for every memory leading to this moment. My childhood is in this old place.

Now my childhood is on fire.

According to the radio, sparks leaped the road and spread quickly throughout West Carson. The antique hitching posts where I used to tie my shoes look like tombstones in the smoke. The ancient cottonwoods are haloed in flame. We're beyond the point of a mandatory evacuation order.

It's so hot in my car and the vent can't filter it out. C Hill is consumed, and the Ashe house isn't far from it. I face a wall of fire to the left of King's Canyon Road and a wall of opaque smoke to the right.

I can navigate by memory. I have to. My headlights can't reach the street signs.

An oak I once climbed explodes, the fire within its trunk escaping with a boom and a shower of sparks. I just drive around the worst of it. I use the wipers to get embers off my windshield.

This isn't safe. I shouldn't be here. I know this. I just need to do a couple more things. *Get Mack's phone, get the keys from Jobson, get the truck. That's it.*

It had seemed like a trivial to-do list when I was in my house on the less-devastated side of town. Now I'm passing old neighbors with their roofs on fire. Embers off the hill are lighting random old homes, and there's just nothing to be done about it.

Carson City is congested, overstuffed with people from Moundhouse and the highlands. A quarter of Northern Nevada's population has been shoved into a single valley. And now the fire's consuming the northwest and blocking the east with southbound roads jammed.

My brother's name is going to be attached to this. If anyone remembers him, it'll be because he started the VC Fire that knocked over this whole line of dominoes.

*Get Mack's phone.*

I can't see the Ashe house until I've turned the corner. Nothing else on Donne Avenue is burning, so I'm optimistic until I see that the ivy scaling the front of the house has caught fire.

A breath escapes me. "No."

I dial 9-1-1, even though I should know better. Every fire-fighter in the state is busy. They can't intervene at an empty building. It doesn't matter, because I don't reach an operator. All lines are busy. When you don't need the police, they're beating down your door, beating down your brother, destroying your life. And when it's finally time to get their help, they're nowhere to be found.

I leap out of the car, determined to do something. Anything.

But I stop just outside the driver's seat. Smoke rushes to fill my lungs and ash stings my eyes. I cough, bend into the back seat, and grab a scarf. I spill water from my flask onto it before covering my mouth and nose.

The fire's catching the foxtails. It's rushing the sidewalk.

*What do I do?*

My former neighbor has a garden hose coiled in his yard. I scramble to attach it to the spigot and twist the faucet while fire licks the fence between yards. I crank the knob all the way up. I aim the hose at the fire and...

Water dribbles. Spurts. Fountains. I press the lever to turn it into a jet and aim it at the fence, wetting it down. The fire's so hot at this distance. It's an iron pressing on my skin. The makeshift mask isn't doing much to keep my throat from searing.

The hose dribbles on the fence, doing nothing. Absolutely nothing.

There's nothing that can stop the fire from climbing up the ivy to the room of my childhood home. The hose can't spare its timbers. It's only minutes before the garage catches too.

I stand outside my brother's house, just a few feet away from Mack's cell phone, and I watch everything burn.

* * *

I take two of the pills Garrett gave me and finish the white Monster before getting back on the road.

*It's gone. It's all gone.*

*Maybe three pills would be better.*

I inhaled the smoke from my burning childhood home, and it's feels like I've inhaled its ghosts too. I'm possessed by every wretched moment I lived in that home. Every house I pass while fleeing is wallpapered in Ronnie's blood. Every lawn is cradling a dying tomcat, and every struggling evacuee is a child in pajamas with a box cutter. "No," I say again to the inside of my car, so quiet that it's like the word seats itself in my throat without ever emerging.

The rear end of another car appears from the smoke.

Traffic has stopped.

I don't press the brakes fast enough, and bumper meets bumper.

The car slams to a halt.

The seatbelt snaps tight against my chest.

I was going slowly, so it's barely enough to dizzy me. But my heart is pounding. I grip the wheel, gaping at the car in front of me.

The driver leaps out of his car. "What the fuck are you doing?" His voice sounds miles away, stifled by the car and my ringing ears.

I don't get out to talk to him. I can't. I gaze at him numbly, jaw dropped, and stare into the face of my dead brother. Somehow, I hit Aaron's car. Aaron is confronting me, shouting at me, wearing an unfamiliar sweater vest.

*It's not real. You're freaking out.*

He shouts something else, but I don't hear the words. I hear Aaron's voice.

*It's time to get the pickup from Jobson,* he says.

My eyes flick to the dash clock. It's almost two o'clock.

"Stupid bitch!" yells the driver. He's an old white guy with a toupee. He gets back behind the wheel of his car.

I rest my forehead against the steering wheel, eyes closed. I focus on taking deep breaths.

Behind my eyelids, I can still see Aaron. I'm lying on the bed in his room. We're children, barely school age, and Wyatt is on the other bed. The windows in that room were tiny, high on the walls, like we were in a basement. The blinds were half-length and red. It tinted their room pink whenever sunrise struck the window.

*Get the pickup, Evie,* Aaron says.

Horns honk behind me. My head jerks up. Traffic has moved, and the car in front of me is gone again. I put Jobson's address into my phone and find his house in suburbia. He's not far away. Nothing in Carson City is that far away.

I drive.

* * *

Jobson lives across from the old hospital in a one-story house that isn't burning. The Range Rover in his driveway looks just like my dad's used to. Red. Rusty. Busted bumpers.

*Dad.*

Another surge of memory strikes me, far more recent than the last. I remember Hank telling me they found Dad's bones at the Ashe house. He said that Aaron had killed him. The specific words won't come to me, but I can easily imagine every detail shouted from my husband's furious mouth. "We found his body, and we know exactly what happened, you little bitch!" Hank screamed last night. "How your parents were fighting! Dad punched Mom, and Aaron came at him with another gun—"

*Hank still doesn't understand.*

They'll never find the truth now. There are no more clues to get from that home. Any evidence of what really happened will get bulldozed with the singed old bricks, torn down to the foundations. Did they remove the bones before the fire caught? Is the last of Dad flaking away to nothingness like his son?

*You're not done with me yet,* whispers Aaron's voice.

I blink and Jobson no longer has a Range Rover parked in the driveway. He has a Ford F-150 with a camper shell. It's open, but he's loaded up, ready to leave. I must be the only thing keeping him from a safe exit from Carson City.

The front door opens and he's there. Deputy Jobson looks monochromatic in the harsh headlights, like the night vision body camera footage. His pupils flash white. He's so big, like Aaron, but he's haloed in a dark energy that my brother never had. There's a Taser at his belt. He looks angry to see me.

I rub my eyes, try to focus on reality. Jobson isn't in black and white. The air is just so hazy, and everything is dark.

"What did Garrett give me?" I ask my hands, holding them in front of my face. My fingers are so puffy. My wrists are too thick. "Is this Xanax?"

*That can't be right.*

It's been so long since I've felt real emotions. Now the toxic ones pulse through my veins, flooding me with a sour burn. Maybe the smoke is poisoning me. Maybe it's been too long since I ate real food. Whatever insulates me from the world is gone.

"Hey!" Jobson calls. "Are you coming or what?"

He's waiting for me to speak to him. He already said something else.

"Did you get the keys?" I ask, mounting the steps to Jobson's house.

The deputy nods once, a jerky motion. "Yeah. A while ago. You should have gotten here sooner."

"I had something to do."

"Wait here. I'll get them for you." He vanishes inside, leaving the door propped open. The air inside smells like murder. I don't know how else to describe it. That wash of cold that oozes down your arms, the scent of rot, the staleness of it all.

*He killed Aaron.*

Everyone's told me to wait for legal justice, but the sheriff absolved him. My brother died and justice shrugged, as I knew it would. "He was a fat asthmatic," said the law, "and Jobson used an authorized chokehold." Why is any chokehold authorized? Why did Jobson never try to deescalate with my brother? Why can the deputy leave and get away with it all?

Jobson retreated into the depth of his pit and expects me to wait outside, breathing the air of death, knowing this man ended my brother.

I slip my hand into my purse. I climb the steps.

I enter Jobson's house.

## CHAPTER 19

## HANK

When I reach the mobile response unit in North Carson, the fire's coming over the hill behind the hospital. It creeps toward the edge of the freeway. Thick bars of smoke on the opposite hill suggest more blown embers, new fires, more places we can't reach with firetrucks. The last northbound lane has been shut down, and getting everyone to turn south is a nightmare of logistics. I should have been here an hour ago.

"The fuck are you doing here?" Cuttino's eyes go narrow when I walk up to him. "Did you check your email?"

His attitude is more than I can take right now. I've been cucked enough. "I've been fielding calls with the Fire Department, stopping to clean up traffic accidents, and had to manage about ten thousand other things on my way here. No, I haven't been on my damn phone! What is it? Did I get reassigned?"

"You could say that." He grabs my arm to pull me aside from the other two deputies. They're conferring with someone from Reno Highway Patrol and don't notice we step behind a cruiser.

Cuttino's energy is different than it was before the party. He's got me pinned in a corner, trapped between a cement post and his car, and every inch of him vibrates with tension. He shivers from his polished shoes to his graying hair. "Look at your email," he says.

My phone's slippery in my hand. I sweated through the pocket of my tactical pants. Cuttino curls his lip when I wipe condensation off the screen before opening my email. In the middle of two hundred thirty-seven automated alerts, I find a report filed by Deputy Jobson, forwarded to me by Cuttino.

"Jobson again?" I mutter, zooming in to read the text on the PDF. It details every secret he knows, from Wilkes deleting the video footage to my off-the-clock interrogation of Jobson. It doesn't mention Cuttino's involvement. Jobson filed it without including him, probably in hope that Cuttino would side with him against us. A risky move. I didn't think he had the balls. "Shit." I turn my phone off and squeeze it in my fist. "*Shit*. Who's seen this?"

"Just me, so far," Cuttino says.

A real risky move. But it must have been Jobson's last swing at me before disappearing.

"What are you going to do about it?" I ask.

His eyes are gemstone bright under the ash-dusted brim of his ball cap. "I've got a better question. What are *you* going to do about it? You and Wilkes are going down if this gets filed, and I'm scot-free. But nobody ever has to see it."

"If you don't act on it, Jobson will forward his complaint to the governor."

"Will he be able to?" Cuttino asks. "Are you going to let him?" He picks the words out carefully so that I can hear that infernal incantation through the blasting wind.

Sickening understanding sinks into me.

Wilkes had warned me Cuttino was a meat eater. He warned me to stay out of it.

"Kaleb," I say. There's nobody to hear us, so I can be frank. "It's one thing to delete things and fire someone to avoid an investigation. But going after Jobson for this…what I'd have to do to make sure he can't smear us—"

"I've got your back if you've got mine. And let's be perfectly clear about this, Hank." He says my first name like it coats his tongue with grease. "If you *don't* clean this up, then you don't just lose *my* back. You lose DeVos's. And he'll make sure to clean up your mess *thoroughly*." He jabs a finger into my chest on the last word. Hard enough to bruise. "You're on thin ice, brother."

I shake my head silently. Not refusing Cuttino, but refusing to believe that Cuttino could be *this* bad. It sounds like he's telling me to kill Jobson unless I want to get killed too. But that's insanity, and Aaron Ashe was my brother-in-law long enough for me to recognize true insanity.

Maybe I'm the problem. I'm the one leaping to death as the only way out of this.

What's likelier, that Eve is right that DeVos has the sheriff's office in his pocket, or I'm losing my mind too?

"I just want to know one thing," I say. "Did DeVos get you to send Jobson to kill Aaron Ashe?"

Of all the reactions I expect, a harsh laugh isn't one of them. "Why? You suddenly missing your brother-in-law?"

"Did you?"

"No, I fucking didn't," Cuttino says. "I don't care about your wife's brother. Don only asked me to delete that footage because of the girl who's in it. She's one of Don's. He didn't want her coming up in the case. Order a hit on some idiot junkie—you've gotta be shitting me."

Tar is creeping through my veins. "Wait. What do you mean, she's one of 'his'?"

"She's his masseuse. All right?"

"The girl in that video's underage," I say.

"Listen to me." Cuttino glances over the top of the car to see the deputies dispersing. It's action time. "DeVos doesn't fuck around with little people. The ones who don't interest him. But he'll do *anything* to protect the people he wants to keep." He steps close enough that I smell alcohol on his breath, and he jabs me in the chest again. "Wilkes folded over the masseuse. Are you gonna fold too? Or are you gonna go clean up Jobson?"

Plausible deniability is a powerful thing. I don't know what's going on yet. I could walk away and argue my innocence whenever Cuttino sends someone else to take care of Jobson.

"The Washoe County Sheriff's Department is searching houses for people who need help evacuating right now," I say, like the words are coming from some devil crouched in my chest. "I could help. Start by checking houses in Jobson's neighborhood." I went over for a football game once. I know exactly where to find it.

And after I cross that line, I'm going to find Eve.

* * *

The deputy's door stands open when I arrive. It's just a crack, left ajar as if by accident. His pickup is in the drive-way. I nudge the door open the rest of the way and enter.

The first thing I notice is a stale smell. Like everywhere else in town, Jobson doesn't have power, so his refrigerator isn't running, but it's stronger than I expect.

When I get into the kitchen, I find his refrigerator door hanging open. Its drawers are cracked by impact, the shelves fallen onto the floor with half his food. One of the chairs in the dinette is knocked over. The other is on the opposite end of the room by the mess of his counters.

Clear signs of a struggle. I draw my sidearm.

"Jobson? Are you here?" My ears are useless for telling if anyone's moving through the house. With this much wind, the fence is groaning outside, the windows whistle, and the walls grumble. Smoky air blasts me as I head upstairs. One of those windows must be open. The idiot's inviting fire inside.

The hallway is dark and all the doors are shut. The first door on the right is a bathroom, easily cleared with a check behind the shower curtain.

The door across from it is Jobson's bedroom. I ease the door open just wide enough to look inside, but it's so dark

I can only see the foot of his bed. I turn on my flashlight. Shadows stretch long, casting silhouettes on the wall. A chair, a computer, closet doors. There's nobody under the bed or behind it. The closet looks like it's been ransacked. Not a struggle, but a hurried evacuation.

That leaves one door left.

It's rattling in its frame, so I think the open window is here. Light shines in the gap underneath. It flickers rapidly, like a body is moving between the window and door.

I set my shoulder against the wall before testing the doorknob. There's no response to the jiggle of metal, so I push the door open. I swing inside, cupping my sidearm.

Curtains billow through the room, long and gauzy. I catch glimpses of a male figure sitting on the window bench beyond them. I've got my gun halfway lifted before I realize his head's tipped sideways, hand dangling limp at his side, one leg out the window. He's not the one making shadows. It's just the wind through the curtains.

I shove the cloth aside to approach.

Jobson is dead. His mouth is open, eyes blankly staring, and blood paints the window frame a few inches above his head. He ate a bullet. The gun rests beside his opposite hand, ashen fingers loosely curled under the grip. "Fuck." I step back and the wind wrests away control of the curtains, shrouding Jobson's body.

I'm suddenly nauseous. I throw myself at the desk, grabbing it by the side so I can hurl into the trash can. But nothing comes up.

My right hand's planted on a piece of paper. It's a note from Jobson, ripped off a legal pad. "I can't do this anymore," reads the note. "I murdered a man. I lied. I've done everything wrong. I'm done and I'm sorry."

"Fuck!"

The word explodes out of me instead of bile. I kick the desk chair across the room with a roar. And I have to scream out all this *pressure* before I can even begin remembering how to breathe.

I want to believe this is a suicide. A suicide would be perfect.

But I can't believe the mess in the kitchen was random. Not when Jobson knew what he knew. He was an obvious target for violence. The problem is that DeVos didn't send someone else to rough him up. *I* was the man sent to rough him up.

I pace in the hallway to calm myself, just for a minute, then radio it into dispatch. "Everhardt here. I'm at Deputy Jobson's house for a-a wellness check, and... He's dead."

"*Dead?*" The voice on the other side is dismayed.

"Self-inflicted gunshot wound."

"We don't have units available, Sarge," says the soft female voice. "I'm sorry. Oh my God, do you know what I just heard, Cassie? Deputy Jobson *killed himself.*" Her voice gets quieter as if she's leaning away from the speakerphone.

I hang up and stare around helplessly.

If there's DNA evidence to collect, we won't find it. If there's gunshot residue on Jobson's hand, we won't detect it. When they publish a list of casualties from this day, Jobson's name will be listed with too many others as a loss in the fire.

It's too perfect.

I pull the cross from my shirt and walk back into the room for a prayer. It's the least any man deserves. I'm halfway across the room when I spot a jewelry box on the floor, right where his chair was before I kicked it. Jobson isn't the jewelry type. A watch, maybe, but not the kind of watch that would fit into a dainty blue-velvet box.

The cross drops from my fingers, swinging at my neck.

My fingers already know the texture of this velvet and which side the hinges rest upon. I had pulled this box out of the jewelry bag before giving it to Eve, taking a last look at the necklace to make sure it was right. The little silver pendant rests inside the box, untouched, unworn.

## CHAPTER 20
## EVE

It's faster to reach the sheriff's office on foot at this point. I'm so tired that I eat one of Aaron's months-old Nutrigrain bars from the bottom of my purse. My blisters burst halfway down Mountain Street, so my toes squelch in blood and pus on every slow-motion step. The world is at the end of a long tunnel, and no matter how hard I try to reach the end, the destination is still miles further away.

With this blanket between myself and the world, I can believe I'm dreaming.

This entire week has been nothing more than a nightmare.

Maybe the entire last decade has been a nightmare.

I'm swaddled in my childhood bed at home, Felix is heavy on my feet, and Aaron's sleeping on the other side of the house. Wyatt is playing with the Nintendo 64 in the living room— the only one who's allowed to stay awake past eight o'clock. My parents are fighting, but it's distant enough I can't hear it.

*Everything is fine. I'm just dreaming.*

My legs move. My body sways. I still have a few more of Garrett's pills in my pocket, and they rattle with every footstep.

* * *

I've reached the sheriff's office.

The front doors are propped open so people can run in and out. There are emergency medical services in the parking lot, and at least forty people are clustered, waiting for treatment. Two children on the sidewalk receive oxygen. Nobody gives me a second glance when I enter the lobby.

In addition to the keys for Aaron's pickup, Jobson yielded his keycard for the evidence locker so I could look for Mack's cell phone. I'm rewarded with a green light when I swipe.

The locker is organized chaos, but I don't have to look far for the evidence from Aaron's house because it's been hastily dropped in the middle of the floor. I shove the door closed and sit with my back against it, cutting through the tape with my box cutter. I toss the lid aside. Inside, I find a copy of Aaron's favorite book, *The Dragonriders of Pern*. Its edges are stained by coffee, even though he didn't drink it. This copy belonged to our mom. I put the book in my purse.

Underneath, there are several Warhammer 40k figurines, and a tube of paper bound by a rubber band twisted tight. It's a thick tube. I peer inside to see that it's obstructed. My box cutter bites through the layers of rubber band. Inside, there's a cell phone. Mack's cell phone. The pages look like they were ripped from a journal. They smell like Aaron's favorite soap.

*This is it.*

I've found another piece of the puzzle from Aaron's treasure hunt.

Mack's phone has battery life, but only thirteen percent. Luckily there's no passcode. When the wallpaper flashes onto the screen, I jolt. Aaron's face is smiling back at me. His features are flattened by the flash, so he looks rounder. He's sweaty and smiling with those big apple cheeks. Warmth beams from him toward the girl under his arm. Mack. He's got his arm around Mack. She's winking with her tongue out and fingers in a peace sign.

*Why does Aaron have an arm around a teenage girl?*

"They're friends," I say. "They were such good friends. Right, Aaron?"

*We met because I was trying to help her escape,* he explains over my shoulder. His reedy voice is chillier than a cemetery on the back of my neck.

I have to catch my breath before I can look for the video of Mack's testimony. It's the second-to-last video she ever took. I can tell because it's twenty minutes long and taken from Aaron's laundry room.

It's a close-up selfie shot with the camera light on. Mack looks sweaty and she's breathing hard like she ran there. "Oh my God," she says through a hand. "Aaron. Oh my God." She fights to calm herself, taking deep breaths. "Aaron told me about the treasure hunt. Someone's going to find this phone, and he wants me to leave a message

with specific information, because someone's going to…"
She sobs again. "Oh my God."

The night that Aaron died, Mackenzie wasn't wearing any
makeup. She looks so young in her hooded sweater.

"Please tell, like, the FBI or whatever that my parents are
selling me to Don DeVos," she says. "The electric company
guy. It's horrible. He passes me between his friends, and
like—I don't think I'm the first girl he's done this to. Please
get the FBI. Okay?"

That's where the video ends.

My thumb moves of its own volition, swiping back to the
video Mack took of Aaron's death.

I've watched the body camera footage so many times that it
shouldn't hurt to see Aaron's death from a new angle. But
this time, every horrible moment is punctuated by Mack's
whimpers. She's in the bedroom behind Aaron when he's
shouting out the window at Jobson. She keeps whispering
things like, "Please stop. Just stop."

When he gets out onto the step, Mack goes to the window.
She records from above when Jobson makes my brother
drop like a tree cut down. She's crying when Aaron lunges
for Jobson, and she gives a muffled scream when the
deputy reacts.

At this angle, I can watch every moment of their struggle.

The deputy starts it, but Aaron doesn't go down lightly. My
gentle brother turns into a thrashing bear. He swings his
fists, he kicks, he bites. His movements are strange. I've
never seen him like that before. His fits have never been
*violent*.

This monster isn't my brother.

It's a hideous miracle that Jobson can get an arm around Aaron's throat, much less hold him down. Aaron keeps struggling until he suddenly doesn't. Mack's sobs are all I can hear on the video. Apparently Jobson could hear them too. He swung around to look at her. "Hey!" The last few seconds are Jobson pushing into the trailer, yanking the phone from Mack's hands, and hitting the off button.

It freezes on the last frame, showing Jobson from below. His face is blurry. He's the real monster here, no matter what it looked like my brother was doing. Aaron may have fought him, but Jobson didn't have to escalate the fight. He didn't have to try to handle Aaron alone. He could have...

No, it doesn't matter anymore.

Aaron's violence doesn't change anything.

But it nudges at something deep in my skull that feels like an alarm bell. Instinct warns me that I *should* care that Aaron was acting as erratic as everyone said, because it doesn't fit in with the narrative I've built.

Something's not locking together. I don't know what.

"What am I missing, Aaron?" I ask.

My brother doesn't offer any insight.

My attention is ripped away from the cell phone by heavy, purposeful footsteps in the hallway outside the evidence locker. It sounds like three different men. I shove Mack's phone into my purse and drag myself to my feet.

There's another door in the back wall. Jobson's keycard works on that one too.

I emerge into the parking lot, shutting the door quietly behind me. I hear the lock to the evidence locker beep from inside. Someone's in there.

I'm not in the same parking lot as the emergency tents. This area is fenced and topped by barbed wire. Cars and trailers populate the pavement between me and the gate. This is the impound lot. It would normally be locked too, but someone's left the chain hanging heavy between fence and gate, promising a noisy passage if I go that way. I don't see any exit, but I can't go back.

It's impossible to walk casually across the lot. I don't look like I belong because I don't. I'm not even sure that I belong in my own skin anymore.

The sky whirls with smoke. The cars around me are dusted gray, as if it's the warmest snowstorm I've ever seen. And still this wind blows. It rips my hair from the clip, blinding me. I almost miss the big white pickup with the SE&G logo on the side. I actually walk past it, hands wrapped around my purse strap, and stop beyond the tailgate when my brain finally registers what I saw.

*Aaron's pickup.* The license plate matches.

I fish the keys out of my purse. They jingle so loudly when I unlock the truck that it feels like someone shaking them at the sides of my head. I slide into the passenger's seat and check the glovebox, the sun shades, between the cushions. I find crumbs and receipts.

Then I find the gun safe under the seat.

My heart leaps as I pull it into my lap. It's not heavy enough to have a gun inside. It's just a little steel box with a four-digit combination code.

Every moment I spend digging through my purse feels like a moment closer to the fire. I'm getting hotter inside the cab as I search for the note Aaron left me at Felix's grave. Dizziness swamps me, a rush of blood through the head. But I find the page.

God, everything is hard.

The string of his license plate is followed by another four digits. 0-7-2-4. The safe pops open when I put those numbers into the lock.

*I knew you'd figure it out, Evie,* whispers Aaron's voice. *I'll have to make harder puzzles for you next time.*

"What next time?" I mutter.

Within the gun safe, I find a recordable CD with "SE&G Security Department" stamped on the label.

The door from the sheriff's office bangs open, bouncing off the wall with a bang. I can't see who comes through at this angle.

"Eve?"

That's Hank's voice.

I haven't seen him since waking up with blood between my legs. The sound of his baritone strikes me in the guts, right where the Nutrigrain bar is weighing heavy, and it feels like I might lose it on the dashboard. I don't know how he found me. He wasn't meant to find me.

"Come on out, we have to talk." His voice isn't far. I slide out of the truck, leaving the door open, and dart to hide behind an impounded Airstream. Hank casts a shadow on the smoke. It crosses the wall behind me. I fold into a ball, purse crushed between my thighs and chest.

The door to Aaron's pickup shuts. "I know you're here, Eve," says Hank with a shivering voice, like he wants to shout but doesn't want to alarm me...yet.

Another man speaks from the door to the sheriff's office. "Sergeant Everhardt?"

"What's up?" Hank replies, his tone completely different. Calm. Authoritative.

"Sheriff Cuttino's on the phone for you."

"Tell him I'm busy with the city health department. I'll call him back."

"Okay," says the deputy.

The gate's just a few cars over.

I'm not so slow that I can't half-crawl across the pavement, grimacing through the pain of my blisters. I get all the way to the gate before the back door slams shut. I freeze with my fingers on the weighty chain.

Hank's not trying to talk to me anymore, and I can't hear him moving at all. My back was turned to the door when it closed. There's a chance Hank followed the deputy inside. I might be alone. This might be time to run.

I yank the chain.

Wrench open the fence.

And I'm on the other side when a fist seizes my ponytail, rips my head back, and pulls me into the impound lot again. Pain prickles over my scalp. I cry out at the momentary free-fall before I'm locked in Hank's arms, staring up at my husband's face.

# CHAPTER 21
# HANK

Evangeline Everhardt *looks* like my wife. The hair in my fist feels like my wife's hair, fine and blond, like the softest silk threads I've ever touched. Even the sounds she makes belong to my wife.

But this bitch isn't my wife.

She's whimpering up at me with big wide eyes like she never has before. Eve doesn't break down. Her innocent mask is so patronizing. The very fact she that thinks I'm stupid enough to fall for it enrages me.

She grieves nothing, fears nothing.

"Hank," she says.

"Shut up." I push her into the side of Aaron's pickup so hard that the metal buckles. She gasps with pain. I block her in with my body. "I'm going to ask you a few questions right now. And I need you to answer them truthfully the first time. My patience is short, Eve, really short. If you keep trying to lie, I'm going to lose it." It's a miracle I've got as much control as I do right now.

"I never lie to you," she says in a tiny voice.

I could hit her. I want to hit her. "Let's start from the beginning," I say. "Who killed Ronnie?"

"She shot herself by acci—"

"Lies!" The word whipcracks through the air, and I know I'm being too loud. They're going to hear us on the other side of the fence. I clench my teeth to bring the volume down. "Aaron killed her. You have to know that he killed her because you were in the room when it happened."

She trembles. Doesn't answer.

"I'm losing patience," I say.

"You told me not to lie to you," she whispers. The skin's stretched tight over her skull, cheeks sucked in and her chin a delicate point.

"The cat. Who killed the cat?"

She closes her eyes. "Aaron killed Felix."

"How?"

"A box cutter," said Eve.

"Was that so hard?" I ask. "Doesn't it feel good to be honest? Now you can tell me why your brother killed your father."

Her entire body is a shiver. "I don't know, Hank. I've got no idea. I-I didn't think he did, I j-just can't…" When she stutters, she sounds like her brother telling a lie.

I drop my ear to her mouth. "Aaron deserved to die. Say it." Eve twists, but I keep close. She can't escape the cage of my arms. "I always told you that your brother was garbage, and I was right. So just tell me that you're wrong. Tell me you're sorry."

"God, I'm sorry Hank. I'm so sorry."

It's not enough. "Say that Aaron deserved to die."

"I never lie to you," she whispers at me, a low hiss under the scream of wind. "And I will never believe that Aaron deserved to die, so if I say what you want, I'll be lying."

I punch the car hard enough to dent the body, and the pain in my knuckles is worth the way she flinches. "This is about you, Eve. You and your fucked-up family. Don't try to turn it around on me!"

"I'm not." Her eyes are squeezed shut, her breath choppy. "Think about what you're doing, Hank. I can't do anything to you—to *anyone*. You're *hurting* me."

"I'm hurting you? How do you think I feel finding out you've been fucking the psychiatrist?"

Her mouth opens, but nothing comes out. Eventually, she manages, "Hank."

I slap her. Not with my open palm, but the back of my hand. If she weren't so small, she wouldn't even stagger. Eve throws herself dramatically against the door of the nearest car, fingers flying to her cheek.

"It feels like you cut into my gut with a knife, Eve," I say.

She slowly straightens, leaning against the car for stability. Eve's jaw is set. One hand has dropped into her purse. "You want to know why someone might kill my father?" she asks. "He beat my mother. And the whole time he did it, he made sure to tell my mom how much he loved her.

Everyone thought they were a great couple. He never left bruises where they could see. But the bruises were there, and wounds claw into your guts. Your guts never heal. The things he did to my mother killed her long after he left us."

"So Aaron killed him to protect Mommy," I say.

"God, Hank! Listen to me for once! I'm not giving you Aaron's motive. I'm telling you that I married my fucking dad, and that's the kind of thing I can say because I've fucked a psychiatrist!"

My sidearm comes out of the holster. I close the space between us to shove my gun into her hands. I pull her tight, letting the muzzle bury into my gut. "Okay. Shoot me. If you think I'm as bad as you say, you should put me out of my misery!"

She's shaking her head, trying to pull free. It's impossible with her hands frozen between us. She's afraid to twitch and pull that trigger.

"I'm going to kill you if you don't," I say.

Her eyes get even bigger. "Hank."

The world is screaming. The wind, the fire, the burn victims, my whole goddamn soul. "Shoot me!"

But Eve doesn't. She just makes these horrible choking noises that, I think, would be crying from anyone else. There isn't so much as a tear. "I get angry at you. Sometimes I hate you. But I never stop loving you, Hank, and I'm not going to shoot you."

"So what is this bullshit with Dr. Glass? *Revenge?*"

"Does it matter, if it stops?" she asks.

*Does it matter?*

There's a man out there that knows what my wife's pussy feels like, and until she climbed on his dick, she only knew mine. Eve knew how much it'd hurt. She did it to punish me because she's a complete sadist.

Yes, it matters. It's the only thing that matters.

"Of course not, baby," I say, pulling her close to kiss her forehead. I take the gun away from her. It goes back into my holster, unfired, just as I'd known it would. She's stiff in my arms, like I'm holding a sapling stripped of its leaves by autumn winds. My arm tightens around her when she tries to leave. "We can forget Dr. Glass." I pet her hair, smooth it down. "If you tell me the truth about Deputy Jobson."

Eve is frozen.

My heart accelerates. I'd expected confusion or a quick refusal. But instead, she's silent, as if I've genuinely surprised her.

"Because I'm trying to think of another reason *this* might have shown up in the place where Jobson killed himself." I hold her against my side so that I can lift the velvet jewelry box between us.

*Now* she looks confused. She even relaxes a little. "What's that?"

She doesn't recognize the necklace I gave her.

I step back to catch my breath, which doesn't help in this smoke, and I end up laughing a little. I don't know why. It just comes out while I rub my fatigued eyes, suddenly throbbing with a headache.

*She doesn't recognize it.*

Eve wore that damn necklace from her brother for years and years, and when *I* gave her a necklace, she forgot about it.

I don't mean to shove Eve.

But suddenly, my wife's on the ground, and my foot's in her gut. I've kicked her in the stomach. She's gasping for air.

"Who's back here?" Flashlights shine over me.

I freeze, lifting a hand to shade my eyes. Emergency medical personnel were passing on the way to the other parking lot—someone heard something. Two men stopped at the other side of the fence, peering in to look for trespassers. All they see is a deputy sergeant standing among the cars. Eve's still on the ground. She's hidden behind the pickup.

"I was on the phone," I say, waving the jewelry box. They're far enough back they won't be able to see what it is. I quickly pocket it. "Everything all right out there?"

They give their assent and return to the tents. I reach down blindly to grab Eve, but she's not there. I have to blink against the smoke to see her throwing her bodyweight against the gate to open it.

"Eve!" I shout.

She's already gone, flying on bare feet across the parking lot. I hurry to follow her and trip over her shoes. Her flats are stained. She's left bloody footprints on the asphalt. She won't make it far on foot. I can still catch her.

My phone rings. I pull it out just to silence the call, but then I see the name on the screen.

It's Don DeVos.

## CHAPTER 22
## EVE

Garrett's waiting outside Comma Coffee. When he sees me coming, barefoot and limping, he meets me halfway. I surrender what's left of my willpower to stand and tumble against him. Garrett carries me to his Tesla Model X, which is almost as big as my SUV. It makes no noise when he turns it on. We sit in the back hatch.

I've always bought cars a few years old, so it's strange to see a modern dashboard. It's half TV. Hank scoffs at these things. He thinks Teslas are moronic and only morons drive them. If he sees me in one, he'll have another reason to be angry.

*My husband wants to kill me.*

"Did Hank do this to you?" Garrett asks, looking at my arm. It looks bad, and it's not half as bad as what I'm keeping under the dress. Every time I inhale deeply, pain lances through my ribs.

"He knows about us," I say.

"Damn," Garrett breathes. "You're lucky you got away from him alive. Don't look at me like that, Evangeline. You know that men who hurt their wives only get worse."

I push away his gentle hands. "It's getting late. Let's leave."

Garrett puts a blanket around me and touches my lip. It hurts. "He came to my house too." Yet he sits beside me, unbruised.

"What did you tell him?"

"Anything to make him go away. I've got everything ready to go. I'm ready to leave with you." What sweet words. It's like standing underneath the cool mist of a waterfall but being unable to feel anything but sunburn. Everything hurts.

I pull the SE&G disc out of my purse. "Do you have your laptop?" He looks like he's going to argue. "Start driving. I'll work while we move."

Garrett situates me in the back seat, where I can stretch out without my side hurting as much. He passes the laptop back before pulling out. We're stuck in traffic immediately, but it still feels safer than the parking lot.

"When's the last time you took the pills I gave you?" Garrett asks.

"It's been a while." Long enough that my brain no longer swirls through memory. Long enough that I don't feel Aaron's presence.

"They help with pain too," he says.

"Is there water back here?" I rasp. "My throat hurts."

"In the back," he says.

He filled several reusable bottles from home. I pop a capsule and wash it down with water, giving myself time to unfurl the pages I got from the evidence room, smoothing them out over my thighs. My legs make a poor platform. My knees touch when I'm stretched out, but there's a huge gap between them, cavernous enough to bare the tendons of my adductors and the upholstery beyond.

The car light makes it bright enough for me to see Aaron's handwriting. These were ripped from one of his journals. I hold the pages to my nose, close my eyes, and inhale the faint scent of my brother's sweat.

"The manifesto?" I whisper. My lips move against paper. Garrett's creaky old laptop boots up. I insert the CD and his ancient machine can't open the files. "What's with your machine, Garrett? Are you computing in 1996?"

"It's more secure to use old equipment," he says. "There are laws about how we store patient files. This way works. Security through obscurity."

"Maybe you're bad at computers," I suggest.

I recognize encryption software that Aaron liked to use, just by looking at the hash on the file names. These are for Aaron and Evie's eyes only. Luckily, the laptop is connected to the network with an Ingotex hotspot. Even with 4G speeds, I can download a program to decrypt Aaron's puzzle piece.

While it works, I read his journal pages.

*I've tried so hard to forget what happened eight months ago, but I can't. GG says I have to process it in order to move on. I couldn't even make myself talk about it, so he told me to write a journal entry with all my memories. Here I am.*

*I was still working for SE&G eight months ago. I was happy. The job sucked, but all jobs suck, and I could deal with it. My meds were stable. I wasn't using. I had money so sometimes I could pay for my stuff without having to use the trust. Sometimes I thought I could even move out of the old house and get somewhere smaller now that I'm alone, and then I could handle it without EV.*

*During the year before the accident, I was doing inspections around Washoe County mostly. Then they sent me out to the Great Basin. It was an overnight thing on my own. I didn't care that the weather was shitty and windy, even though I hate the wind. It's nice working alone. SE&G had to maintain a lot of old power lines because sparks started wildfires in another county. Things burned. People burned.*

*I worked down the line one at a time, going the opposite direction of a guy at the other end. We were supposed to meet in the middle around breakfast the next day, and I was running behind. The lines needed too much work. Maybe I was starting to rush. Maybe I missed something important. Maybe I started that fire. Maybe I deserved to lose fucking everything. I hate this. So much.*

*Fuck SE&G, I didn't miss anything. I did it all right. That equipment was so old. When it sparked, I did what I was supposed to do. I called the SE&G emergency line and told them there was a fire. I was supposed to leave with my truck. They said they'd send someone to stop it as soon as possible.*

*But they didn't send anyone. I waited ten minutes while it spread. The fire was just getting bigger. So I called the fire department, and they sent me to the Bureau of Land Management, and nobody had heard anything from SE&G.*

*Nobody was coming.*

*I thought if I could keep the fire from traveling it would be okay, so I went in to pull some loose sagebrush away and shovel sand on it. I'm stupid. I'm so stupid.*

*My hands are melted from this. Because I grabbed the wrong thing. Because I got too close.*

*It didn't even hurt at first.*

*Now I never feel anything in my hands but pain, and I have to take the Vicodin if I ever want to sleep. Four Vicodin and an Ambien at night, every night, just so that I can get some rest. It doesn't stop the nightmares; it just means that I don't wake up when I'm back out in the desert getting my hands melted, screaming while nobody comes to help.*

*I wasn't supposed to get hurt, but SE&G didn't care that I did. They just want everything to burn. They're monsters. Fuck them.*

*She's going to have to take care of me forever. EV deserves better than that. But I'm selfish because I can't tell her to get me a nurse when seeing my sister is the best part of my day, every day.*

I feel dampness on my cheeks. I'm surprised to wipe away tears.

It's no manifesto.

"What are you reading?" Garrett is watching me through the rearview mirror.

"Part of Aaron's journal," I say. "He thinks that SE&G didn't respond the night of the accident because they wanted to let everything burn."

"Why would they want to do that?"

I pull the other pieces of the puzzle from my purse. There's so little, it's pathetic. I have the first note. I have the accounting papers in addition to a couple of crumpled articles I yanked off his cork board. There's also an unused syringe of naloxone stuck in the corner of the lining. It's not part of the hunt. Just a reminder of what I've lost.

I flip through the accounting papers, brow furrowed as I try to make sense of the numbers he circled. When I stare at the paper, all I can see is Mack's video. My brother acting like a wild animal. I'm so stuck in my brain that I can't tell where we are. "Where are you driving?"

"South," he says. "We can go to South Tahoe."

"Don't. Pull over." He turns onto the side of the road. We're near the Casino Fandango and its lightless neon. I get out of the car so I can limp into the front seat, taking everything with me. "I think these ledger printouts explain what SE&G was doing. I just don't understand it. There's no explanation."

"Let me see." Garrett shifts the accounting papers across the car and onto his lap. "I'm in private practice. I know a few things about accounting." He takes a minute to read, then turns the paper to show me. "What's this part here mean? What's a Wildfire Security Credit?"

"Wildfire Security…" Aaron had articles about that. I pull one of them out of my purse, crumpled up with tissue. "That's from a bill Assemblyman Frank wrote after the Bighorn Fire. Do you remember that?"

"How could I forget?"

A series of fires had devastated the Great Basin, out between here and Elko on the east side of the state. They mostly went ignored in the news at first. Then their fires had eaten a little town tucked in the mountains near Truckee. More than twenty people died when the only road out was blocked by a fallen tree. The town of Lone Well was scorched off the map.

"The Wildfire Security Credit uses taxes to clean up SE&G fires." It's not hard to pull up the text of the bill online. I zero in on a section of the bill about Wildfire Security. "Look here. They get funding approval from the state a year in advance. So for next year's Wildfire Security fund, they'll have to give a projection from this year's burns."

Garrett leans in to keep reading, his arm brushing mine. "This is from *last* year. They've projected Wildfire Security funds for the next five years, and look at this interest rate. The company's getting a huge boost from investing instead of performing maintenance. I don't think they've got the capital to recover from this fire, much less prevent the next one."

"They won't have to pay for this one if they prove they didn't start it." My chest hurts. "They're planning to convince a court that Aaron committed arson. They don't accept liability, and they get richer. But they underestimated Aaron. He collected evidence."

"Paranoia's got survival benefits," Garrett says.

"Aaron found more than a pay raise for Don DeVos while he was investigating." I hand Mack's cracked phone to him. "Look in the camera roll. Last video."

The decryption program on the laptop finishes, and I finally open the folder. There are dozens of files in it.

When I click open the first one, I find screenshots of security footage. It's not until I start going through the whole slideshow that I realize what I'm seeing.

Garrett fumbles with the phone for a minute, but gets Mack's video to play. I can hear her quavering voice while I click through the pictures. "Please tell, like, the FBI or whatever that my parents are selling me to Don DeVos. The electric company guy."

The first image is too blurry to make out, but the second is an external shot of Don DeVos's house where Mallek is walking Mack inside. I *think* that's Mack. She's petite and young enough.

In the next pictures, I see several different parties. Not all are at DeVos's house, but all appear to happen at expensive locales, like villas and cabins. They show this poor woman entering a bedroom with different adult men a dozen times.

Mack's voice continues on the video. "It's horrible. He passes me between his friends, and like—I don't think I'm the first girl he's done this to."

The tightness in my chest just keeps getting tighter as I continue clicking. There are faces I recognize among these pictures. Local celebrities of different kinds. The guy who sells all the cars. The last governor. There are a few from Silicon Valley, just a quick skip over the border. And then I stop on a picture of the new sheriff, Kaleb Cuttino, who Hank has been working with all week. He's got a hand up Mack's skirt.

"Please get the FBI. Okay?"

I shut down the images, feeling nauseous. None of the other pictures had caught assault, only the grim walk toward inevitable rape.

"Aaron couldn't prove SE&G was starting fires, so he proved its CEO is a human trafficker," I say.

A sudden surge of dizziness tells me I'm going to vomit. I'm nauseous all the time these days. If I eat. If I don't eat. When I take my pills. If I lay down too long or stand up too quickly. That might be the greatest curse of all this—the fact that as I do it more, it happens more easily, even at times when I shouldn't be sick.

The feeling triples, quadruples, and Garrett produces a plastic bag just in time. I can't stop myself. He's right *there* when my stomach empties. It's mostly acid, and I cry out at the burn on my smoke-torn throat.

A cool hand spreads over my back, rubbing my spine. "I feel sick too," he says quietly. "I had no idea DeVos was like that. I'd heard stories, but..." His hand slides to my lower back, where it remains.

"If you heard, why didn't you do anything about it?" I asked.

"There was no proof, just gossip. What are you supposed to do about that?"

I don't have an answer.

We all know that there is a secret code about these things. There's no record my father ever hurt my mother, nothing the police would find, but everybody around the neighborhood knew. Other kids whispered about it. Sometimes the neighbor's mom would go out of her way to give me cookies and pat my hair. Even then, I knew what pity looked like.

"You look angry," Garrett says. "I thought you'd be happy you were piecing it together."

"This absolutely provides motive for killing Aaron," I say. "But Jobson didn't kill Aaron deliberately. That was an accident."

"Are you sure? How's your judgment been lately?" His fingers smooth over my brow.

I want to slap his hand away, but the words penetrate as much as the coolness of his skin.

My judgment hasn't been great. I've been in an uncontrollable tailspin. I walked into Jobson's home, where I knew a murderer would be waiting for me, and I talked to him alone while he wore a gun at his belt. I confronted DeVos at his office when Aaron's workers' comp was denied. And I'd begun an affair with the man sitting beside me with his hand on my forehead as if checking for fever, looking at me like I'm his future.

"I don't know," I finally say. "I'm hurting. I'm not thinking clearly."

"Let me grab painkillers. I've got Vicodin."

"No. Tylenol." I don't take Vicodin. I'd rather hurt now than lose myself in an abyss like Aaron had.

Garrett digs through his briefcase, looking at different pill bottles. While he's distracted, I login to Gmail and send the photos from the CD to Mack's cell phone. She's logged into her seldom-used Facebook account. I post everything. Mallek walking her into DeVos's house. Cuttino with his fingers up her skirt. The video with her tearful plea for help. The only caption I post is, *HELP ME.*

It takes barely a moment. I've closed out of everything by the time Garrett comes up with an orange bottle. "I have Percocet."

"I already took the Xanax. You said it would help me hurt less."

"The Xanax relaxes you through the pain. The Percs take it away." He puts the pills into my palm and holds my hand as tightly as my gaze. "Your injuries are serious. You're not going to be able to function if you're doubling over every time you cough, and you're not going to get addicted with one dose. You're not Aaron."

"Take them back." Trying to argue with him makes me cough again. This must be what it feels like to get stabbed in the back.

"This is almost over," Garrett says softly. "I'll still be here for you after. I won't let you fall. Okay?"

He's so gentle and persistent that I believe him.

The pills are big. My stomach sees them as a hostile force, and I gag but keep them down.

"I love you, Evangeline," Garrett says. My hand is over my mouth, and I'm shuddering with nausea. But he looks at me, brushes my hair behind my ear, and says he loves me.

Garrett starts the car again. "Let's go. We'll head to the FBI field office in Reno and get these to Wyatt. It's what Aaron wanted."

"Yeah, you should go," I say, ejecting the disc. "Do you have an extra pair of shoes? I'm going to DeVos's house."

"No." He grabs my arm. I think he's going to hurt me the way Hank does, but he says, "I'm not going to let you go alone."

Even a faint smile is so foreign to me that my cheeks ache at the effort. "Where did you come from, Dr. Glass? You're such a Boy Scout."

He laughs. It makes him look boyish, unrestrained. "Blame it on the fraternity Ro Epsilon Chi. Those guys drilled the motto into me. 'Purity in loyalty, joy in union.' Aaron wasn't just a patient, but a friend. You mean everything to me. I'm loyal to you, and if you let me, I'll do my damnedest to bring you joy."

When he does the Ro Epsilon Chi salute—at least, I think that weird fist over his head is a salute—he looks so dorky. He still remembers the stupid motto. And he is one of the only people left who cared about Aaron half as much as I do. The other might be about to die in DeVos's house.

"You need to know something about Aaron," I say quietly. "About me."

He frowns. "What is it?"

I grasp for the ability to tell him the truth. Those secrets that Aaron and I promised would be buried with our bodies. If I'm going to do this, leave with Garrett, abandon Hank, then he needs to know everything. But I think he won't understand. He's not like us.

Twenty years of suppressing memories and parroting the same stories to anyone who will listen is difficult to release.

"I'll tell you another time," I say. "We should get going."

## CHAPTER 23
## EVE

The highway is barricaded to prevent people like us from going places we shouldn't, so Garrett and I take a service road to approach DeVos's house. "There's a trail through here big enough to drive on. I've hiked it a few times," Garrett says, leaning over the steering wheel to wipe ash off the inside of the windshield. He punches the air conditioning button to turn it off and closes the vents. "The trail is on the side of the hill, not a lot of trees. We should be able to get through even if the brush is lit."

When he turns off Carson Street, we plunge into a neighborhood turned endless by darkness. His headlights cut narrow circles through the black smoke. There are fewer house fires since the buildings are newer, but the drainage ditches blaze. They're filled with rabbit brush gone dry in a hot summer, and they ignited like dryer lint. Embers skitter across the road.

Garrett turns the car off the road to climb onto the trail. We're boxed in by smoke, both that which rises from the valley and haloes us from the hillside.

"See? Not so bad here," Garrett says. "This goes behind WNC, over the pass, then comes out in the foothills where DeVos lives. We'll have Mack out of there in twenty minutes. You don't have to worry."

I'm not worried. I can't feel anything. That Percocet has kicked in, and I'm empty within the world's softest edges.

My purse rests beside me. It's fallen open.

Garrett glances at it. "Is that a box cutter?"

"It was Aaron's," I say. "He left it for me."

"Why?"

I close my purse, the leather buttery-soft against my fingers. "I don't know. I'm still missing his manifesto, so I don't know if he explained it to me there."

"What if there's no manifesto? What if he was really hallucinating?" Garrett says the words I fear to think.

Some slimy reptile of a thought slithers through the back of my mind, leaving a trail of chills.

I'm missing something.

*You still need to find the manifesto, Evie.* It's Aaron's voice, this whisper, back with me once again. I look over my shoulder, but the SUV is filled with Garrett's boxes. And of course, my brother is dead. He can't guide me through all the answers.

He's right, though. I have to find the manifesto.

"Oh my God," Garrett mutters as we turn a corner.

A burning tree has fallen into the road. The bushes on the shoulder have caught too.

"Go through it," I say.

He turns round eyes on me. "What?"

"You have to keep moving. Drive through it."

Garrett sets his shoulders and hits the gas. He turns to hit the broken bottom of the tree, where there are fewer branches to burn. The trunk scrapes along our flank, turning under the impact as we teeter on the side of the cliff. His wheels grip the ground, but it feels like we're going to roll anyway.

Then we're through.

"Oh my God," he says. "Oh my God." It's so hot in the car he's soaking with sweat. His hair is plastered to his forehead.

"You're almost there, Evie," says Aaron. His voice is more distinct now. It sounds real. His presence *feels real*.

I have to look around the car again, but he's still not there.

"What's wrong?" Garrett asks.

I shake my head, force myself to face forward. My brain is sliding.

*It's the Percocet.*

We drive for twenty minutes in smoke and shadow until Garrett navigates to DeVos's house. Every light in the front of the woodsy mansion is turned on. His garden is lit by spotlights. An air conditioner is humming. The only difference now is that misters spray from under the lip of the roof, dousing the lawn and walls to keep them moist. Rainbows shimmer in the water.

The fire cannot touch this house.

We park and run through the sprinklers to get inside. Reaching the front door leaves ash streaking gray down my skin, purified from the hazards of the outside world. The front door is unlocked, as if waiting for someone to exit, but his den is empty.

"I think they already evacuated," Garrett says.

"Let's see if Mack was abandoned. I'll check this floor. See if you can find a basement."

I'm consumed by surreality on my walk through the hall behind DeVos's poker room. I know this place, and I know I've been here before. But my recognition mostly stems from the horrible photographs on that CD.

This is the hallway where Mack walks to get "passed around." Where wretched old men seek their happy endings at the hands of a victim then laugh about it with friends.

*I hate him. I hate them all.*

It's strange *feeling* hate like this. My mind is elevated to new levels, making connections I ordinarily do not, and letting a buzz of real emotion seethe out of my core.

Some of the doors in this hallway stand open. I check the first of them, digging my nails into the frame to help me stand as my legs turn liquid. The room is dark beyond, unlit.

Hallucinations fill the shadows.

Waking dreams form Dad standing over Mom in my childhood kitchen. The floor is tiled black and white, the refrigerator avocado green. I can see it all. It's *real.*

My mother is holding an empty box of Oreos. "Where did they go, Sean?"

Dad's voice is indistinct. It's been too long since I heard him, so I only remember the rumble of his anger. *I ate them. I can eat them if I want. I pay for everything in this house, you dumb bitch.* My father's shaking his fist. His feet make earthquakes. Their voices are distant, muted.

"Aaron bought these with his allowance, Sean. The Oreos are his favorite snack," she says.

I've turned from the door before I can see Dad hit Mom. I always looked away, too small to intercede, too scared to use my voice. But in a way, I looked away because my mother deserved it. My father was disgusted by her, and I shared in it with him.

Guilt. I'm feeling guilt.

"It's not your fault," Aaron says. "We all survive in different ways." He's still nowhere to be seen, but his voice has gotten clearer, coming from over my shoulder as if he's watching events unfold too.

I'm alone in the hallway.

When I look back, there's nothing but an unoccupied room in Don DeVos's house. Some kind of half-bathroom.

Voices call to me from the next door.

*Over here, Evie.*

"I'm coming, Aaron."

I follow his voice to the next room. I open the door to find a massage table, neatly stacked sheets, and a laundry basket. It smells like coconut oil.

Aaron stands beyond the table. He's not the adult I've lost, but the child I loved. He's so much taller than the petite little Evie gazing up at him. I can see myself as I was. I wore a Barbie shirt with frilly sleeves. My shorts were long enough to be capris on my spindly legs. Back then, Mom used to let my hair grow long but never brushed it, and it was always tangled into a massive knot at the nape of my neck.

"Give me the box cutter, Evie," Aaron says. The little girl gives it to him. Her hand is bloody. He uses his shirt to wipe her clean and then says, "I won't let them know about you. They won't understand. We'll just have to keep another secret between the two of us."

We had already agreed that nobody would know that Aaron left a gun for me to find.

Just as they would never know I pulled the trigger on Ronnie out of curiosity.

"Felix isn't hurting anymore," I say. The voice I hear belongs to a little girl.

"I know, Evie," he says. "I know."

"Dad won't hurt Mom anymore," I say.

"I know, Evie. I know."

When I step around the table, I see a body on the ground too large to be a cat's. It's Dad. He's a big man, tall to adults, a giant to children, and now he's in the fetal position in a pool of blood. He's been shot in the chest.

*Dead.*

"It's okay to cry, Evie," Aaron says.

"What if I'm not sad he's gone? What if nothing makes me sad?" I ask him. "The only thing I ever feel is anger."

"Don't tell anyone. They can't know."

I'm keeping an eye on Dad's dead body while Mom gets some bags and shovels, planning to conceal the evidence under the bricks. "We have to finish before Wyatt comes home from his friend's house," Mom says. Our oldest brother would call the cops. He's like that. *Not like us.*

While Mom fetches shovels, I dig inside Dad's body. I use that box cutter to try to get through his ribs and see if he ever had a heart. I don't get very far. The wrong tool in a small hand isn't capable of doing such a thing. Aaron convinces me to surrender the blade again. When Mom sees the damage inflicted on Dad, she doesn't even ask which one of us did it.

All of that and so much more is contained in the massage room.

We would never speak of the truth again, not even in private. These secrets would die with us.

I can shut the door on it all.

There are more doors further down the hallway, infinite memories to explore. But I can't reach the next one because a man staggers up from the opposite end of the mansion, lurching toward me with a bottle of scotch hanging in one hand. At first, I cannot tell if he's real.

"Mallek?" he bellows at the sight of me.

It's Don DeVos.

And I'm not hallucinating.

I should be afraid. Like most men, he's taller and heavier than me, and a toddler could beat me at arm wrestling. But I'm still disconnected from the floor under my feet. I'm not sure I've got anything left in my body but bones. The idea of being hurt by him doesn't scare me because I've already been skinned and butchered and left without a single nerve to transmit pain.

"You're not Mallek," he says, stopping a few feet away. His eyes are rimmed red. His shirt's stained. "Where's Mallek?" As if I should have an answer to that.

"Where is Mackenzie?" I counter.

"Mackenzie? You're here for Mackenzie?" He points at me. "I remember. You're Hank's lady. I thought he took care of you."

Conversation escapes me. Reality is too fractured. "Where have you put her?"

"I was just coming to find my girl." His eyes connect with a door further down this endless hallway. This one is locked from the outside. He's been keeping Mack in a prison with fine whiskey and expensive cigars.

"You're going to keep using her?" I ask.

His laugh smells of alcohol, even from here. The odor radiates from the damp patches in his armpits. "I think you're confused. I also think you're trespassing…again. I'm going to find Mallek and have him remove you permanently." That isn't the kind of dirty work DeVos does himself.

"You're not getting away with this," I say. "I know that you've been letting fires burn so you can increase your company value on the back of A.B. 76. I know that you ordered Jobson to kill my brother to make him the perfect silent scapegoat. And I know you're letting the Carson Valley burn now so you can hide what you're doing to Mack."

He laughs again, shaking his head. The mirth is draining out of him. He's sweating harder, cheeks almost the color of the fire seen through his tinted windows. "Yeah, I'm making money off wildfire recovery. This is America. It's legal. We passed a law."

"Starting fires and letting them burn will never be legal!"

DeVos's eyes glint darkly. "You're going to have to prove that. And it's going to be tricky because I didn't intend Carson City to burn. It's one thing to take down a few old single-wides, but it's another to wipe out a legislature that's a big fan of me. And hide Mackenzie? Why the hell would I have to hide little Suzie Q? She gives *great* massages. Her family knows what's up, they get paid, everyone's *fine*." He takes a step toward me. "Everyone but you."

"You can't use Jobson to kill me too." I take a step back. "He's dead."

*I killed him.*

"Don't think about it," Aaron says behind me. "You did what you had to with Jobson. Now focus on what happens next."

*Focus on Don DeVos.*

DeVos's laugh is its darkest yet. He takes another drink and says, "I don't even know who this Jobson is. I talked to a friend about taking care of Ashe, helping him shut up about infrastructure, you know, and I've got no friends named Jobson." He smiles gleefully. "My pill guy whipped up something good for Ashe. How do you think I had the stuff to drug you the other night?" His voice is taunting, cruel.

My tongue seems to float within my teeth as memories of Hank's assault on me rise like bodies from the bottom of a frozen pond after spring thaw.

*Should I feel like this?* I've never taken such painkillers before, but surely I'd know if it would leave me disembodied. If Percocet allowed me to see through DeVos's jacket, his shirt, his ribcage, all the way to his raisin of a heart, then someone would have warned me.

DeVos is suddenly in front of me, looking down from so high that he might as well be hanging from the topmost spire of a church. The weight of his presence presses on me. "You're blown out of your mind right now," he says, peering into my eyes.

I'm holding the box cutter inside my purse. I'm watching DeVos for movement.

*You're so small, Evie, you have to move faster than them,* Aaron says. *You have to kill him too. You have to kill them all.*

It's what Aaron wants me to do.

I let DeVos run his fingers down my shoulder, touch my arm, graze the side of my breast. "No family left, right? Dead parents, dead brother? And you've got a good body." My thumb slides the box cutter open. "I know a few guys who like them old. Maybe I'll take you *and* Mackenzie to—"

The world explodes.

A pinhole opens in DeVos's chest, high and to the left. Blood spurts from his back in a wider radius. Bullet holes are sometimes like that, I've heard. They vibrate and expand and rattle around and come out messier than they go in.

DeVos's body tumbles. He goes from the highest of highs to the lowest of lows in the ungraceful dive to his grave. He bangs against the wall, his foot slips at a funny angle, and he hits the carpet on one knee. I glimpse his exit wound. That glossy red is what I remember with my cat too. I'd dug around in Dad's body until I found glints of white bone. I've seen all of this before, and whatever I should feel can't reach me in my oblivion.

Garrett stands at the end of the hall, backed by the light from DeVos's little casino. He's holding a gun. No longer aimed, but not quite dropped. "Evangeline," he says. "Are you okay?"

DeVos is at my feet, struggling to roll over, hand pressed to his chest. His gaze is unfocused. He's not long for this world.

"I'm alive," I say loudly, ears ringing.

"I can't believe I shot him." Garrett drops the gun before joining me.

I didn't even know he had a gun. "Why did you do it?"

"Because," he says, looking surprised, "he was going to kill you." But he lifts his hands to look at them, and I see a horror in his features I can't relate to. I didn't feel horror after killing Ronnie. Or after Dad died. Or after Jobson. Horror doesn't make sense in my senseless world.

But now Garrett is like me. This man loves me, treats me well, and kills for me. I don't have to understand his feelings; I understand the experience. Garrett shot Don DeVos, and we stand over him together, holding hands, as the man bleeds to death.

# CHAPTER 24
# HANK

Cuttino is neck-deep in chaos when I return to the checkpoint. The traffic jam on the north side of town has gotten worse. Half the cars have open doors, their drivers and passengers emerging onto pavement to ask what's wrong. Nobody can get anywhere. The fire is everywhere.

When I approach, Cuttino's already red-faced. He shouts at me. "If you're going to tear me a new hole over the traffic, don't start! We're already doing everything we can about the semis. One more bitch screeching in my ear won't make the bulldozers get to Washoe Valley faster!"

"Semis?" I ask.

"Two of them overturned trying to turn south. One was trying to pass the other and..." He slaps his hands together. "Fuck, that's the last thing we needed. This day can't get worse." He snags me by the jacket and pulls me away from the crowd again.

I elbow him off me, hard. "Jobson is dead." Before he can reply, I continue. "It looks like death by suicide. There's a note."

Cuttino nods. "Good, great, fine. Perfect."

I'm not sure if he thinks I did the killing or not. I'm not sure that it matters anymore.

"DeVos called me," I say. "He wanted me to tell you…" Trying to get the words out feels like reaching a gauntlet down my throat to forcibly extract my heart. "He said you fucked up. He said you've got about fifteen minutes to run."

"Fifteen minutes, starting when?" Cuttino asks.

"About twenty minutes ago," I say.

He's apoplectic. "Why didn't you call me? What did he say I did? I didn't do anything!" Before I can answer, his phone rings and he checks it. I can see the screen. It's the governor. Cuttino shoves past me to take the call behind the back tents.

Silence ripples over the deputies in the parking lot. It's contagious. One cluster falls into a hush, then a man turns to whisper to a nurse, and her group goes quiet too. Every face is illuminated by cell phones. I hear someone crying.

As soon as I open my phone, I find a dozen Facebook alerts, and over ninety-nine on Twitter. I'm logged into the sheriff's department's social media, and I open Facebook to find that our page has been tagged in the comments on a viral post. Something that's already been shared over ten thousand times.

A girl named Mackenzie Reese posted a photo of Kaleb Cuttino. He's groping her. The text above the post says "HELP ME."

My eyes lift above the crowd to Cuttino, pacing behind the SUVs while on the phone. He's ashen.

I don't recognize Mackenzie Reese's photo until I read the Reno Gazette-Journal article. Despite her Facebook profile's claim that she's eighteen, Mackenzie is a seventeen-year-old from Carson City who has been missing for days according to friends.

This is the girl that Eve wanted me to look for.

She's a minor.

She's with DeVos in a picture dated from last year, when she was sixteen.

Cuttino assaulted her.

But there are more layers to this that make me feel like the Earth's gonna split open and eat me whole. This girl's being held as some kind of sex slave by DeVos, so she was in that house with me while I was playing poker. I took DeVos's money. I drank his beer. I shook his hand, apologized when Eve made a mess of herself, and went after Jobson on his word and a whiff of a threat.

*I didn't see anything happen. I had no idea. I'm not complicit.*

But suddenly I understand why Wilkes stopped playing ball. *Grass-feeder. Not a meat eater.*

Cuttino rips off his hat and barks into the phone and hangs up. By the time he gets back to me, there's murder in his eyes. "DeVos can't ditch me," Cuttino says. "Telling *you* to get rid of *me*? After some stupid fake picture? Fuck no. I'm going to talk sense into that asshole. He can pull some strings. He can make the governor give my job back."

I just stare at him, wordless. I'm too busy screaming in my head.

*You sexually assaulted a sixteen-year-old.*

There's no fixing this. No string-pulling will make this disappear. And it's not because Cuttino can't get away with it in the system—he can. But he can't take back every wretched thing he did to that child, and there are higher powers who know. *God knows.*

He storms to his car, and nobody tries to stop him. I follow behind. When he gets in, I do too.

"Coming? Good," Cuttino says. "Someone else will fix *this* fuck-up." He jerks his head at the traffic jam, indicating the disaster on the freeway.

We peel out of the parking lot. The road up toward the college is as packed as Carson Street, so Cuttino drives up the sidewalk and bike lane, slapping the switch for emergency lights. There's nowhere for people to move so they can get out of our way. The sirens send them flying in every direction—over benches, plastered against walls, into traffic.

Cuttino's barely looking at the road in front of us. "Don said the girls are always eighteen. And it was just massages. There's nothing wrong with getting massages from an adult woman! She's the one who jerked me off. She wanted it. She was supposed to be eighteen fucking years old!"

He yanks the wheel, and we shriek past the college onto a wide dirt road, or maybe it's some kind of trail. I fall against the door and nearly hit my head on the glass. I fumble to get my seatbelt on, bracing myself against the back of the seat.

"Besides, Don shares his perks with everyone," Cuttino says. "It's not like I'm doing anything I shouldn't. And if I am, about a hundred other guys must be up to the same fucking thing! Why call me out? Just me? That little bitch

Mackenzie is out to get me, I'm telling you. And when I'm done talking sense into Don, I'm going to make her say sorry."

He doesn't seem to notice or care how much is on fire around us. It's getting hot in the car and the air conditioning's still running, so it sucks the smoke right into circulation. "Slow down, you're going to run us off the road," I say.

"Shut up, Everhardt," Cuttino says. "I haven't forgotten you. After everything I've done for you, you're in this as deep as I am, right? You'll fix this. We're gonna fix it."

He guns it and drives off the end of the paved road onto a trail wide enough for cars. We're following tire tracks from a car that traveled this road before us. Somehow, I know that Eve was in that car. It's like I can smell her on the air outside. Like she's beckoning to me from DeVos's house, urging me to find her. I'm going to wring every last drop of truth out of the bitch I call wife.

Cuttino's looking at me with those wild eyes, not at the twisting trail. "If I don't get through this, it's your fault. You're gonna pay, Everhardt."

"You're—" I start to say.

A sudden sense of momentum takes the words from me.

The road swerves in front of us. Cuttino overcorrects the wheel.

The world goes black.

* * *

I wake up an instant later.

I'm upside down, everything hurts, and my vision's blurry.

*Cuttino flipped the car.*

I groan, reaching up to touch my forehead. The roof of the car crumpled to a couple inches above my hair. My seat-belt's holding me, the strap aching against my collarbone. I'm bleeding. There's a friction burn on my arm. "Dammit…Kaleb. Kaleb, are you alive?" My neck's gone stiff so it's hard to turn. Cuttino's not in the seat beside me. The windshield is shattered, and there's a burning tree beyond.

*Get out, Everhardt.*

I manage to unbuckle my seatbelt and my body collapses against the roof. I kick the door open and crawl outside. I'm surrounded by brush, and the fire's moving in fast. We must have hit something, spun off the road, gone down an embankment.

We brought a tree down the hill with us. It's burning too.

Cuttino cries out from the other side of the wreck. "Everhardt!"

I limp around the car. My right leg got banged against the dashboard, and I nearly lose balance when I see the sheriff. He got thrown from the car. He's halfway under the burning tree. Now that he's awake, he's screaming at the burn against his lower legs, slapping at the ground as he tries to pull himself free. He coughs, gags, chokes.

"Everhardt! Get me out of here!"

The man's all blood and soot and panicked fox eyes glinting from the middle of it. I could get in there and pull him out. Could I do it without burning myself? Life as a burn victim is beyond torture, a vicious, painful half-life. There's a reason that Hell is filled with flame. It's the kind of punishment people like Aaron and Cuttino deserve.

"I guess I'm a grass eater," I say.

Then I climb up the hill, back to the trail, away from Cuttino.

He keeps screaming. The wind's loud enough that I don't have to hear him by the time I reach the dirt road, wheezing and weak.

But there's no doubt in my mind that he can't escape that tree. I can imagine his last minutes under the trunk, smothering and melting and knowing that I let him die. And in that moment, I feel like I'm God, turning my vengeful gaze toward Eve.

# CHAPTER 25
# EVE

With DeVos dead, I keep searching for Mack.

She's down the hall behind a door I can't open more than two inches. It bumps against something soft but immobile.

I peer through to see a young man dead on the floor, naked except for underwear. His skull's been bashed with something so many times that the back is pulp. His ponytail is caked black, tangled with chunks.

Mack huddles in the rear corner of the room with Mallek's gun. She's wearing clothes stripped off the dead body, his pants rolled up, shirt hem tucked in, everything too big for her petite form. Mack turns the gun on me when I squeeze through the narrow entrance.

"Wait," I say, holding up my hands.

"Oh my God, Evie!" She drops the gun and leaps to her feet. "I didn't know what else to do! I didn't think anyone was coming back for me. Rob said he was going to tie me up and leave me here and..." She sobs, lifting her bloody hands. Hers are bigger than mine were for my first murder, so many years ago.

"You didn't do anything wrong. And nobody is going to find out." I am Aaron now, gentle and tall, standing over a scared little girl.

Mack has a bruised eye and split cheek. I pull the mini first aid kit out of my purse so I can sterilize it and apply a bandage.

"Why *did* you come back for me?" Mack asks, holding still while I fix her up.

"My brother wanted you safe." This is about Aaron. It's always been about Aaron and *only* Aaron.

"Thank you," Mack says. She tenses when she sees Garrett over my shoulder. He's come inside after us.

"He came with me," I say. "We've got a car. We can get out of here. You're safe now, Mack, and nobody's going to hurt you again."

* * *

I don't know I'm lying until we leave DeVos's mansion.

The road to the front gate is obscured by smoke and burning branches, our only known exit gone in flame. There's no quenching these flames, no chance that fire-fighters will save us.

"There's an access road out back," Garrett says. He turns to leave, but I linger on the front step, thinking about DeVos. He was going to tell me something before he died, and it won't stop nudging at the back of my mind.

He said that he didn't use the police to kill my brother. He used his "pill guy."

*You're almost there, Evie,* Aaron says. His voice seems to come from my chest now. He's inside of me, frantic, making my pulse rise. I press my hands against my heart. Without Aaron's necklace, the only thing under my palms are the topography of my bones.

In the billow of smoke over the gates, I can see facial features. Dark eyes. A cut jaw. It's not Aaron, but someone else…someone who still stands between justice and me.

*What am I missing?*

"Evie?" Mack prompts. "Are you coming?"

Her voice is a shock of reality. "I'm coming."

I chase Garrett and Mack to the back of the house, their shadowy forms racing ahead of me down an endless hall.

I've been in the solarium before. Its big windows are streaked with soot. Garrett enters a lounge beyond with a big fireplace and walls covered in memorabilia. The sight of it makes me more nauseous. I don't have to remember what happened here to know that *something* happened. My bones hurt with it.

The ghost of DeVos stands in front of the fireplace, his hand on the mantel, fingers curled around a snifter. When he turns to smile at me, there's nothing in his eye sockets except shadow.

*I know some guys who like them old,* he says.

My stomach clenches, and I brace myself on the back of a chair, digging my hands in. "How do you know the access road will get us out of here, Garrett?" I ask. "What if it just leads to a cell phone tower and it's a dead end?"

"I've looked at maps, and I know the area," Garrett says.

Something catches my eye in the shadows. It's an oversized photograph of DeVos with his fraternity brothers. The men in it are holding their fists above their heads in a weird gesture that I've seen tonight. And their motto is written across the bottom of the picture. *Purity in loyalty, joy in union.*

"What are you doing by the fireplace? We have to go," Garrett says.

I turn on him slowly. "You knew DeVos…didn't you? You knew how to get here. You were in the same frat."

"Evangeline," he says warningly.

I press my hands to my forehead. Hadn't Garrett mentioned a medication adjustment for Aaron? The only time I'd seen him behave half so strange had been when his medication was wrong, but Garrett was more careful than that.

*Unless he was doing DeVos a favor.*

A terrible thought surges. "Where did you get the money to build a psychiatric hospital?"

"We have to go." Garrett reaches for me.

I jerk away before he can touch my hand. I back up to the photo of the fraternity, afraid it will vanish into my drugged hallucinations if I move too far. "Mack, go start the car," I say. She runs out the door, and when Garrett turns to watch her go, I take another step back. Further away from him. He has long arms. I need as much space as possible. "We're going to talk before we go anywhere, Garrett."

He still looks patient but worried. "This isn't the time to talk. There are two dead bodies, a closing wildfire—"

"Did you deliberately mis-medicate Aaron?" I ask.

"No, of course not."

There's an imperceptible pause before he replies. He blinks twice while speaking, and then he licks his lips. Garrett has never made me uncomfortable before. Now, with the way he's looking at me, my skin is crawling, and I know I was wrong about him.

He steps toward me, and I step back again.

"Tell me the truth," I say.

"Okay, yes, I knew DeVos." Garrett rolls his eyes. "Everyone knows him! He supplied major funding for the psychiatric hospital, but that doesn't mean—"

"When I was eighteen years old, I started looking at colleges." I'm grinding the purse straps in my hands, squeezing so tight. "Mom realized that once I left, she'd be alone with Aaron. She couldn't imagine taking care of him for the rest of her life. She planned to send him to assisted living."

Garrett stops approaching me. His hands are out like he expects me to lunge and bite.

"One of her cousins runs a home in Tennessee that would take Aaron," I say. "*Tennessee.* That wasn't anywhere near home or any of the colleges I wanted. But my mom was set on it. She filled out the paperwork, wrote a check, and got drunk. Really, really drunk." I can still see her on the floor.

Mom's back is resting against a chair behind Garrett as if she's really there—as if she ever could have been in a home like DeVos's. Mom was a fat woman with rolls over her rolls. Once she got down, she didn't often get up. I can smell her toxic sweat and the rotten grape stench of wine.

"She hadn't even told Aaron he was going to leave the next day. She said she'd wire the money in the morning, fax the paperwork, and buy the plane tickets. She kept yelling at me to bring another glass of wine." I rub my forefinger and thumb together, remembering the crumble of pills between my fingers. "I put other things into her wine."

Garrett's hands drop. He straightens. No longer threatening.

"She didn't wake up. So I shredded the paperwork and forged a suicide note," I say. "I took custody of Aaron and that was my life. I gave him everything because that's what I owed him."

I still can't believe I went so far.

But I had been angry, so angry, and everything had hurt worse since we buried Dad in the side yard. I used to sleep on the bricks and wake covered in caterpillars and tears. Dad hurt Mom, but Mom hurt me. She hurt Aaron. And she killed the man who brought us into this world in a stroke of selfish passion.

I learned too many lessons from my mother.

She was the one who showed me how to cover a murder. Lie to the police, repaint the laundry room, bury the bodies deep.

"Did Aaron know?" Garrett asks.

"I've never told anyone." But that doesn't mean Aaron didn't know. The two of us are one soul, and he provided all the best parts of me. It was impossible to fool him. Still, I chose to give him reasonable doubt. I didn't burden him with one more secret.

"God, Evangeline," Garrett says. "I'm so sorry."

"I understand we sometimes make terrible, unforgivable decisions." I make sure to give him my biggest eyes. "I can't undo what I've done. I can only move forward. But I can't move forward with you unless I know the truth."

"God," he says again, glancing over his shoulder. "Okay, Evangeline, I just have to preface this by saying I didn't plan for Aaron to die. And at no point did DeVos order his death. It was an accident."

He comes nearer and I let him. I want to see his eyes.

"Aaron gave me his manifesto for safe-keeping," he says. "I wasn't supposed to read it, but I thought it might give me insight into his mental state. When I saw his accusations toward DeVos—which was only the fire scheme at the time, nothing about sex trafficking—I confronted Don personally. We were in the fraternity together. We'd had a few dinners together. Don told me the accusations were true but overblown. Aaron was a dangerous obsessive, and Don wanted me to 'do something about that.'"

"And you did," I say.

"He agreed to fund the psych hospital. It meant I could provide desperately needed mental health services to an underserved region. Whatever Aaron went through, it would help thousands more just like him."

And give Garrett a huge pay raise with a beautiful house. All he had to do was sell my brother out.

"I changed his meds," Garrett says. "At worst, I figured he'd have to do some time in the hospital. DeVos could clean up the evidence, and nobody would believe Aaron's accusations. His evidence would be meaningless."

My drunk mother is still on the floor between us. Aaron is facedown beside her. Neither of them are moving. I rub my eyes but they're still there, real as ever.

"You were on the phone the night we were together," I say. The night when Garrett took me on his kitchen floor, entering my body, claiming me. "You called the cops on Aaron, didn't you?"

"Aaron texted me asking for help to hide a friend, Mackenzie, I guess. I sent Aaron the best help I could offer. Yes, I called the police."

Jobson slumps against the lounge window, a hole in his head and gun in his hand.

Ronnie skips a path to the solarium doors.

I'm surrounded by bodies.

"I'm sorry, Evangeline, I'm so sorry," Garrett says. He buries his face in my hair. His breath is hot and wet. "The guilt's killing me. I never meant for it to go that far. And I never dreamed DeVos would keep someone captive, or that he'd burn the city down, or—"

"You're so innocent." I can't make it sound like a compliment.

He strokes my back. "We all make mistakes, but I don't know how I'm going to live with this one when you two mean so much to me."

"Did you ever hurt Mack or another one of DeVos's girls?" I ask, letting my arms wrap around his shoulders.

"No. God, no. I wasn't in that circle. You know I'm not like that."

"But you did kill my brother."

"Jobson killed him," he says. "A horrible accident."

I twine my fingers in Garrett's hair, pressing our cheeks close. Hot tears streak from my eyes. I can't remember the last time I cried, really cried. "You knew the statistics," I whispered. "You've quoted them to me. People with mental illnesses are sixteen times likelier to be victimized by police violence. Right? You called the cops, even though you knew."

"Yes, Evangeline, but—"

"One last question," I say. "These pills you've been giving me. What's in them?"

"Xanax. Percocet. They're only—"

"Am I sane right now?" I put my mouth right next to his ear, so I barely have to breathe the words out. "Or have you poisoned me like you poisoned Aaron?" I'm seeing visions, hearing voices, and it all feels so *real*.

"I would never do that to you," Garrett says, his arms smoothing around my waist.

I put the box cutter through his jugular.

His reaction is slower than you would expect. Maybe it's because I'm still holding him so close, so tenderly. The truth is that I'm too weak to push him away. Shock has slapped my bones to dust. Garrett's blood courses warm over my hand, and when his fingers come up to feel the wound, he first brushes against my knuckles like a lover would.

Then he shoves me away. Even now, he's gentle.

Garrett collapses at my feet.

"Why?" he gurgles. I think he says, "Hank…"

"You're a coward," I say.

His blood is black on the carpet. Garrett lets me roll him over, shaking his head, trying to say my name. He's still looking for me to change my mind and run away with his bleeding corpse. He wants this to be okay.

I shove his knees apart and kneel between them. Garrett lifts his knees in an attempt to protect his tender parts. I sit on one before gouging the razor high in the inner thigh. Right where I hope the femoral will be. His pants quickly soak. This time he tries to take the box cutter out of my hand, but not until I've gotten through another vein. His hand is weak on my wrist. His eyes lose focus and roll back.

His face is ridiculous, and I burst out laughing.

I slap my hand over my mouth, capturing the sound. My chest hurt when it came out.

Then my shoulders start shaking. Fresh tears flood from my eyes. My cheeks are so hot that I'm surprised they don't sizzle at the dampness. I throw my head back and realize that's definitely a laugh, as if I'm riding a roller coaster and terrified for my life but enjoying every moment. I'm not enjoying it. I've been possessed by a flood of feelings that have been waiting for Aaron to rest in peace.

They're all dead now. Jobson, who strangled him. DeVos, who disabled him. And Garrett, who betrayed him.

Aaron can rest.

I take the keys from Garrett's pocket. I take one last look at his face. *It shouldn't make me laugh, why am I laughing?* And I leave him gurgling his last breaths on the floor.

When I stand up, I see no more ghosts. I hear no more voices. I am still foggy, the world still slithering around me, but it has lost the edge of madness. I've never felt saner in my life. I step out into the sprinklers that keep DeVos's lawn damp, and I can breathe. Finally. I can *breathe*.

A luxury sedan, sleek and black, roars up to the side of the house. Mack skids to a stop next to me. "Jesus Christ, Evie, is that blood?" she asks, hanging out the window. "Are you okay? Where's that guy?"

Water from the sprinklers weeps down my bruised flesh. I'm still laughing. My streaking mascara stings my eyes, and my ribs ache on every breath. "He killed Aaron," I tell Mack.

She clenches her jaw. "We can't let the cops find us here."

"Don't worry," I say. "I'm married to the cops."

# CHAPTER 26
# HANK

How many hours do I walk after Cuttino burns to death? Day and night have no division in the ocean of smoke. I know where I should be in the foothills, but nothing looks right. The world has been drained of color. The wind has finally stopped, and the smoke shoots straight up, carrying licks of flame toward the trees. My body throbs with pain. I'm alone in the smoke with my pain and my God.

"Yea, though I walk through the valley of the shadow of death, I will fear no evil," I mutter, over and over, a hundred times. "You are with me; your rod and staff, they comfort me."

Whatever anger I brought with me is draining away. The hurt and insult of it all fades with the heave of my lungs, the shuffle of my feet. I dream of falling into an ocean. Just letting the wet swallow me up and pull me deep.

"Yea, though I walk through the valley of the shadow of death, I will fear no evil..."

DeVos's gate is standing open when I arrive. A small comfort when it looks like he's already lost a garage and a shed to the fire which consumes the right side of the property. When I spot his house, my heart sinks. The lights are off. The sprinklers aren't running. I stop, sagging with an arm against a tree. It doesn't seem urgent that I get to that house anymore.

Hell, I don't even know what I was going to do when I got there.

A car engine roars. A Saab comes around the side of the house and stops beside me. The door swings open. My wife steps out. She's as beautiful as the day I met her, waifish and blond. Yet something is wrong. It's not just the muddiness of her legs or her sodden clothes. It's the smell of blood. It's the black stains on the hem of her dress.

It's that box cutter in her hand.

And Eve is openly sobbing.

"Hi, honey," she says, chipper despite the tears.

I don't know how to react. I can't seem to get angry.

Eve only has one emotion for every occasion, so I've never seen her cry. I've wanted it. Before, it seemed like if she cried, it would be some concession. An apology for everything she's refused to give me over the years. A change of heart.

This crying feels different.

The world's flipped the wrong way. Up is down, Heaven is Hell, and the valleys are burning. Anything seems possible. I've never been scared like this in my life.

I'm *scared.*

It's a strange, hideous feeling. The idea of putting my gun into her hands is unthinkable.

"What happened up there?" I ask, edging backward.

"What do you think, Hank?" Eve asks. "They died. Everyone died. DeVos, Mallek, Garrett."

"Jesus Christ."

"They died in the fire," pipes up a voice from inside the car. I bend down to see Mackenzie driving the car, wearing oversized men's clothes. The kid is alive. She's safe.

"All those lives for her?" I ask in a low voice. "Really?"

Eve comes closer. "Some deaths make the world a better place."

"God makes those choices," I say, knowing it means nothing to my wife. She was a holiday Catholic. I'm not sure she ever believed. I should have known something was wrong with her. "How am I supposed to sleep beside you, knowing that you're like…" I can't put a word to it.

Her face turns redder, her nose wrinkles. "Do you want to divorce me?"

I'm so deep in shock, I can't tell if I do. "I love you, Eve. I've always loved you so much it hurts."

She wipes at her eyes and seems surprised to find tears. "I know who you are, Hank. And now you know who I am too." She laughs at her moist fingertips. I've never heard Eve so shrill. It's like the emotions she never had returned at once, gushing from her with jagged edges. "If you ask me, our marriage has never been stronger."

Eve smiles at me. It's eerily beautiful, this smile. She's the shadow of death with the grin of a skull, and she's still so slender, with such soft hair, and a long neck that I've kissed a thousand times.

She looks like Aaron.

He's all I can see. That's his smile squishing her cheeks. He had the same soft hair. And the madness in his eyes—that's the madness that Deputy Jobson faced.

*She killed them all.*

The fact that I briefly contemplate letting her get away with this is its own kind of madness.

Clarity drives me to pull the handcuffs off my belt. "Put your hands over your head," I tell Eve, and I don't wait to see if she listens.

She moves. She's lifting the box cutter.

My body slams into hers, shoulder into gut, and I drive her to the ground. She's bones underneath me. Just a sack of bones like her dad's. But her hands are still scrabbling for her box cutter, fallen to the side, and that means she's a threat.

I roll Eve over, twist her arms behind her back.

She screams, "Hank!"

From the car, Mackenzie screams, "No!"

I cuff my wife. "You're under arrest for the murder of— Jesus Christ, Eve, a lot of murders. You've killed so many people."

Her eyes stare into space, face smashed against the rotting leaf litter that forms a bed under us. One of her eyes tries to fix on me but can't. She's squirming. "You can let the fire take it all away," Eve whispers. "We can be together."

"You need help, honey," I say, "and I'm going to make sure you get it."

# EPILOGUE

**Eight months later**.

The Glass Memorial Psychiatric Hospital was built on a
hill overlooking Carson City. It was easy to clear the site
for construction after the wildfire turned the land black,
leaving nothing to do except scrape off the top with bulldozers and lay foundation. Don DeVos's estate committed
to several sweeping philanthropic projects, and the GMPH
was the shining diamond of them all. Anyone driving into
town from Reno would see the huge, reinforced windows
that formed its outer walls, suggesting the patients would
have a clear view of Washoe Valley's glorious vistas.

Someday the vistas would be glorious again, once everything had time to grow back. Seemingly half the city had
been leveled by the fire—the wealthy half on the west side,
specifically, to which state legislators committed millions
in repair funds. For now, the GMPH overlooked a
scorched valley. And the visitors' room in the maximum
security wing provided a view of nothing but a few strips
of clear-blue desert sky through windows too high on the
wall to reach.

There, Evangeline Everhardt met with her brother Wyatt Ashe. They could interact with each other across a table in a locked room so long as Eve made no sudden movements. She kept her hands spread across the top of the table where the guard could see them. The individual bones in her hands jutted through her skin.

"You need to eat more of the food, Eve," said Wyatt softly. "They're worried about your weight."

"The food in here is full of salt and sugar. It's unhealthy. I won't eat it."

"The dietitians make sure you're getting balanced nutrition. You don't know better than the dietitians."

"I just don't like it," said Eve clearly.

"Discharge stays off the table if you won't be compliant with the psychiatrists. Diet, medication, treatments—"

"It's nice to see you, Wyatt." She interrupted him with a genuine smile. "I don't want to fight every time I see you."

"No, I don't either. I'm sorry." They never really fought. Wyatt didn't have the heart to push Eve, the last member of his family, especially now.

He'd provided a lawyer when Hank arrested her. The district attorney had filed charges against Eve for only one crime—the murder of Deputy Jobson. Eve was evaluated by a psychiatrist and Jobson's house burned down with all the evidence, so the lawyer had an easy job. The judge had taken one look at the opiates in Eve's blood work before sending her to a maximum security facility in Clark County. It had taken a court order to get Eve transferred back to Carson City once the new mental hospital opened.

*Opiates*. Eve had gotten on drugs, just like Aaron, and Wyatt hadn't noticed. The guilt had deprived him of sleep for eight months.

"You look nervous, brother," Eve said.

"Not nervous," Wyatt said. "Worried. I'm always worried about you these days."

"Why would you be nervous? It's not like being in the psychiatric system murdered our other brother." Eve's smile was so empty.

Wyatt sighed. "Tell me you're at least going to grief counseling." Eve's care team theorized she had suffered a mental breakdown after Aaron's death. The therapist insisted Eve would be ready to go back to normal life once Eve accepted that.

"I attend," Eve said.

"Do you participate?"

Eve smiled.

"Okay," Wyatt said, sighing again. Every time he came, he brought new clothes for Eve, none of which fit, as well as books, magazines, and games that she didn't seem to play. She didn't move to take the bag from him when he offered it. "Here are some new notebooks in case you want to do some journaling. Your psychiatrist strongly recommends it."

"Has the body count changed?" Eve asked, talking over him. "How many people do they say died in the fire now?"

"Two hundred fifty-seven," Wyatt said. "Still. It's not going to change."

"Then Jobson died by fire. DeVos and Garrett, too. Every death attributed to Aaron Ashe's act of arson. Most of the people who died were seniors, weren't they? Or disabled? The frail ones. He killed all the frail ones like a complete monster. Only a monster would start a fire that killed so many people, and a monster like that deserves to die."

Wyatt wasn't supposed to feed into Eve's obsession. He massaged his temples, closed his eyes. "Can we talk about the books you've been reading?"

"Did you find Mackenzie?" asked Eve.

"Yes. The social worker said she'll be here today. That's why I came first. I still don't think seeing Miss Reese it's a good idea for your recovery, and neither does your team. You shouldn't talk to her."

"I just want to talk to Mackenzie," she said, steadily and pleasantly as ever. "Thank you. But it's been nice seeing you too. Maybe I'll feel more like talking next week."

With his shoulders slumped, Wyatt stood. "Sure."

Eve asked, "By the way, how's my release from the hospital coming along?"

"Great," Wyatt said, working to inject a positive tone into his voice. "I'm working on it through every channel I have."

He was not.

Something dark in Eve's eyes suggested that she knew it, too.

"I love you," Wyatt said sincerely. "I'll be back as soon as I can visit."

Eve said, "I love you too," and Wyatt thought she meant it. She'd just never meant it as much as she did with Aaron.

He didn't realize how sick he was feeling until he stepped out into the waiting room where other visitors milled. Mackenzie was among them. Wyatt had found her in a Reno foster home, where the teenage girl had been taken after the DeVos incident. Her parents were still being held pending trial for their daughter's sex trafficking. In the meantime, Mackenzie was going to a private high school under a different name.

Wyatt hadn't expected the social worker to pass along his message, much less permit Mackenzie to accept Eve's invitation, yet there she was.

Mackenzie didn't recognize Wyatt. Wyatt almost didn't recognize her. The clothing her foster family provided was simple—T-shirts and jeans. Mackenzie wasn't in makeup. Her hair was cut chin length. She looked nervous as she waited for her turn to speak with Eve, bouncing her knee.

Wyatt left without speaking to her.

Mackenzie's fingernail polish was driving her crazy. The cheap stuff her foster parents bought chipped too easily. She scraped at it with her thumb while she waited her turn. The psychiatric hospital was uncomfortable. The bland walls, the hard chairs, the number of people wearing pastel uniforms.

"Next guest for Evangeline," called an orderly.

Mackenzie stood up. She entered the meeting room.

Eve looked up at her, hands still flat on the table where the guard could see them, and Eve smiled. It wasn't the hollow smile she'd given her surviving brother. "Hi Mack," said Eve.

Mackenzie slid into the chair across from her. "Only one guard for you? Damn, you should be insulted."

Eve laughed. "Tell me how life's going for you. Is the foster family treating you well?"

"I dunno," said Mackenzie.

"You say you can't talk about it when I call you," said Eve. "Now you don't know. Are the parents a problem?" There's a hard edge to her otherwise pleasant voice.

"They don't make me do stuff for money. But it's boring, and I hate the little bitch sharing my bedroom, and the dad yells at me. You happy to hear that? I'm not happy to be living in it." Mackenzie folded her arms and slumped in her chair. "It's nice to see the face that goes with the voice. I appreciate how you've been checking up on me." She wouldn't look directly at Eve when she said, "I like having someone who listens when I can tell the truth. You're the only one who really knows."

"You're the only one who knows Aaron didn't kill all those people," Eve said quietly. The guard outside the door, a tall man in uniform, was distracted watching another patient passing in the hallway. Eve slipped a notebook page across the table to Mackenzie.

Mackenzie unfolded it. She frowned at the pencil markings. "What is this?"

"How do you feel about treasure hunts?" Eve asked.

Slowly, the girl tucked the note into her pocket. "Like you used to do with Aaron?" Mackenzie asked. "Are the stakes as high?"

"Depends," Eve said. "If you want. But there's at least nine thousand dollars in it for you."

"*What?* Nine thousand—"

"Shh. DeVos cut me a check before he died, trying to get me to shut up. The money should be yours. Figure out the map and it'll take you there."

"Then what do I do?" asked Mackenzie.

"It could be a college scholarship. A down payment on your first apartment. Or you can use it to finance a special project."

"Like what?"

"Over two hundred people died in the fire and history will say it was Aaron's fault," said Eve. "Some of the men responsible died. Some of the men who hurt you died too, but not all of them. Maybe we could talk some more about that. What to do about it."

Mackenzie remembered killing Mallek. Her heart raced. Her blood burned hot. She was once again overcome by enough fear, loathing, and rage that her hands shook and tears stung her eyes. She had never hated anyone as much as she'd hated Mallek while killing him.

Mackenzie felt like Eve could read her mind.

"The first time is the hardest," Eve whispered. "But if they're sick, if they're hurting, if they're evil—it gets easier every time."

"You're crazy," said Mackenzie softly.

"Don't you feel like you're going crazy?" asked Eve. "Knowing what you know? Seeing who gets hurt for it? Who gets blamed?" She spoke normally when she said, "Twelve. Sixteen. Nine."

"What?" Mackenzie asked.

"Twelve. Sixteen. Nine," the woman repeated. Her smile was so warm. "Will you come visit me again soon?"

Mackenzie stood up, feeling so strange, as though her body had turned to smoke. "Yeah," she said, "maybe I will."

* * *

Sheriff Hank Everhardt was in the lobby when Mackenzie left. He was a handsome man in his mid-forties with several shiny burn scars and a sheriff's badge. He had been made the interim Sheriff after Cuttino's accidental death in the fire. Soon there would be an election, and the polls suggested he'd be selected. He always wore the badge on his belt beside his gun and his Taser.

Mackenzie didn't even notice him. She hurried into the brassy sunlight as if she couldn't escape the institutional setting quickly enough.

"What do you think Eve said to her?" Wyatt asked. He was standing aside with Hank, absorbing sunlight through the psychiatric hospital's overlarge windows.

"I don't want to know," Hank said. "Have you listened to her talk lately? She's totally snapped."

"What does this mean for you and Eve?" asked Wyatt. At Hank's darkening expression, Wyatt said, "I just need to know if Eve's going to have someone in Carson City to take care of her. If I need to transfer to a closer job. I won't judge you, whatever you say."

"It's up to God to judge me," said Hank. "My wife's a trial He sent that I couldn't rise to meet. I already filed divorce papers weeks ago. That's the second reason I'm here. I was hoping to pick them up with her signatures today, but the therapist said Eve won't sign."

Wyatt scrubbed a hand over his thinning hair. "Damn."

"You don't have to worry about your sister, you know. This is a good facility named after her dead boyfriend. They'll take great care of her. She's exactly where she belongs."

"She's my sister." Wyatt shrugged. "I have to worry about her."

"All you Ashes are the same," said Hank. "Don't be like them. Cut your losses." He shook hands with the FBI agent and turned to leave.

"Didn't you come to visit her?" Wyatt asked. "Isn't that the first reason you came here?"

Instead of responding, Hank simply waved as he walked out the doors.

Mackenzie was sitting in the front seat of Hank's patrol car, playing on her cell phone. When the social worker asked for a law enforcement officer to provide transportation, Hank had taken the job himself. He figured the girl would appreciate a familiar face. Someone who had technically rescued her from DeVos's house, not to mention his crazy wife.

The girl was grateful. She showed it in her smile when Hank slid into the driver's seat.

"How was the conversation?" Hank asked, pulling out of the parking lot.

Mackenzie shrugged. "I don't know."

Hank said, "You're almost done with school now, aren't you?"

"I'll graduate this year," she said, "and then college, maybe. I don't know." She was nervous, her hands fluttering. She asked, "Is it okay if I vape in your car? I'm so nervous. It helps me calm down." She glanced at Hank through the veil of her hair. Mackenzie had a backpack on the floor between her feet.

Hank said, "You need to quit."

"I know, I know," she said. "It'll kill me. Everyone says it. But I have a really bad craving right now."

Hank didn't say anything. Mackenzie's hands crept to her backpack. She pulled out her vape, and still he didn't say anything. He kept watching the road. He didn't look at her, because then he wouldn't have to tell her to stop. He smelled the faintest hint of menthol.

Mackenzie rolled down the window of the car without asking. She pursed her lips to blow vapor out the gap, and the wind tossed her hair off her neck. She had fine curls at the nape. She was slender but curvy in all the right places. A beautiful young woman just starting to bloom.

"Tell me Mackenzie," said Hank, "do you like to play poker?"

# ACKNOWLEDGMENTS

My first and biggest thanks must go to Jessica Alvarez of BookEnds Literary Agency.

Thank you to my family who survive with me.

To the readers who have supported me through many wild years of a weird career, especially the Army of Evil.

And of course huge thanks to those who offer advice and kindly talk me down from my ledge of crazy whenever it gets too high: Yasmine Galenorn, Melissa F Miller, Bree Bridges, David Dalglish, Deanna Chase, Christina Garner, Kate Danley, Michael Wallace, Robert Duperre, Scott Nicholson, Krista Ball, Nathan Lowell… I could keep going because I'm blessed to be surrounded by grounded people. I couldn't do it without y'all.

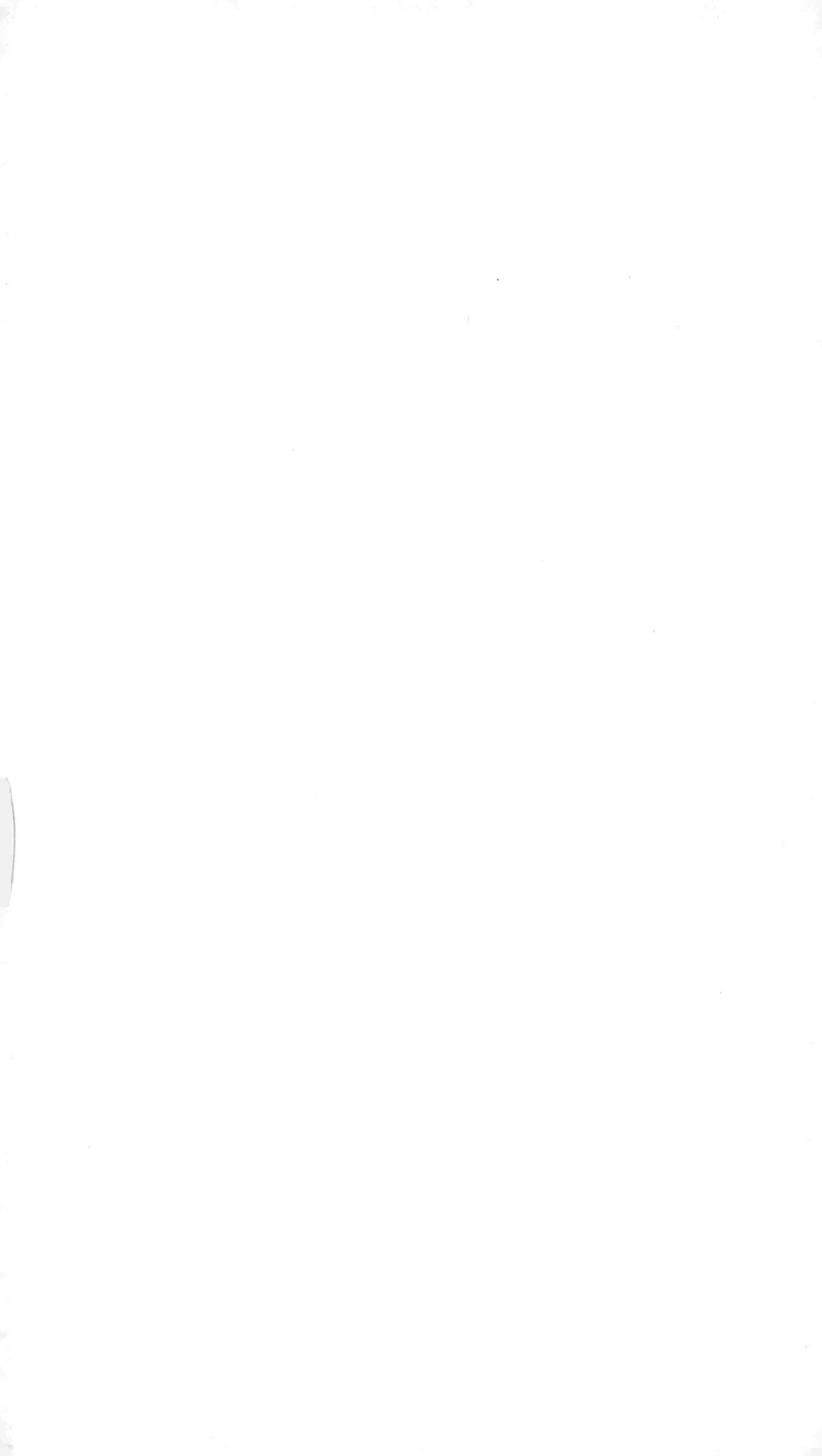

# ABOUT THE AUTHOR

SM Reine is a New York Times bestselling author who has written many novels and sold two million-something books. She is married more happily than her suspense novel would suggest and lives near Reno, Nevada with two human offspring, a cadre of animal babies, and an excessive number of typewriters.